VIOLET VENDETTA

CHARMING MYSTERIES

JOANN KEDER

Edited by: Amber Richberger
Cover Art by: Molly Burton, Cozy Cover Designs
ISBN: 978-1-953270-29-0

"You are worth finding, worth knowing, worth loving. You and all your one million layers. Always hold that close."— Danielle Doby

CHARACTERS, IN ORDER OF APPEARANCE

Feather Jones—paranormal investigator and co-owner of Kindred Spirits

Gemini Reed—co-owner of Kindred Spirits

Jayden Ko—owner of Ko Industries and leader of P.I.N.K.

Tug Muehler—Feather's fiance and owner of Tug Bars

Olive Thomas—co-owner of Tug Bars

Howard Beachmont—Gemini's neighbor and friend

Leo Reed—Gemini's husband

Trent Mathews—nurse

Gladiola Crabbitz—neighbor of Gemini and Howard

Eli Crabbitz—Gladiola's nephew

Mr. Beasley—past leader of P.I.N.K.

Alistair Violette—client of Kindred Spirits and

member of N.A.G.S. Rocky Boulder—new police chief
Azalea—host at The Bleeding Rose
Cassie—Feather's client at Featherworks Hair Salon
Lulu Rodriguez—Jayden's secretary at Ko Industries
Quentin Zahn—true crime enthusiast, perpetual thorn in the side, and neighbor of Gemini and Howard
Hetty Zahn—Quentin's mother
Ruthmarie Reed—Gemini's dead mother-in-law
Millicent—dead girl who helps Feather
Pheobe Pepper—member of P.I.N.K.
Sophia Reed Floris—Gemini and Leo's daughter
Maeve McCullovy—Millicent's dead maid
Maxine Smart—FBI agent
Opal Hughes—Cassie's mother
Patience Thistle—local historian, story hour reader and annoyance to anyone over ten

CHAPTER 1

FEATHER

The Bleeding Rose hid behind the Charming Small Animal Veterinary Clinic. It was camouflaged by a large azalea bush and a commercial trash bin with the words "Charmed to serve you!" spelled in peeling green paint across the top. A faded, red metal door with a sign that read "No Trespassing!" written in ominous, stretched letters warned the curious away.

Feather glanced to her side, where her partner, retiree Gemini Reed, stood. There was no time to ask how or why someone who lacked her own gift of paranormal sight stood beside her. It was a well-worn rumor that an "average" person would experience a shock much like that from an electric fence if they dared enter.

When she blinked, she and Gemini stood beside a booth, where a man—whose appearance was blurred like that of an anonymous witness being interviewed on a television show—sat smoking a long cigarette. A smell, something sweet and slightly spicy, reached her nostrils and made her gag.

"What are we doing here?"

The man dabbed his cigarette on the corner of a red ash tray before bringing it back to his lips. At least she assumed he had lips. "Feather Jones, your talents are well known. You're simply the best, my dear."

"Who are you?"

"You'll find out soon enough, sweet girl. What you should be asking is why I've chosen you. Isn't that the real issue?"

The room grew cold, ice cold, and Feather's teeth chattered. She glanced over at Gemini and was shocked to find her frozen stiff. Icicles hung from her silver hair, and her bright, blue eyes were open wide. Her hands were outstretched as if asking for help.

Feather touched Gemini's hand, hoping to warm her, but instead her friend's hand crumbled to the floor. Feather gasped in horror, but there was nothing she could do as the rest of Gemini's body followed suit.

In Gemini's place, another frozen human appeared. A woman dressed in a blue rubber catsuit and wearing a brunette wig was frozen with the same look of terror in her eyes.

Feather recognized her immediately. It was her

mentor and trusted friend, Jayden Ko. She'd never seen Jayden, who was normally in control, look so helpless before. Jayden's eyes were filled with fear and one hand grasped something, though Feather couldn't make out what.

She turned to the mysterious figure and yelled, "Why are you doing this? I demand that you tell me what you want!"

Looking down at her own body, she realized her hands were disintegrating, just like her friends'.

"Stop! Stop right now! This isn't funny!"

A disconnected laugh echoed around her as the entire room crumbled. She tried screaming but nothing came out. There was no choice but to wait for her own demise.

"Feath? You all right?" Tug Muehler, Feather's muscular fiancé, shook her shoulders, his brow furrowed with worry.

Ignoring his concern, she pushed herself into a seated position. "Tug? Was I dreaming?" She opened and closed her small hands and was relieved to find them still quite functional and attached to her body.

Now that it was safe to snuggle, she pulled Tug close and nestled her head into the spot between his armpit and his chest. He was her safe place. She used her thumb to feel the band of her engagement ring, something that gave her comfort.

After several minutes of bliss, Tug kissed the top of her purple, pink, and blue head. "Are you going to tell me what that was about, or should I make some completely off-in-left-field guess?"

"Just a silly nightmare. It must've been those enchiladas. You're never going to let me in the kitchen again, right?"

Tug gave her a warm, reassuring smile and chuckled. "It's a legit mistake. I mean, if I hadn't done it before, I might think whipped cream could replace sour cream myself."

"You're being too kind, babe." She playfully tapped his chest. "It will be a long time before the sugary taste of whipped topping-filled tortillas leaves my taste buds. You went above and beyond boyfriend duty when you ate three of them."

After explaining the dream as best she could, Feather jumped out of bed to get ready for work. When she had showered and dressed—into a plaid button down shirt, jeans, and combat boots—Feather joined Tug in the kitchen. The smell of Tomelets, Tug's version of omelets that included goat cheese, orange peppers, bacon, and green onions, met her nostrils and reminded her stomach that two small bites of dessert enchiladas wasn't enough.

As they ate, she thought back to the unsettling dream. Feather Jones, Paranormal Investigator, was used to disturbing dreams. After all, it was the only way spirits could trick her.

"I can't shake the thought that there was more to

this than your average nightmare," she said between bites of toast.

"You said there were no ghosts. Who else can get into that noggin?"

"Probably no one. It's acceptable to have a normal person dream every now and again."

Tug swallowed the last of his second omelet and looked up at the clock, which used a painted likeness of Choco Chump and a Lemon in Love Tug Bars wrappers as arms. Feather gifted him the clock when he trademarked the name of his protein bars.

"We need to roll. Olive and I are going to Charmless State Prison today. The warden wants to talk about a contract to provide bars to the inmates."

"That's wonderful, babe!"

The thought of Tug and Olive inside the barbed wire fence of the most notorious prison in the state terrified her. Olive would inevitably say something inappropriate and get them into trouble. For the umpteenth time since he'd announced the huge contract between Tug Bars and the prison, she shoved her worries aside. It was probably her fertile imagination and nothing more.

The cold rain came down in sheets, and Feather resented having to give up her seat next to the heater, but it wasn't worth the fight to try and keep it.

They pulled up to the curb in front of Charming Acres Retirement Community and watched as an enthusiastic woman bounced in her pink polka-dotted rain boots. She waited not-so-patiently while Feather got out of the front seat and held the door for her.

"Goodness, girl. You need better rain gear." Olive yanked Feather's coat wide open, adding to Feather's morning irritation. "This ain't no weather for sunbathing."

Olive Thomas, a compact woman with short hair dyed to match Feather's, always insisted upon sitting in front. She had a massive crush on Tug and made no secret about it, despite the fact that she had a serious boyfriend.

Olive was her usual chatty self. "Did you watch the season finale of *Detective Dirk Dandy* last night? Woo-eee. Shocked old Titus right off his chair. Good thing I've been using hand weights when I walk around the warehouse."

Olive rolled up the peach-colored sleeve of her rain jacket and flexed her bicep. "Lifted him up without even losing my breath."

Feather watched as the windshield wipers moved rhythmically back and forth, back and forth, back and forth. It was mesmerizing today, perhaps because she'd had a restless night. Or, more likely, because she had no interest in Olive's television show.

"Titus? What happened to George?"

Feather could never be sure if Tug was genuinely

interested in her banter or just being polite. She always forgot to ask him.

As her attention returned to the windshield, she was shocked to find a face staring back at her. A giant head undisturbed by the wipers' movement stared hard.

She glanced down at her arms, which showed the tell-tale signs of spirit involvement. Each hair stood on end, almost as if she'd encountered a strong bout of static electricity.

"Psst. Babs in Four C said she'd seen him out cattin' around."

The conversation in the front seat continued. Tug and Olive were oblivious to the drama happening right in front of them.

"Sure enough, I caught him night before last, slinking out of Dorinda's place. That was that."

"I'm surprised, Olive. You and George have been an item for almost a year. Didn't take long to find your new Mr. Right. I guess you're in high demand."

Olive blushed, clearly pleased.

Feather Jones, we're coming for you. Be ready!

Feather shook her head. She'd learned that the more interest she showed to a negative energy, the more it wanted. She wouldn't even give this wind-shield guy the satisfaction of speaking.

They pulled into the second parking space in front of their warehouse. Tug Bars were manufactured in the back and Kindred Spirits Detective Agency resided in the spacious front office. Tug offered to pave the rear entrance for Olive's benefit, but she insisted she could walk just like everyone else.

Tug left the car running, waiting patiently for Olive to gather her purse and check her hair in the mirror. The giant head no longer appeared, but the windshield wipers screeched as though they weren't wipers at all but nails dragging across a chalkboard.

"Shut it off, Tug!"

Both he and Olive turned around and stared at Feather with surprise.

"Sorry, babe. I didn't know the radio bugged you so much."

"It was that song. Not my favorite."

At least it was over. She'd tell him the truth later.

As soon as Feather stepped out of the car, a new piercing sound assaulted her. Slapping her hands over her ears, she glanced helplessly at Tug and Olive, who were still discussing Olive's favorite show.

"You guys can't hear that?" she screamed.

They both stopped and turned around. Tug walked briskly to the car and grabbed hold of Feather's elbows, looking her in the eye. "Are you okay, babe? You've seemed off since you woke up."

More than anything, she wanted to tell him. He was her rock. But today he was signing the contract with Charmless State Prison. Tug Muehler didn't need the weight of her troubles on his shoulders.

Tolerating these strange occurrences seemed like a small price to pay for his clear conscience. Hopefully. Maybe Gemini could run her home if needed. "I'm fine. It's probably a weird imbalance or something."

CHAPTER 2
GEMINI

"Gem, this neighborhood is in terrible trouble!"

Retiree Gemini Reed's normally unflappable neighbor, Howard Beachmont, stood on her porch shaking like a leaf. Though she'd seen him at arguably his worst, when he was distraught about being arrested, he'd never looked quite so scared.

Howard was a handsome man of seventy with a short salt-and-pepper beard, green eyes, and a good head of hair. His dark, bushy eyebrows made him appear menacing to those who didn't know him, but he had become a good friend to Gemini.

She shivered in her blush-colored sweater as she held the door open. It was a blustery northwest coastal day, and the wind from the open door went right through her.

"Come in, Howard! Tell me what happened while I make you some tea." She held the door open for him as angry, wind-driven drops of rain assaulted her. "Did you lose your raincoat too?"

His wet face was taut. "No. I didn't think I'd be outside so long. You know me, I check the forecast three times every day. I have to make sure all of my vegetation is receiving precisely the right amount of nutrients and moisture."

She disappeared into the bathroom, returning with two fuzzy green towels. Gemini used one to wipe the back of Howard while he wiped his front. Howard removed his rubber gardening shoes, the ones Gemini had given him last Christmas. They'd already begun filling with water. "Indoor and outdoor use!" she'd told him. So much for that.

"I'm so sorry to drag all this water over your hardwood floor. We're in an awful predicament, though, and I felt I needed to come right away."

Gemini stared at him, shocked. "What's gotten into you, Howard? Nothing flusters you!"

The tea kettle whistled a cheery tune, and she turned abruptly to remove it from the heat. "Mint Melody, I presume?"

She reached into a drawer where an extensive collection of teabags were categorized by flavor—spicy to the back, fruity to the front. Mint on the left.

"Today I'd like something simple. An English

Breakfast with a squeeze of lemon, if it's not too much trouble."

Gemini shook her head. "The perfect choice for a dismal morning. I'll make one for myself." English Breakfast, in the front because it was so common, of course.

A glimmer of a memory flashed through her head. As a newlywed, she and her husband Leo had fun decorating their home. When his parents came to see it for the first time, his mother brought a box of English Breakfast tea. "That's all you'll get from me," she grumbled. "At least until I'm sure this marriage is going to work out."

Why on earth did that pop into my head? Gemini wasn't in the habit of thinking about her long-dead mother-in-law. Just as quickly as the memory came, it drifted away.

Luckily, she'd baked strawberry scones when she awoke, anticipating a trip to Howard's later in the day.

After placing the steaming cups of tea and the plate of scones in front of Howard, she sat directly across from him. Placing her chin in one palm, Gemini looked her friend directly in the eye. "Howard, I need you to start from the beginning."

He cleared his throat and crossed one knee over the other. "I don't need to remind you that Gladiola Crabbitz is becoming a habitual thorn in our sides."

Gemini rolled her eyes. Ever since Gladiola

bought the house directly behind Gemini's, she'd been nothing but trouble. "All because we were acting as officers of the neighborhood association and inspecting the property before she moved in."

"She was so friendly the day I encountered her and her realtor. We chatted about flowers and fine coffee and she seemed a perfectly lovely woman." Howard shook his head. "I don't know what changed."

"*We* happened." Gemini scowled. "It really burnt her biscuit that we were on her property. Even the fresh-baked cookies I brought as an apology didn't soften her up."

"You missed yesterday's performance, courtesy of Gladiola's dog walker. Thug broke free of his leash and terrorized children for almost an hour before the dog catcher arrived. If I'm not mistaken, the dog walker had a hint of glee in his eye."

She went through yesterday's schedule: groceries, haircut, then work at Kindred Spirits Detective Agency. It was clear to her how she missed all of the commotion.

"The Neighborhood Allies of Greenberry Section had enough. We decided to fine Gladiola."

Gemini opened her mouth to protest. She was

the secretary for N.A.G.S. and received no notification of such a meeting.

"We knew you were doing detective work," Howard said, as if reading her mind. "It was left to me to inform you of our peaceful actions."

A loud snort erupted from her otherwise gentle mouth. "Whatever your intentions, I'm sure it didn't end peacefully."

Howard rubbed his hands on his pants and looked down. "The dog catcher had just captured Thug when the police arrived. Gladiola was making a horrible fuss. She called her nephew, who arrived just in time to threaten the police chief. Chief Boulder didn't take kindly to that."

"I'll bet."

"All the fuss caught the attention of Mr. Beasley, who volunteered to negotiate between the association and Mrs. Crabbitz. I wasn't certain the poor old fellow had the stamina to stay upright that long."

Feather confided to Gemini that Mr. Beasley was a formidable leader of P.I.N.K., Paranormal Investigators of the Northwest, Level K, the local organization of paranormal investigators. Despite his frail stature and unassuming demeanor, he possessed more paranormal abilities than everyone else in the group, at least before his recent retirement.

"And what did Mr. Beasley say to our unhappy friend?" Gemini reached for a scone and was pleasantly surprised when she bit down. "The cream cheese icing really makes these pop! I'd like to tell my daughter that she was wrong about that addition, but, well, you know I have to pick my battles with my darling girl. Brandon's mother told her it's in poor taste to use cream cheese. The nerve!"

Howard nodded in agreement as he took another sip of tea. "This is a wonderful blend, Gem. You'll have to show me the box before I leave."

"Don't keep me in suspense, dear man." She glared at him expectantly. "What happened with Mr. Beasley?"

"Oh, yes. He was quite composed as he went through the reasons why Thug needed more room. Gladiola's yard is too small for a dog of that size and energy, and the poor dog walker, who by now was sobbing on the curb, couldn't be expected to walk him again. Eli agreed to take the dog with him, thankfully. There was something strange about the interaction, though."

He took another sip and placed another scone on his plate. "Just one more."

Gemini made a circular motion with her arm, signaling him to continue. The recent sleepless nights were catching up with her, and her level of patience had sunk to an all-time low.

"Mr. Beasley spoke in a low tone that I'd not heard before. He said something to the effect of, 'You won't win, sir.' Eli's eyes were the size of snack plates, and his face turned the color of my best ruby beets."

Eli was probably a member of P.I.N.K. too.

"I don't like where this is going." Gemini shoved the last of her scone in her mouth and tried to enjoy it, even though she knew the story wasn't going to end well.

"You know, Gem, I think much of Gladiola's behavior stems from loneliness. Her husband passed away last year and she occupies herself by making others her business. It's probably not about upsetting the rest of us at all."

Gemini mulled that over. The investigator in her knew to wait for all the facts before reaching a decision. "We'll see. I brought her cookies that first week and she accused me of trying to poison her! That's just rude!"

"Eli put the dog in the back seat of his car, waved goodbye to his aunt, and everyone thought the excitement was over. When the crowd disbursed, Gladiola turned her anger toward me.

"I have to tell you, Gem, by that point, adrenaline was coursing through my veins. I couldn't help myself. Every frustration I'd had with the woman for the past four months came tumbling out of my mouth. And not in a nice way."

"Oh dear. How did she react?"

"Not well."

Gemini felt her blood run cold. "And?"

She observed Howard's face, normally lightly tanned, was pasty. He motioned for Gemini to come closer as he lowered his voice to a whisper. "She said, 'The past always catches up, no matter where you try and hide.'"

CHAPTER 3
FEATHER

Feather let her hands drop, even though the piercing sound still cut through her skull like a sharp knife. Her fingers were white due to the continual pressure she'd placed on her ears. Yet the relentless, piercing sound continued its assault, echoing ominously and causing ripples of discomfort to flit across her face. Her eyes, once tightly shut in a futile attempt to block out the noise, now opened wide. She bit her tongue and did her best to remain calm. *Think happy thoughts, Jones.*

Tug, Gemini, Jayden—they all loved her unconditionally. The cases where she'd made life better for some and death better for others always filled her soul. *Yes, she could do this.*

She waved goodbye to Tug and Olive through gritted teeth and watched them walk inside before bringing her hands back up to her ears. The rain was coming down sideways, but she didn't care. A wet head was better than bleeding ears. There had to be a way to make this stop. Maybe a change of scenery?

Unfortunately, when she walked into the office of Kindred Spirits Detective Agency, the sound amplified. Gemini was typing away but paused to swivel around in her Work Ahead Office Supplies Luxury Seater.

"You won't believe what's going on in my neighborhood!"

"What?" It was embarrassing not to be able to understand her partner.

Gemini frowned before mouthing, "The new neighbor I've been complaining about scared Howard to death!"

Feather shook her head and pointed to her phone. As soon as Gemini finished typing and pushed send, Feather felt sick. These people had been harassing Gemini and Howard for too long.

I'll help you figure something out just as soon as I get my hearing back.

Gemini nodded and typed back:

Now what can I do for you?

Her silver-haired partner's wide smile changed to a look of concern, her mouth drawn in tight at the corners.

She wished she knew. This hadn't happened

before. It wasn't physical. Maybe she needed the help of another paranormal investigator? Feather shrugged.

Send Jayden a message. She'll know what to do.

It was as if Gemini read her mind. Jayden Ko was not only the CEO of Ko Industries but also Feather's mentor and the most intuitive woman she knew.

Quickly, she typed out a description of the noise. Her ears were hurting so badly that she wondered if she would lose all hearing permanently.

Almost immediately, her phone buzzed in her hand.

New clients coming in soon. No time to talk. Try earbuds. They might block the sound. Let's talk tomorrow, doll! J

Last month, Olive won earbuds in a cake walk at her retirement center. Insulted by the lack of dessert in her bounty, her boyfriend George told her to give them away and he would buy her a fancy cake. "What do I know about those techy things? You might as well take them, Feather."

He had bought her a two-layer angel food cake with orange cream frosting on one layer and strawberry cream cheese on the other. A delighted Olive thought it the perfect exchange.

Feather pawed through her junk drawer. They

were gone. She felt a warm hand on her shoulder and looked up at her partner with tears in her eyes. Gemini patiently closed the drawer and opened another, the drawer Feather used to keep extra staples, hidden unhealthy snacks that weren't Tug Bars, and discount coupons for Lupe's Lunch Loot Delivery.

Reaching to the very back, Gemini pulled out the earbuds and handed them to Feather.

Tears rolled down Feather's cheeks. She felt so alone, so out of touch with the world. She hated herself for showing emotion, even in front of one of her best friends.

Quickly, she found a music app and began listening. The piercing sounds were drowned out by Gary Polka's "Swingin' Rap To My Favorites". She'd never been so grateful for awful music in her life.

She gave Gemini a thumbs up and, thankfully, Gemini returned to her desk. It wasn't that she didn't feel grateful. Feather still couldn't communicate with others because one obnoxious sound was being drowned out by another.

After a recent Sip'n Paint Feather had reluctantly attended with Jayden, she'd discovered how much she enjoyed the process of creating something new. The next day, she approached Gemini with the idea of painting a mural on their wall. As was always the case when she had a new idea, her partner enthusiastically agreed. Gemini and Leo owned a paint and hardware store when they lived in Fassetville, so Gemini was eager to help her pick out just the right paints.

So far, Feather's mural depicted Gemini and Feather. Well, it would, once she finished painting the background. There was more to come and, when the time was right, it would come to her. The best part about painting was not what she created but the calming effect it had on her.

She was lost in thought when she felt a warm hand on her shoulder and jumped. With last night's horrifying dream still fresh in her mind, she was afraid to turn and see who it was.

An envelope appeared in front of her, placed by a well-worn hand with a small, heart-shaped diamond on the fourth finger. Gemini mouthed "Sorry!" and returned to her desk.

"Probably a retired magician who thinks he's smarter than the rest of us!" Feather yelled. She was positive it was much too loud, so she chose to end the conversation there in hopes of saving Gemini's ears.

Suddenly the polka music stopped. Feather picked up her phone and looked at the screen. It was still playing. These earbuds must've been the cheapest they could find.

It was at that moment she realized that the music

stopped as well as the piercing sound in her ears. Thank goodness!

"I assume you received my invitation?"

Feather spun around, recognizing the voice from her nightmare as it echoed through the room.

CHAPTER 4

GEMINI

Gemini wedged herself between them, holding the invitation Feather had cast aside. "Indeed we did. You're Mr. Violette, I presume?"

She hadn't taken it seriously. The overly-curly handwriting stating a Mr. Violette wanted someone "taken care of" seemed like a childish prank. While she was studying local ordinances regarding angry neighbors, he snuck in.

Dressed in a long violet cape with matching pants, Alistair Violette was equal parts intriguing and amusing. His angular jaw and arched brow reminded her of the old Dracula movies she'd watched as a child.

"My partner and I couldn't help but wonder what this is all about. Who is it that you wish to be... dealt with?"

Mr. Violette chuckled softly, a mischievous glint in his eyes. "Ah, my dear detectives, the task at hand is quite peculiar indeed. You see, there's a rambunctious group of garden gnomes that have taken up residence in my prized azalea bushes."

Gemini and Feather exchanged puzzled glances before Gemini managed to ask, "Garden gnomes, Mr. Violette? We are a reputable organization. Last month, an interview with Feather was featured in *Soul Hunters Monthly*."

Just as Gladiola Crabbitz and her threats seemed unreal, so did this situation. Maybe someone was playing a prank on them. Howard said there were people in the city offices with odd senses of humor. "Are you sure you want to hire us? We don't come cheap. You could easily find a neighbor child who could track them down for you for no more than a few dollars."

Mr. Violette nodded solemnly. "This job is far too complex for children, Mrs. Reed. These mischievous little creatures have been tormenting me for weeks. They rearrange my garden furniture, spill tea on my prized begonias, and even hold raucous parties at midnight! It's an absolute nightmare."

"Do you have any... suspects?"

Feather looked sincere, which puzzled Gemini. Surely she saw through this poor, lonely man's theatrics.

The mysterious man leaned forward, his voice

lowering to a whisper. "The mayor... is an avid collector of porcelain figurines."

"You want us to 'take care of' the mayor over porcelain figurines?" Gemini repeated with a healthy dose of skepticism. "That hardly seems like a reason to want someone dead."

Mr. Violette laughed softly, taking a sip of his coffee. "Ah, my dear Gemini, you underestimate the dark underbelly of the porcelain world. There are rival collectors, fierce competitions, and a black market that would make your head spin."

Though she was used to odd people coming through their doors, it bothered Gemini that he knew her name. This was taking the prank a step too far. *Stop being silly. He probably saw our picture in the paper when they featured us in the Charming Business Spotlight.*

Feather's eyes widened. "So, someone wants the mayor out of the picture to gain control of the porcelain trade?"

"Exactly," Mr. Violette confirmed without a trace of humor. "And it's up to you, dear detectives, to uncover the culprit and save the mayor from an untimely demise."

"Can we get back to you, Mr. Violette?" Gemini wasn't in the habit of kicking potential clients out of the office, but if he didn't leave soon, Alistair Violette would be the first. "My partner and I like to discuss our cases privately before agreeing to take them. Of course, there is a hefty retainer fee and you'll need to sign a detailed contract."

Alistair smiled, displaying a row of white teeth. She swore they were pointed but forced herself to look away.

"Yes, you may discuss the validity of my case. In the meantime, I'll leave my card with you."

Gemini reached for the purple business card, but he pivoted and handed it to Feather instead.

Wrapping his cape around his body in dramatic fashion, he exited their office.

"Cheese and crackers! We've had some Offbeat Ollies before, but this one takes the cake!"

"Or the gnome!" Feather quipped.

"Should I send him our standard, 'Sorry, we're too busy, here are the names of other investigators' letter?"

Feather shook her head. "He is a little off, I'll give you that. But there is something about him that is drawing me in."

Gemini slapped the desk with one hand. "Feather Jones? You can't be serious!"

"Don't worry, I'll handle this one myself."

Gemini couldn't believe what she was hearing. Feather's middle name was skeptic. Why was she falling for this?

"What were you going to tell me earlier? When I walked in?"

"Oh, we've got some nasty neighbors. Remember

my telling you about Gladiola Crabbitz? In addition to calling the police about my poisoning her with my mother's cookie recipe, breaking and entering, and stealing the bed sheets on her clothesline, the police called this morning to ask if I'd thrown weed killer on her lawn."

Gemini wasn't sure how much she should say, given Feather's unusual demeanor and the fact she just recovered her hearing. "But you really should get back to the mural. Before the paint on your palette dries."

Feather nodded, setting Alistair's business card on the desk.

Gemini noticed with dismay that her partner clasped her hands over her ears as soon as she set the card down.

CHAPTER 5

FEATHER

"Do you want anything?"

Feather felt guilty over convincing Gemini that she wanted to sample Tug's newest bar, Butterscotch and Brownie For the Win. Waiting for her friend's bathroom break could prove costly. Alistair clearly had some kind of power over her. "Maybe a coffee. As long as Olive didn't make that nasty flavored stuff again. Blueberry cream cheese was a coffee too far."

Gemini nodded in agreement. "I'll make you a fresh pot if I smell produce."

"Oh, and Gem? Can you talk to the new delivery driver about his paperwork? Tug and I haven't gotten anywhere with him."

Feather's high-pitched voice and wide smile were more emotion than she usually expressed in an entire week, and it was exhausting.

"You think he needs a little of the Reed charm?" Gemini folded her arms and leaned against the door frame. "I dealt with all kinds of employees at the paint store. If I can't get what I want from him, no one can."

"Thanks!" Feather rose from her desk and waved to Gemini as she walked away. *That was overkill, Jones.*

As soon as Gemini disappeared down the long hallway, Feather grabbed her phone and dialed the number on Alistair Violette's business card. She used the speaker function on the phone as she transferred her weight, back and forth, back and forth, between her combat boot-clad feet.

After a few rings, a deep voice answered. "So you've found yourself wondering, 'How does that man control my hearing, and what does he really want?'"

Feather huffed. "The mayor has been my client. He may have an eye for women in short skirts, but he's no gnome thief."

Alistair laughed with a deep, sinister cackle. It was the same voice she'd heard in her dream. *Nightmare.* It was a nightmare. It sent a chill down her spine.

"What's your game? I don't have much time before Gemini returns."

"I was truthful about one thing. I do need your help with the elimination of a particular person."

"Gemini already told you. We aren't that kind of agency."

"You'll join me this evening, 8:30 at The Bleeding Rose." He acted as though she hadn't just given him a polite brush off. "I'll be in the back booth. You'll want to hear what I have to say. It involves someone in your life."

She felt another chill down her spine. This time, it wasn't induced by Mr. Violette or an otherworldly being. "And if I say no?"

The air purifier, a recent expensive purchase Gemini made, began its muted hum. Only now, the hum was more of a roar. Feather's ears started buzzing again. She wasn't used to anyone in the living realm playing these kinds of tricks. "Okay! I get your point!" she screamed. "I'll be there at eight!"

The sound in her ears immediately stopped.

"Not just you. I need your partner as well."

"Why? Gemini has a sick husband and a dangerous neighbor. She doesn't need to add murder to her worries. Leave her out of this."

As she spoke, Gemini caught the glass door with one foot and somehow maneuvered herself inside the office holding two coffee cups. She flashed a bright smile, oblivious to the deal Feather was making with Alistair Violette.

Gemini set a napkin on Feather's desk containing two bar samples before giving her two thumbs up.

Feather smiled and returned the gesture. "Yes, Mr. Violette, we'll be there this evening. But that's no guarantee we'll take your case."

Gemini frowned but turned and began working at her computer.

Once Feather was done on the phone, she pushed a button on her fancy chair that moved her the few feet to Gemini. It was a ridiculous detail on an already-ridiculously expensive chair, but Gemini had insisted. The settlement the Reeds were granted after Leo's intentional overdose was to be used to help those she loved.

After Feather glided across the protective plastic on the floor and leaned her arms on Gemini's desk, she playfully glanced up at her partner. "Go ahead and ask. I know you can hardly contain yourself."

Gemini waited a full minute to answer. "You purposely shooed me away, didn't you?"

There was no point in denying it now. "Yes. Mr. Violette was very... persuasive. He wants us both to meet him tonight at The Bleeding Rose. At 8:30. I'm sure that once he understands I handle the paranormal end of our detective business, he'll decide your presence isn't needed. Gnomes aren't a two-person job."

Gemini brought her coffee cup to her lips. Feather couldn't tell if she was hurt or just lost in thought.

"How did you get back here so quickly anyway?

You threw me off my game, sister." Feather's eyebrows rose as she waited hopefully for Gemini's response.

"He's gone. Tug says he showed up an hour late this morning. Again. Tug told him that was his one and only warning. The next thing he heard was the man's tires squealing as he left the parking lot."

Feather took a bite of the bar. It was the Caveman Coconut she'd sampled two nights ago. "Needs chocolate chips," she'd suggested. Feather was pleased he'd taken her suggestion to heart, as he usually did. "That makes six delivery drivers in less than a month. Poor Tug."

"Why on earth would you agree to take that creepy purple man's case? He's clearly off his noodle."

"I'm sorry I lied to you. I just wanted to protect you from this weirdo, and I thought I could handle him myself. We don't lie to each other and I promise never to do it again."

Gemini's face filled with doubt. "Well, all right. But there is another issue. I'm in bed by 8:30. That's when I feel like staying up late."

Feather nodded with understanding. "I promise we won't be out late. I'll have you home by 9:30. If he needs to talk longer than that, I'll come back alone. You can even sleep in tomorrow. You are the boss, after all."

"Is that safe, hon? I don't like the idea of you

being out by yourself either. That's practically the middle of the night!"

Feather forced a somber, though she wanted to burst out laughing. Gemini's heart was always in the right place, even when she didn't fully understand the situation.

"I wouldn't be able to live with myself if something happened to my best friend simply because I refused to accompany her."

They were both back to their respective computers when the bell over the door jingled again. Feather's body tensed.

"Ladies, I see you're working hard."

They both let out a sigh of relief when Chief Boulder, the new police chief, greeted them by removing his large, white cowboy hat. "What a nice surprise, Chief! Did you come to collect on our promised donation for Carb-a-Palooza?"

She opened her drawer and sifted through a considerable assortment of paperclips, staples, pens, and gum before removing an envelope. "Here you go, Chief."

"Thank you, Mrs. Reed. I'd forgotten myself." He cleared his throat and gently stroked one side of his impressively bushy mustache. "I'm actually here for something else."

"Oh, right."

Gemini dropped into her padded chair with a *shoosh.*

"What is it, Gem?"

"Remember last week at bridge, when I told you about our neighbor, Gladiola Crabbitz? She's decided that Howard and myself are up to no good. I'm concerned she might do something rash."

"Now, Mrs. Reed, that's a bit premature, isn't it? Mrs. Crabbitz phoned me just yesterday to tell me that you and Mr. Beachmont have tried to harm her nephew's dog. She's concerned the two of you may harm her as well."

Gemini's mouth gaped open. "Are you kidding?"

Chief Boulder shook his head. "Wish I was. She also mentioned your attempt to poison her with some cookies? Said she's called the station numerous times, but nothing's been done."

"I bring all of the new neighbors baked goods! She wasn't home, but I included a note explaining that if she didn't want them to give them away. Cheese and crackers! This woman is unreal!"

Feather knew all about this one. "You've only been here six months, Chief. But everyone in town will tell you Gemini is the best baker around. The only poison here is the words coming out of Mrs. Crabbitz's mouth. Gem brings us goodies all the time. Not once have I been poisoned."

"Didn't think there was anything to her claims, but I had to check. Do you have any of the cookies in question here?"

Gemini jumped up from the desk. "In the break

room. It's a different batch than the ones that, you know, contain the poison."

She didn't wait for his response. As soon as Gemini was gone, the chief turned to Feather. "Was wondering if I could hire you?"

This was a strange turn of events, one Feather wasn't prepared for. "Sure. When Gem gets back—"

"Not her, just you." His voice lowered at least an octave, and she had to lean forward to hear what he was saying. She'd never known a mustache to suck up that much sound.

"I need you to check out The Bleeding Rose. I've been getting reports of someone plotting a murder."

"Here you are, Chief! One dozen secret recipe cookies!"

Feather jumped back, feeling guilty even though she hadn't done anything wrong. "He's lucky it's early in the day or Tug would have eaten them all by now!"

Gemini shoved a plastic bag into the chief's hands. It was obvious she wanted to get rid of him.

"Thank you, ma'am. And you can call me Rocky. There's no need to be so formal."

When he'd left, Gemini tapped her index finger on the desk. "I'm holding you to 9:30, even if you're hanging on every word Mr. Violette utters."

"Got it. No hanging on words."

"Pick me up a few minutes early. I need to buy some fruit for a new muffin recipe."

"I will!"

After she left, it occurred to Feather that Gemini would drive right by Chunky's Grocery, Gemini's market of choice.

CHAPTER 6
GEMINI

"This week has been full of stuff and nonsense, dear heart."

Gemini spooned the last of Leo's butterscotch pudding into his mouth and gently wiped the corners with a napkin.

"That awful neighbor, Gladiola, that I've mentioned several times, banged on my front door this morning until I opened it. I was ready with a kind word and a smile, but she wasn't interested. Instead, she complained that my kitchen light was too bright and it gave her a sick headache. Can you believe it?"

She brought a cup of water to his lips and poured a tiny amount inside his mouth.

"In other news, I haven't been to a bar since you and I met. Do you remember?"

Her eyes glistened at the memory, as if it

happened just yesterday. "It was our third date and you insisted on going to a bar to watch the Oregon Ducks game. I kept my raincoat on, thinking I'd get splashed." She chuckled. "Wasn't I surprised to discover the Ducks played football and they weren't ducks at all but young college men!"

She leaned her head on his shoulder. "I just wanted you to know about this bar situation. I'm not on the prowl for a young, heavy-drinking beau if that's what you're thinking. It's purely for business. We've always had a 'no secrets' policy and I'm not about to upset the apple cart now."

"Knock, knock."

A six-foot-five man with sandy-blond hair entered and pulled up a chair beside them.

"My partner said those were the best combination of butter, sugar, and flour he'd ever had!" Trent Mathews, a nurse at the Charming Care Center and one of Gemini's favorite people, playfully slapped her leg.

"I haven't seen you for a couple of weeks. Refresh my memory?"

"Yeah, we went to the Grand Canyon. We took your cream cheese brownies and savored every last crumb."

Gemini turned back to Leo and spooned another tiny bite of pudding into his mouth. "Ahh. Yes. That recipe is a keeper."

"I've known you long enough that I can suss out a mood and you, girlfriend, are in the middle of one."

She turned to face him. "It's that obvious? My sleep has been sporadic and we had a strange man come in today wanting to hire us to track down his lost gnomes."

Trent crossed one giant leg over the other and laughed. "You're not serious!"

"I'm afraid so. This man was so out of his gourd, I didn't give it a second thought, but Feather says we need to hear him out. She's picking me up this evening to meet him at The Bleeding Rose."

Trent's jovial expression sobered. "That's not a safe place for you, Mrs. Reed. I've heard crazy stories ever since I was a kid. There are ghosts all over that place, and they aren't the fun kind you and your partner find."

She swallowed hard. "What kind of ghosts?"

"Well, you know I don't gossip, but..." Trent did little but gossip. "There were rumors that a high school kid wandered in there by accident. He was never seen again. Well, at least the living version. His ghost haunts the place now."

"Oh." It was nothing more than children's games. "Well, I'm curious, not as much about Mr. Violette but as to why my partner treats this like a real case. I didn't come out of retirement to find garden gnomes."

"Remember last month, during Carb-a-Palooza,

when the Name Your Noodle Trivia Contest was halted abruptly?"

She and Feather had volunteered to give out free bottled waters with their logo on them. "I do recall that. What happened?"

Trent leaned in close enough that she could smell the delicious cucumber mint soap she'd given him in his holiday gift basket. "A guy came up and threw red sauce on Lasagna Lovin' Lifeguards. The entire team looked like something from a horror movie."

Gemini nodded, unsure where this was going or how it was connected to her trip to The Bleeding Rose.

"Chief Boulder arrested the guy who did it, but the next day, it was like it never happened. My cousin was in charge of that event so she called to find out who he was. No one at the station had any information, so she cornered Chief Boulder. He said he'd been out of town all weekend and didn't know a thing."

"I'll grant you, that's strange. But I'm still unsure why you're telling me this now."

"My cousin held on to the one piece of evidence she collected during the chaos. It was a sauce-stained napkin from The Bleeding Rose."

"I'm sure it was a coincidence. Purely coincidence."

CHAPTER 7

FEATHER

The Bleeding Rose had a reputation for being a haven for the supernatural community, a place where secrets were whispered between the shadows. Feather told Tug it was just a place for people to go and feel like they were important. In reality, she felt anything but and didn't want to risk others with her gifts seeing her for the fraud she was.

Feather pushed aside the vines and knocked on an old metal door as she stuffed her insecurities deep down inside, pushing her fears away at the same time.

"Jones?"

There was no peephole. "How does this person know it was you?" Gemini tried to peek in the tiny hole.

Feather pointed up, where a security camera

tracked their every move. At that moment, the door buzzed and clicked open.

An unusual-looking woman stood at the podium. "Hey-ya, gals. Welcome to The Bleeding Rose."

Her less-than-enthusiastic voice didn't match her wild getup. She was wearing a drop-waist emerald green dress adorned with intricate beadwork, sequins, and fringe that swayed with her movement. Long strands of pearls cascaded down her neck. Glancing down, Feather noticed fishnet stockings and metallic heels. She really worked the part.

"Hi. You're Azalea, right? I've heard people talk about you."

"Probably. I ain't the type to go out quiet. Ya know what I mean?"

There were all types in the paranormal world. Some, like Feather, who kept her true identity hidden in public. Others, like Azalea, went all out. She was probably the life of Halloween parties, giving tarot readings and offering psychic connections. Those people were always more show than substance.

"We have an appointment with—"

"Alistair. Yeah, I know. But we have to follow protocol. Over here."

Gemini and Feather followed Azalea's instructions and moved beyond the podium. "Stop! Right there's good." Azalea cleared her throat. "The patrons here are an eclectic mix of individuals who have dedicated their lives to unraveling the enigmatic and unexplained. They gather to share stories, theories, and cryptic clues over glasses of absinthe and specialty cocktails with names like Ectoplasm Elixir and Spectral Sour. The bar's resident mixologist is rumored to have a sixth sense for crafting the perfect drink to match your mood."

She paused, though it wasn't clear if she was waiting for their response. "The scent of ancient books mingles with the rich aroma of espresso, creating an atmosphere that's both comforting and haunting." Azalea made dramatic gestures as she spoke, as though she were a poor actress making up her own stage directions.

"In one corner, a group huddles around an old Ouija board, attempting to make contact with spirits from beyond. At the center of the room sits a vintage playing loops of grainy footage capturing eerie apparitions and mysterious poltergeist activity. The jukebox, seemingly possessed, occasionally emits tunes that resonate with the supernatural theme— haunting melodies that linger in the air like phantom echoes.

"In a back alcove, a bookshelf holds a collection of well-worn tomes filled with accounts of spectral encounters, ancient rituals, and the arcane arts." Azalea sighed. "Feel free to peruse them, at your own risk."

She looked down at her chipped, black finger-nails. "Any questions?"

"No, we're good. If we could just see Mr.—"

"You gotta sign in first."

A large leather-bound book with yellowed pages sat on the bar where Azalea gestured. As her arm swung around, the pages of the book flipped quickly before coming to rest on a blank spot.

"Neat trick." Feather wasn't impressed.

"Wait—it ain't just any Jones. It's THE Feather Jones! Just wait 'til I tell the gang who decided to join us." Azalea bounced, causing her jewelry to rattle.

The woman let go of Feather's shoulders, apparently just realizing she didn't come alone. "And you brought your grandmother? I thought your family didn't support your gift."

Gemini was relieved the room was dim so the blush in her cheeks wasn't obvious. "I'm not her grandmother. My name is Gemini Reed." She offered her hand to the woman, whose nametag she was now able to read. "Azalea, it's so nice to meet you."

Feather touched Gemini's shoulder. "This is my partner at Kindred Spirits."

Azalea clicked her tongue as she examined them. "You don't say! You gals are the talk of the para-normal community! You're one of a handful of para-detective agencies actually making money! I guess you came to show off a bit, eh?"

"Actually, we came to meet someone."

"There's only regulars here tonight. Weeknights aren't the most exciting."

The formerly pleasant expression on Azalea's face clouded. "You're not looking for that creepy guy in the back booth, are you?"

They followed her gaze to a circular red booth on the opposite side of the room. Though it was hard to make out his expression, it was clear the man who darkened their doorstep was seated there, waiting for them.

Azalea jerked Feather's arm before she could move beyond the check-in area. The hushed voices that had temporarily paused when they entered were speaking again.

"You be careful, Feather Jones. There's all sorts of darkness surrounding him." She made a dramatic circle in the air, using one arm and then the other. "I almost kicked him out because we have a strict, no-bad-juju rule." Azalea pointed above her head, where an as-yet unread sign declared, "NO

-dark magic
-spirits with an attitude
-outside food or drink
-bad juju

Feather nodded solemnly.

After they'd signed the book, Azalea showed

them to Alistair's table. By the time they reached him, it felt like they'd already been there all night.

"Welcome, ladies," he said, his voice resonating with an otherworldly charm. "I'm delighted that you've decided to join me."

Gemini eyed him cautiously. "Mr. Violette, we're here to listen to what you have to say, but we need to know more about this situation and why you've approached us. Neither of us want trouble with the mayor. I took the liberty of chatting with him myself."

Gemini opened her over-sized, blue-striped bag and pulled out a garden gnome wearing a purple wizard's hat. "There you are. He was happy to hand it over. Oh, and there are five more in his backyard. None that seem to hold any value to him. Knock yourself out."

Alistair Violette leaned forward and folded his hands together. "Congratulations, Mrs. Reed. You passed the test."

"What test?" Feather and Gemini asked in unison.

"I wanted to see just how far Mrs. Reed would go to protect the mayor. I'm pleased her loyalty is beyond reproach."

Feather wasn't sure what kind of game he was playing, but whatever it was, she was losing patience. "You have exactly thirty seconds to explain yourself. After that, we're leaving, with or without answers."

There was a twinkle in Alistair's eyes. "I've been watching you for some time, Miss Jones. Your paranormal detective work is beyond reproach." His eyes darted between Feather and Gemini. "You too, Mrs. Reed. As long as we don't count your attempt to scare off the goblin in Mrs. Peabody's bathtub drain."

Feather stole a quick glance at a red-faced Gemini. "That was an... unfortunate oversight on our part. We're still relatively new to the business."

Alistair leaned back in his chair, steepling his fingers. "Unfortunate, yes, but also highly entertaining for those of us who got wind of it."

Feather sighed dramatically, a playful smirk on her face. "It was the first time we'd encountered a bath bomb in our investigation. It was an honest mistake."

She had called Jayden in a panic, "The spirit is bubbling up in the tub and won't respond to me! Help!"

"Rose scented, if I recall correctly?" Alistair added with a chuckle.

Now she was plain mad. "Neither of us want to rehash this."

"We don't," Gemini added. "You've got your gnome and if there's nothing else..."

Alistair turned the gnome upside down and

pulled off a price sticker. "Thirty-five dollars. Prices at the Chunky's Market aren't what they used to be."

"That's where you went on your way home!"

Feather gasped. She was at the same time relieved and irritated that Gemini didn't confess that was her plan when she left work early. Feather reached over and patted her visibly upset partner reassuringly. "It's just fine, Gem. You proved what an upstanding person you are."

"Which is exactly the reason I need Mrs. Reed for our plan to work."

Gemini stood abruptly and placed the strap for her purse over her body. "It's after nine. You promised I'd be in bed in fifteen minutes. This poor man is lonely. I can sympathize, and tomorrow I'll put together a list of organizations where he can meet—"

"What a pity. And here I was, ready to help you with those pesky Crabbitzes."

CHAPTER 8

GEMINI

When Gemini first moved to Charming, she volunteered to serve coffee and treats in the break room of Featherworks Hair Salon. It was just as much about providing a listening ear to women with no outlet for their worries as it was about Gemini Reed gaining an outlet for her baking addiction.

Many times, people would speak of The Bleeding Rose in passing, but she never took them seriously. One story was more outlandish than the last. "I've seen the long dead come back to life there," one especially unreliable source reported.

"They drink the blood of men with blond hair," another insisted. "I've seen them!"

One time after they'd met for lunch, Olive offered to show her where the infamous club was located. They walked down a side street until they reached an alley. Olive pointed to an almost invisible door, half-covered with bushes and trash, The Bleeding Rose's entry.

As Gemini was about to continue, Olive stuck out a protective arm. "This is as far as we go, Gemini. There's bad vibes practically screaming from a loudspeaker, and this old gal isn't inviting another curse into her life. No sirree, I've broken my last mirror."

Tonight, as soon as they entered the bar, Gemini smelled the oppressive combination of stale smoke, liquor, and fried food. When Sophia was little, she liked to bowl with her friends at a local bowling alley that had the exact same smell. Sophia's bowling days ended when she refused to put on shoes that anyone else had worn.

"I understand your skepticism, but there are forces at play that go far beyond the realm of what's considered normal. The person I need your help with, they possess powers that threaten the balance between the supernatural and human world."

A giggle escaped Gemini's mouth before she could hide it with her hand. "Sorry. You make it sound so dire. It's just a gnome. I'm sure the mayor would just hand it over."

Feather leaned forward, her voice filled with a surprising amount of compassion. "We've encountered many beings with extraordinary abilities. What makes this person different?"

Alistair Violette's eyes bore into Feather's, and

for a moment, Gemini wondered if the poor girl would get up and run.

"This person has the ability to manipulate life energy itself. They can drain the essence of others, leaving them weak and vulnerable. If left unchecked, their power could cause unimaginable chaos."

Gemini and Feather exchanged a knowing glance. This wasn't as far-fetched as they had originally thought. Kindred Spirits Detective Agency had encountered similar cases in the past, where individuals misused their supernatural gifts for personal gain or harm.

Gemini spoke firmly, her voice laced with determination. "Mr. Violette, we'll consider assisting you. However, we need to establish a few conditions before we proceed."

Everything in her screamed to turn and walk away. Yet her fierce loyalty to a young woman with a spiky rainbow of hair and combat boots kept her feet planted right where they were. "First, if we find that they pose a genuine threat, we'll take our findings to Chief Boulder."

Alistair Violette leaned back and crossed his arms. He almost seemed... amused. "I respect your commitment to justice, however misguided it might be." He reached into the pocket of his cape and pulled out a roll of bills. "This will change your minds."

Feather stood so abruptly that the table jiggled. Gemini caught her water just in time.

"Mr. Violette, or whatever your real name is, we don't need the money. If you had any kind of powers, you'd know that—"

Gemini grabbed Feather's forearm and scowled up at her. The last thing they needed was for this man to know her financial situation.

Feather sighed. "Give us the name and we'll investigate. But Gem's right, we have to do it our way."

His gaze traveled from Feather to Gemini and then back again. "As you wish." Alistair opened his napkin and pulled out a small piece of paper. He slid it across the table to Feather.

When she opened it, she gasped. "You're wrong!"

"I promise you, this person needs to be neutralized."

"I won't do it!" She stood. "Come on, Gem, let's get you home."

Somewhat flustered by the change of events, Gemini tried to think quickly. "And what was this deal you were proposing? In regards to Gladiola Crabbitz?"

"She is an acquaintance of mine. I'd be happy to intervene on your behalf. I could end your troubles," he snapped his long fingers, "just like that."

This was absurd. She'd had some doozies before, like the time she was hired to find out if a man's cat was cheating on him. (She was. She got plenty of affection and expensive food from the neighbor two doors down.) But this didn't even have a ring of truth to it. This man was simply nuts.

"Feather and I will take the matter under consideration. Meanwhile, I'll put together a list of activities in Charming. I'll call you tomorrow with our decision and this information."

As Feather exited the booth, the paper Alistair slid over to her fell on the floor. Feather was already bolting for the door, so Gemini took a moment to open it and read the name.

Jayden Ko.

CHAPTER 9

GEMINI

Feather let out a shaky breath, her hands trembling ever so slightly. "I can't believe someone would ask us to do something so... so terrible," she whispered.

Gemini turned and placed a comforting hand on Feather's shoulder. They hadn't spoken a word on the way home. Both were lost in their thoughts. "We made the right choice, sweetie." She used the gentle voice normally reserved for calming down Olive. "We didn't start Kindred Spirits to be instruments of harm. Mr. Purplepants can find another agency to do his bidding."

Feather nodded, a glimmer of determination returning to her eyes. "You're right, Gem. We have a responsibility to use our gifts for good. Let's focus on the cases that truly need our attention."

"*Your* gifts, you mean."

"We both have gifts. Half of the cases that come to me are solved by my partner." Feather's mouth softened into a crooked smile. "Besides, Kindred Spirit would just sound dumb."

It became nothing more than a harmless joke by the next morning. They had tears in their eyes while reenacting Alistair's Dracula vibe when Tug walked into the room.

"Why do I always seem to come in after the joke?"

He wrapped his muscular arms around Feather and lifted her small body off the ground. She responded with a big kiss, her new engagement ring sparkling under the fluorescent lights of their office.

Gemini sat and began working on her email, though it wasn't an easy thing to do—concentrating when that much passion was in the air.

After they'd kissed for at least ten minutes and Gemini had typed "Dear Sir" ten times, Tug set Feather down. "Now, is someone going to fill me in?"

Feather and Gemini exchanged uncomfortable glances.

"I already figured out something was wrong last night, when you came home as white as a ghost."

Feather swallowed hard. "We had a weirdo here is all. We're bound to attract a few. When we met him last night, he put on a real show."

Tug carefully examined his fiancee's face. "Nope. There's more to this story. I have exactly," he looked at his exercise watch and frowned, "I have ten minutes before I have to make a delivery to Flex's House of Muscle and then," his hands pattered on the desk, "I have to drop off our biggest order to date."

"Yes, Olive has given us the lowdown. Four times, I believe."

> Gemini, we've got an order for two thousand Tug Bars! Can you believe it? I'll have to stay out way past my bedtime all week!
>
> Ooh, if tongues at Charming Acres Retirement Community won't be wagging!

"What happened to your new delivery driver? I helped him fill out his tax information and he seemed very enthusiastic."

Tug's eyebrows made a V as he shook his head. "Gone. Didn't bother showing up today. That's the third time this month. I offer good pay and benefits. I don't get it."

"You've been working so hard lately, babe. This is really unfair."

"Yeah." Tug rubbed the back of his neck with one hand. "It'll be another late one tonight."

"Tug Bars are really taking off. All due to you."

He gave her one of his disarming half-smiles. "And to your support. Couldn't do it without that beautiful face to come home to every night."

He gave her a peck on the cheek.

They both watched him leave, Feather with an adoring smile and Gemini with worry. "Tell me," she insisted.

Feather turned around. "What?"

"Tell me."

Feather sighed heavily. "Okay. I parked the car and sat for a few minutes before going up to our apartment. I knew that Tug would figure out right away that something was wrong unless I calmed myself somehow. So I popped on some meditation music. Or at least that's what I thought."

"What played instead?"

"I thought maybe there was something wrong with my phone, because the sound was slow and squeaky, like a car with bad brakes."

Gemini placed her chin in her palm. "Sounds terrible. I'm so glad my generation never had to worry about electronics."

"That's just how it began. I tried changing to a different song, but every track was the same. Then a man whispered, 'You're the only one who can stop her. If you don't want more deaths, she must be stopped.' It was Alistair's voice. I'm just not sure how he did it."

Gemini cleared her throat and tapped her fingers on her desk. "I read the paper after you ran to the car. I know it's Jayden Ko. Do you think... do you think..."

"That we should take this case? Absolutely not."

"Then I'll call him now and let him know our decision." Gemini swiveled around in her chair and looked up Alistair's number. She called several times, but each time she got the message that the phone had been disconnected.

"Oh well. At least we don't have to worry about him anymore. He's probably found someone else to scare."

Gemini hoped her voice didn't belie her uncertainty. Everything that had been happening was too much to be a coincidence.

CHAPTER 10

FEATHER

There was no way she could keep this from Tug any longer. She waited up 'til he returned from a night of baking. "How'd it go? Was Olive any help?"

"No, she had bingo tonight. It was just me. How was your night?"

His back was facing her and Feather couldn't help but feel a little shut out. There was no reason for her insecurity, she chided herself. *None at all*. She was the partner keeping secrets.

That night, as they lay in bed, each propped on an elbow, she let loose the entire ugly story.

"Let me get this straight. You've made a deal with this purple guy to kill Jayden. And you've made a deal with, well, yourself that you're going to figure out why and prevent harm coming to your mentor."

Tug shook his head. "You've really got yourself stuck in the mud with this one, babe."

Feather nodded and bit her lip. "I wanted to make sure that Alistair didn't look any further for an assassin. How could I turn him down?"

"I'm not judging you, babe. I'm just wondering how long it will be before the guy realizes he's been duped."

"That's what worries me. He's got all sorts of weird connections, but so far, he doesn't seem suspicious. And the worst part is that he wants to involve Gem."

"Over my dead body!" Tug shot up and threw the covers off. "I'm going over there right now to tell this Alistair dude to stay away from both of you. If he wants someone else to do his dirty work, it won't be the two most important women in my life."

"Babe, the last thing I need is to worry Alistair is trying to manipulate you too. Please don't get involved." She gently pulled on his arm until he was back at her level. Feather covered him with the fuzzy lavender blanket Gemini gave her for her birthday.

"Why don't you just tell Jayden? Shouldn't she be in on the secret?"

"I can't! If she finds out, she might try and protect me instead of herself. Every time I have a crisis, she's been my protector. Now it's my turn to do the same for her."

Tug pulled her in close. "One of the many

reasons I love you. But I have to circle back to my original question. What's going to happen when he finds out you're working both sides?"

Feather had thought about it, though she didn't allow her mind to go to that awful place. There was a solution and it would present itself soon. That was what she'd learned from Jayden.

Tug kissed her fingers one at a time, stopping when he reached her ring finger. "When are we planning to make our engagement public? I mean, you have this gorgeous ring that you hardly wear. If I were insecure, I'd think you were afraid to marry me."

Their cozy bliss was disturbed by the buzz of Tug's phone. He rolled over to see who it was. "Olive. I should take it. Last time she called me this late, she was locked out and when she knocked on windows she yelled, 'I'm not here to rob you!' No one let her in."

Feather rolled her eyes. "Get it. I need some sleep to prepare for my visit with Jayden tomorrow. It's going to take every ounce of concentration I have to keep her from reading my thoughts."

FEATHER CLOSED her eyes and reimagined her favorite dream. She and Tug were perched on a large, blue boulder on the side of a babbling rainbow-colored brook, alternately laughing and kissing. It was a slight alteration of a recurring dream she'd had as a child, when Fruity Boats cereal were her favorite breakfast. Multi-colored boat-shaped pieces covered in sugar, of course, filled her lonely mind with much-needed escape.

Over the years, the story changed but the colorful location remained the same. Teenage Feather Jones, who drank cheap Tulley Valley wine, sat on the blue boulder hundreds of times. Some days, her handsome eighth grade calculus teacher would join her. On others, the friends she wished she'd had filled her blanket.

She closed her eyes and opened her mouth, ready to receive a juicy strawberry. Instead, a metallic taste filled her mouth. When Feather opened her eyes, a gruesome sight awaited her. On top of Tug's muscular body was the head of Alistair Violette. He laughed at the way he'd tricked her.

Feather spat the strawberry on the ground, where her beautiful rainbow-colored scenery had become a barren black-and-white landscape. "You're not allowed in my dreams! I don't even allow ghosts in this space!"

"You can't hide from me, Feather Jones. I'm much too powerful."

Open your eyes, Jones. Do it now.

Feather sat up and wiped the drool from the side of her face. Light poured through the window, reminding her that she'd forgotten to pull down the room-darkening shade the previous night. Glancing beside her, she saw that Tug's side of the bed was empty, without even a rumpled sheet to mark his existence.

She'd have to shake off this disturbing encounter without his help before she went inside Ko Industries Tower. It wasn't optional. Feather Jones was about to perform an incredibly challenging feat. She was going to prevent her psychic mentor from reading her thoughts.

Feather flashed her driver's license at the security desk and continued toward the bank of shiny black elevator doors. She marveled at the elegance of the building, from the marble floors and walls to the massive murals of the women who shaped Charming, Oregon's history. Her favorite was the mural of M.C., an entrepreneur with three children and no money, who started a successful toy company.

She pushed the button for the elevator on the end, the only one that went all the way to the eleventh floor, where Jayden Ko occupied the entire space.

The doors opened and Bill or Phil, she couldn't remember exactly, smiled and nodded as he used his special key to access the penthouse. It was a good thing she no longer needed an appointment to visit Jayden. What would she give as the reason for her visit? *To decide whether her friend should be murdered?*

As she stepped into the elevator, serious-faced men and women in business suits stared at her like she didn't belong. That was just fine. She wasn't, in fact, anything like them. Thanks to Tug, Gem, and even Olive, Feather knew her place in the world.

She felt a tap on her back and whipped her head around.

"Feather? I'm Cassie. You did my hair last month."

Cassie had gorgeous, long, brunette hair hanging in ringlets below her shoulders. It was highlighted with blond and lavender strips, just as Cassie had requested.

"Oh! I remember. You came in with your dog. Peaches, right? I didn't know you worked for Ko Industries."

Normally, Feather frowned upon animals coming in to the shop. She'd dealt with more than one customer whose "he's friendly, he doesn't hurt anyone" dog bit another customer. But Cassie's Pomeranian was the opposite. He slept on her lap the entire time, never making so much as a squeak.

"I work across the street, but my boss has me running paperwork over here almost every day. I've been telling all of my friends about you," Cassie gushed. "Most of them are disappointed when they can't get in. You are booked out for months!"

"I only work two days a week now. The rest of my time is spent—"

Feather paused. She still felt secretive about her second profession as a paranormal investigator, despite the fact that they'd hung flyers and handed out business cards all over town. "You have to be comfortable in your own skin at some point, doll," Jayden had told her.

"I help my boyfriend with his protein bar business. Tug Bars. Maybe you've heard of them?"

Cassie's face went blank, but a man standing beside her said, "They're in the break room on every floor. When nobody's looking, I put a few in my pocket for later."

The entire group chuckled as the doors opened to the tenth floor. Most of the staff exited, including Cassie. At the last minute, Feather held the door open and handed Cassie her paranormal investigator business card. "Just give me a call and we can work something out. I don't mind coming in on my day off to do hair if it's someone I already know."

Cassie stared at the card and then at Feather as the doors closed.

Are you happy now?

My granddaughter has lost weight. Tell her she needs to dump that worthless boyfriend and start eating real food again.

I'm off the clock now, Mavis. The next time Cassie comes for a cut and color, we'll have a chat.

I'm going to haunt that creaky old house until you do.

The doors opened once more, this time on the twelfth floor. Jayden's office consumed the entire floor and contained an apartment, a full gym and recreation area, and a dining room complete with a private chef.

"Lulu! Is she in?"

Jayden's secretary glanced up and nodded. One of the perks of being a close friend of Jayden's was that Lulu never turned her away.

She knocked on Jayden's door and waited.

"Come in, doll. I've been expecting you."

CHAPTER II

GEMINI

"Gemini, you're positively jumping out of your skin today. What gives?"

Howard stuck a flyer between Mrs. Wilty's screen and wooden door. Though Mondays she attended water exercise class until noon, it was best to leave her a flyer while they were out and about. They didn't need another neighbor bent out of shape.

"You know me well, friend." She rolled up another flyer and handed it to Howard. "It's the guy we met at The Bleeding Rose the other night. I can't get him out of my head."

Howard stopped abruptly. "You went into The Bleeding Rose? It's got a reputation as a rather—"

"Seedy place, I know."

"I was going to say colorful, but we're probably getting at the same thing."

She nodded before they continued walking again. "We told him that under no circumstances would we take his case. He wants to bring harm to Jayden Ko."

Gemini didn't ordinarily make a habit of sharing the details of cases with anyone. Well, on occasion she would share with her daughter, Sophia, but the need to unburden herself today was too great.

"How many ways could that go sideways? Gem, this is dangerous territory. I think you should contact Chief Boulder and inform him. Wouldn't you feel terrible if harm were to come to Miss Ko and there was something you could have done to prevent it?"

She stopped in the middle of Raspberry Drive, placing one hand on either hip. Today's cloudy weather left her shivering, something that worsened when she wasn't moving. A short-sleeved deep purple button-up blouse was no match for the cool marine winds.

"Of course I would!" Gemini cleared her throat for emphasis. "So very."

Howard placed a flyer in a mailbox decorated with baseballs. The owner had a smooth-as-silk voice that he used to announce baseball games before his retirement.

"Apologies. Are you asking for advice or a listening ear?"

She handed him another rolled-up flyer. "The

latter." She explained, as best she could, the story of Alistair Violette visiting their office and their subsequent bizarre meeting at The Bleeding Rose.

"And why would you entertain his delusions, even for a minute? Wait, don't answer that. I'm sorry for doubting you, again. You're planning to investigate his backstory, I hope." Howard turned and continued to walk.

"Yes. But we have also accepted his offer. Well, I didn't. My sense is that Feather returned to accept his offer on our behalf."

He stopped abruptly and squinted. "Gem, you're many things, all of them positive. You're no murderer."

"Cheese and crackers, Howard! Of course we're not going through with it! Jayden Ko has guided Feather through the process of becoming a paranormal investigator. She's been nothing but kind. I'm afraid Feather is cooking up some plan to pretend she's going through with it but has no intention of killing anyone."

"That's a nice rosy picture you're painting. How do you know it's true?"

Gemini tapped the screen of her phone. "Tug put a tracking app on all of our phones, so that when we're in the middle of an investigation, we can keep tabs on each other."

"I don't mean to throw sardines on your salad,

but why wouldn't Feather just turn hers off if she didn't want you to know where she was going?"

"I thought of that too."

They began walking again and the conversation paused while she stuck a flyer in the mailbox of 414 Raspberry Drive.

"We haven't had a case where any of us were in danger for at least," she looked up at the sky as she thought, "six months. Feather was irritated to be tracked in the first place. I took a chance that she forgot all about it and I was right."

Howard picked up a rock on the porch of 418 and set the flyer underneath. "What comes next? And how did your purple man expect to help us with the Crabbitz couple in the first place?"

She had conveniently left that part out of the story. While Howard was open to most of the shenanigans in her life, he would draw the line at flat-out hocus pocus.

"Don't know." She bent down and placed a flyer in a repurposed metal box painted with colorful green plants and the number 420.

"Well, that certainly casts a pall over the day, doesn't it?"

There was something comforting in Howard's voice. She couldn't be sure why she felt so safe around him, but he always understood when she needed support. Not unlike her own Leo.

"Mr. Violette's offer aside, what should we do, Howard? I hate to sound like an insolent child, but I'm tossing and turning at night."

Howard removed his Fighting Saucy Salmon cap. The local basketball team utilized the image of a fierce fish swimming in a restless ocean inside a glass. "I think what we do, Mrs. Reed, is finish our door-to-door canvass. Someone has to know what Gladiola is up to, and once we have that information, we'll set this investigation on the back burner while we figure out what to do with your Mr. Violette."

She nodded enthusiastically and continued walking down the middle of the block until she reached 422 Raspberry Drive. "I've never met these people. Have you, Howard?"

Howard shook his head. "No time like the present. We could use another ally. Why don't you see if anyone is home?"

A home partially obstructed by a mixture of out-of-control wildflowers, weeds, and blackberries, Howard used one arm to hold the foliage back while Gemini carefully stepped over stickery branches to make her way to the front stoop.

Once he joined her, she knocked. They found that it usually took several knocks before suspicious neighbors came to the door, and this inhabitant never attended block parties.

On the fourth knock, as she was rolling up a flyer to leave in the door, it slowly opened.

"Hello, I'm Gemini Reed. I'm your neighbor from—"

"Know who you are." The disembodied voice appeared to be attached to a younger man, as yet unseen.

"Oh. I'm afraid you've caught me off guard. I can't remember making your acquaintance, Mr...."

"Quentin. Just call me Quentin."

"All right then, Quentin. We're dropping off flyers about an upcoming neighborhood meeting. We'd love to have you there." She thrust a flyer into the darkness in front of her, half-wondering if that particular appendage would still be attached when she withdrew it.

When nothing happened, she turned around and shrugged at Howard. He nodded and joined her on the broken cement stoop.

"Quentin? I'm Howard Beachmont. Also your neighbor. I've lived in this neighborhood for almost twenty years. How long have you been here?"

"What is it you want? My mother and I don't like strangers."

"We wanted to ask you some questions about Gladiola Crabbitz. Have you met her?"

He didn't have a chance to finish before the door swung open, revealing a man dressed in a thick, fuzzy sweater and wearing square wire-rimmed glasses. Behind him, a tiny, hunched-over woman with long gray hair hanging past her waist appeared. "I'm Hetty. You can call me Hetty."

"I've got this, Mother," Quentin snapped. She shrugged and retreated.

Quentin eyed Gemini suspiciously and then turned toward Howard. "You know then?"

"Yes, of course. That's why we wanted your opinion."

Gemini let out a slow breath. Howard was so good on the fly.

Quentin opened the door wider but didn't offer to let them in. Instead, he folded his thick arms over the belt of his rust-colored corduroy pants.

"Gladiola hosted a meeting of her own. She was worried the two of you are a danger to her and her nephew."

Gemini gasped. This was worse than anything she'd heard before. "Then you can understand why we're so upset. We hope you'll come and hear our side of things too."

Quentin took another step outside, nearly knocking Gemini off the small cement pad. "You do know we have an FBI agent in the neighborhood?" He leaned forward and pointed to the next house over. "I'm in sixteen true crime online groups. Maxine always appreciates my advice."

Quentin smiled proudly as his body twisted one way and then the other. "We think Gladiola has a secret she doesn't want anyone to know. That's what we think."

From somewhere other than the doorway, a disembodied voice added, "It was a block meeting, son. A secret one, and now you've gone and blabbed it to the suspects. Gladiola says the two of you are in cahoots with some developer who wants to put up apartment buildings on your properties. Got the block worked into a suds."

After ascertaining the location of the mystery voice—an open window behind a thorny blackberry bush—Gemini glanced helplessly at Howard and then back at Quentin. "When did this block meeting happen?"

"It was before the one you missed, Mrs. Reed." Quentin's mouth lifted slightly in the corners. "We were all sworn to secrecy. Maxine and I felt there was something fishy going on."

"That's odd. Neither of us have any plans to move, or to sell. I can assure you both we're here to stay."

Hetty made a small chirping noise. Gemini couldn't be sure whether it was a happy or angry sound.

"Well, I don't know." She slammed the window shut, forcing a rush of air containing the scent of too many cats and not enough litter boxes up their noses.

"I'm sorry about her." For the first time, Quentin appeared to warm up to them. "She's funny around new people. That's why I moved in, so she wouldn't have to deal with the public. If you need any help, just ask. Maxine and I would be happy to assist you in any way we can."

Quentin reached into the pocket of his corduroys and handed Gemini a glittery gold business card that read "Quentin Zahn, True Crime Aficionado".

After they thanked Quentin and were out of earshot, Gemini turned and stared at Howard. "I'd like to say that's the strangest thing that's happened to me all week, but sadly, it's only one of many. Now what?"

"At least we have confirmation that Gladiola Crabbitz is poisoning our neighbors' minds."

He stepped aside, allowing Gemini to make her way back through the tall, stickery brush. The last stop, Maxine Smart's home, was in direct contrast to Quentin's. The lawn was neatly manicured and a pot containing purple and orange pansies sat on the porch. After knocking without a response, Gemini tucked a flyer underneath her peach-colored welcome mat.

Walking back toward their homes, the sound of a speeding car caused them to pause. When it became apparent the car wasn't stopping, they retreated to the perfectly-manicured lawn of Maxine Smart.

The car veered up on the sidewalk and screeched to a halt, barely missing the fire hydrant.

Gladiola Crabbitz got out and slammed the door so hard it made Gemini jump. Gladiola marched up Maxine's driveway, her black heels clacking as she shook a flyer above her head. "You're slandering me!" she screeched. "You two are causing trouble and I won't stand for it!"

Spit flew from her mouth as she raged. Luckily, it missed its intended victims. Having never spent any time close-up with Gladiola, Gemini took a moment to study her. A round-faced woman with large, dark eyes and pink lipstick, she appeared to be in her mid-50s. Her hair was piled high on her head in a style they used to call a beehive. She wore pearls around her neck and a simple, fitted blue dress. This woman could have walked out of a magazine ad from Gemini's youth.

"Your name isn't mentioned once, Mrs. Crabbitz," Howard replied calmly. "We're simply inviting neighbors over for a gathering, that's all."

Gladiola narrowed her gaze. "I'm a widow. It's been two years since my George died and, ever since, people have been out to get me. That's why my nephew moved in. We both know what you're doing and you won't get away with it."

"Our flyers are no different from yours," Howard retorted. "Just informing our neighbors of a gathering. As far as I know, we're allowed to hand out invitations."

He pointed to the crumpled paper to make his point.

Even though they hadn't done anything wrong, Gemini's face turned crimson and guilt coursed through her veins. In her time working as a legal secretary for Fleagal, Feelgood and Flem, her son-in-law's law firm, she learned that in order to diffuse a potentially difficult client, diversion was best.

"You're dressed up." Both Howard and Gladiola turned to glare at her.

"What?"

"I said you're dressed up. On your way to a special event?"

Gladiola looked like a sailboat without wind. "I... I'm going to a luncheon, if you must know. It's for widows. We take care of our own."

Howard nodded.

"I'm sure it's a comfort for you, dear." Gemini touched Gladiola's elbow for emphasis.

After a few moments of awkward silence, Gladiola turned abruptly. "I'm leaving," she called over her shoulder. "But understand that I'm watching you both."

As she drove off, Howard waved. Gladiola didn't look at them.

"Gemini Reed, you've won my undying admiration. Again."

"Accolades aside, we've got to come up with a new plan. Gladiola has discovered our secret meeting, so one of us needs to have another brilliant idea."

SLEEP WAS in short supply that night. Between Gladiola's paranoia, Alistair's murder request, and Feather's unusual behavior, she understood why. Gemini just couldn't figure out how to fix it. She was going through the list of herbs one of their clients had suggested for combating sleeplessness when an odd thing happened.

It sounded like her cupboards were opening and shutting continuously, as though someone were looking for something but couldn't find it. Brandon, her son-in-law, offered to install a security system, but she was pleased with the one Tug and Feather gifted her. They were alerted to a break-in just as soon as it happened. Which begged the question, what was happening now? They should have called.

She lowered herself slowly to the floor, remembering just which boards squeaked and avoiding them. In her bedroom, she kept a baseball bat. Tug jokingly taught her how to use it, just in case. "You've got a heck of a right-field homer in you, Gem," he had mused.

As she crept to the kitchen, she thought of Sophia and how, at Gemini's funeral, her daughter would stand before those gathered and, almost gleefully, explain that her mother refused a high-dollar security system. "I told her so," she would utter with a not-so-subtle dig to the woman in the coffin.

Gemini reached for the light switch with one hand while wielding the bat with the other. Tug said that wasn't how it was done, but that was her only option.

She quickly flipped the switch and swung the bat, narrowly missing the candy jar where she kept the Sugar Shells for her grandson.

There was no one in the room. It would have been a huge relief, had she not seen for herself cupboard doors banging open and closed. Blinking twice to make sure she wasn't really asleep, she called, "Who is playing tricks on me? Whoever you are, I've got a security system. The police are on their way."

When no one replied, she chided herself for not bringing her phone in with her. As she turned to retrieve it, she felt a cold chill go down her spine and a rush of air in one ear.

Once again, Gemini raised her bat, turned around, and swung with all her might.

"You always were quick to anger. I told my Leo he should have married that nice Catholic girl from

Piney Falls. I would've had ten grandchildren instead of one."

The bat dropped to the floor as Gemini blinked rapidly. "Mother Reed? Tickle my feet and call me Suzy! How is a dead woman standing in my kitchen?"

CHAPTER 12

FEATHER

Feather cleared her mind and waited. When it came to the spirit world, she had learned how to invite them when she was ready to listen. She envisioned a little shop with a flashing OPEN sign.

As soon as she heard a ball bouncing across the floor, she opened them to find a young girl with long spiral curls dressed in a white pinafore covering a dark dress. Her high-pitched giggle was infectious, causing Feather to giggle softly too.

Millicent died during the 1918 Spanish Flu epidemic and was always in search of a playmate. Feather gave in on the days she wasn't busy, or, more accurately, when she needed help from the other side.

"Sweetie, I'm going to play ball with you for ten minutes."

The child paused and cocked her head to the side. "For why? You want me to testivate again?"

"It's 'investigate,' and yes. You did such a good job last time that I knew you were the right detective for this job."

Millicent dropped the translucent ball and sat cross-legged next to Feather. "Is this another secret that I can't tell anyone?"

Feather nodded. "All good detectives know when to keep a secret. Are you a good detective?"

"I'm the BEST!" Her emphasis on the last word caused a sharp wind to whirl around the room, even though none of their apartment windows were open.

"For this assignment, I'll need you to sing."

"What song? My Babby taught me this one..."

Her tiny, off-key voice would have been cringe-worthy if Feather didn't enjoy Millicent so much.

"La...la...Joe's in the garden, begs your pardon, he's—"

Feather raised her hand in the air. "That one is perfect. I'll tell you just when to sing for me, but first, let's play catch!"

JAYDEN LOOKED RESPLENDENT AS ALWAYS. Today's on-point look included a navy blue catsuit with silver stripes. Her long nails were painted silver and black and her lipstick was black.

"You didn't call before you came, like usual. What's up?"

Feather plopped down in the chair. *Now, Millicent!*

"Oh, I've been getting some really strange clients lately. I was hoping you could give me some advice."

Jayden winced but continued. "My vision seems to be a little off today. Maybe you could spend a minute clearing your mind so I can help you better?"

"Sure." Feather closed her eyes and went through the motions of meditation. *La...la...la...da's in the garden, begs your pardon...*

Between Millicent's loud, off-pitch singing and Feather's undeniable guilt over tricking Jayden, there was no way she could clear her mind even if she wanted.

"What about now? Are you getting anything? Feather?" Jayden's voice broke.

Her eyes snapped open. Jayden sat with her head in her hands, uncharacteristically morose. If there was one thing to count on, it was Jayden's composure. She never let it be known if she was sad or mad, or anything in between. Feather's heart sunk. The last thing she wanted was to bring her friend and mentor to a state of mental collapse.

"What's wrong? Is it me? I'm so sorry. I didn't mean to—"

"It's not you, doll." Jayden reached in her desk drawer and pulled out a tissue, carefully dabbing her eyes. "I've got a new client and, ever since we signed the contract, things haven't been the same."

Feather reached across the desk and grabbed Jayden's hand. "You can tell me anything, Jayden. You know I won't betray your confidence."

It was the same thing Jayden had said to her hundreds of times. Somehow, it was much more difficult to be on this end of the conversation.

Her mentor looked as though she were sizing up a prospective employee, searching Feather's face for any signs of deceit. It hurt.

"This client is retired and spends her time going on archaeological digs. During her most recent dig in Costa Rica, she found this."

Jayden opened an envelope sitting on her desk and pulled out four large photos of a small bowl. It was clear that, at one point, it had been painted green with some kind of symbol rimming the bowl. There was something familiar about these photos, but Feather couldn't place where or when she'd seen them before.

"What's this? Is it some kind of good luck charm?"

"She's not sure. But ever since she brought it home, she's had ghosts visiting her. I guess that's the wrong way to phrase it. She's had angry spirits torturing her every night. She's taken to sleeping in a hotel most nights thinking they can't get to her there."

"Why doesn't she return the bowl? Wouldn't that end all of this?"

Jayden nodded. "It would, if this were a run-of-the-mill haunting."

"But you don't believe that."

Jayden grinned. "You've come to know me too well, doll. Yes, I suspect this is a curse. Much more difficult to get rid of once you're afflicted. To make matters worse, I seem to have caught the same bug, so to speak."

Feather couldn't believe what she was hearing. Jayden was the most experienced paranormal investigator she knew. If she wasn't immune to this curse, no one was safe.

"My gifts have been out of whack. Yesterday, I had a vision of Lulu falling to her death. She dropped out of an open window at the rooftop restaurant on the corner. With every drop of attitude I'd hired her for, Lulu informed me that she'd fallen last night."

"You were right on target!"

Jayden shook her head decisively. "She fell getting out of her car. Scraped a knee. I'm sure my spirit friends are having a good laugh."

"Oh."

Jayden stood abruptly, staring out an impressive bank of windows to hide her tears from Feather.

Turning her back didn't hide the fact that her shoulders were heaving. It hurt Feather's heart. The thought of someone insinuating Jayden was a hired killer was madness. She was barely able to keep her life on track at this point, let alone harm someone else.

Feather had run out of supportive words. "What can I do for you? How can I help?"

A warm smile encompassed Jayden's lovely face. It was the same one Feather relied on every time she was at the end of her own rope. "You're a sweetheart. There's nothing right now, but..."

"Lean on me, Jayden. I've done it with you a hundred times!"

Jayden sighed. "Okay. I hate to make this more of an issue than it is, but... there is someone following me. I noticed them three days ago, when I was dropping my catsuits at the cleaners. It all began when I took this client."

She reached in her drawer and pulled out a small circular object on a key chain. "I want you to take this. If something happens to me, push this button."

"I'm not high ranking, I'm only a—"

"At this point, I don't know who to trust, but I do trust you, doll."

CHAPTER 13

GEMINI

Gemini spun around. She couldn't believe what—or who—stood in her kitchen.

She hadn't thought about Mother Reed in years. Hers was the only funeral Gemini had attended where she had to stifle a smile the entire service. The woman was rude, argumentative, and disrespectful of her son's marriage. If there was a line, she'd find a way to cross it. When she died, Gemini looked in the coffin and found it was the first time she didn't want to choke the woman.

"Yes, I'm dead. But not dead enough to miss your annoying self-talk."

Gemini was rarely at a loss for words, but she was truly gob smacked. Ruthmarie Reed appeared to have stepped out of Gemini and Leo's wedding album, 38 years ago.

Her short, dark hair was cut at severe angles around her round face, and her bangs hung in a straight line over unruly eyebrows and thick-framed glasses. Luckily, Leo resembled his father.

Gemini remembered how she and Leo giggled at the reception about the giant corsage she insisted on pinning to her sea foam green mother-in-law's dress. "It's my day to be treated like royalty. My only son gets married once. Or maybe twice, by the looks of her."

Tonight, Gemini couldn't help but stare. Every single detail about her mother-in-law was the same, as though they'd stepped back in time. Ruthmarie's wiry eyebrows went every which direction and one eye glanced to the right while the other peered into her soul. Nothing had changed. She was even wearing the fluorescent pink lipstick the photographer begged her to remove.

And now the smell made perfect sense. Ruthmarie used the most offensive perfume—a combination of black licorice and pizza.

"Mother... Ruthmarie, I've never seen a ghost before. I don't mean to stare. You look—"

"Like I did at my only son's wedding?" She placed her hands on her ample hips and glared. "That's the deal. I could pick my favorite look if I agreed to help you. You can bet I didn't ask to come back as the 104-year-old raisin who left this world the first time."

When she laughed, Gemini flinched. It was a shrill sound Leo used to liken to a crow being beaten to death.

"What's so funny?"

"That I had to think about it before agreeing to help you."

Same old bitter woman.

"You must know about Leo. I assume you've been watching over him?"

Ruthmarie's face softened slightly. "Oh yes. My darling boy and I have lovely conversations almost every evening."

"I don't understand. Leo isn't dead."

"He's not, but his mind is in a state of limbo. Inside here," she thunked her temple with a meaty finger, "my dear son is still as sharp as ever."

There was a glow around her cranky mother-in-law, and Gemini wondered if she'd turned over a new leaf upon entering the other side. Ruthmarie's words comforted Gemini. It validated what she knew: The man she loved was still in there somewhere, even if the doctors tried telling her he may never fully recover.

"The kettle is boiling."

Gemini whipped around and, in the next instant, her kettle whistled.

"We have to get busy. They could decide to snatch me away at any moment." Ruthmarie's voice was sharp. "Make your tea and be quick about it."

It was the same, bitter woman who did her best to break up their marriage. Ruthmarie had an eternity to work things out, and it didn't seem like she was in a hurry to get started. It didn't matter. This dream would end soon enough.

She poured a cup of chamomile lemon and sat down. "Ruthmarie?"

A finger tapped her on the shoulder and she jumped, spilling onto her favorite robe. Laughter. Again.

"Stop that! If you're here to help, then help!"

Her mother-in-law appeared in the chair across from her, the usual smug look of satisfaction covering her ghostly face. It occurred to Gemini that not only was this ghost wearing clothing that hadn't fit her in decades, she was exactly the same age she'd been that day.

This Ruthmarie was 54, not the elderly woman who clung on to life until every ounce of joy had been squeezed from the staff at the care center. Now, she appeared younger than Gemini. One more slight.

As if reading her mind, Ruthmarie muttered, "You didn't age well. I'm glad Sophia takes after her father's side."

It had been a long time since she'd had to raise her inner shield to prevent these jabs from hurting her. She'd been too quick to praise her mother-in-law for becoming a better soul. "Get on with it!"

Ruthmarie harrumphed. "Still rude, I see."

Gemini looked away, taking a sip of her tea. That was the last time she would allow this woman, ghost or no ghost, to get under her skin.

"I'm here to inform you that Gladiola Crabbitz is interested in destroying you."

It was Gemini's turn to chuckle. "Tell me something I don't know. If you came back just to give me that tidbit, it was a waste of fancy wedding clothes and that awful hair color you used."

The church had reeked of formaldehyde on their wedding day, a byproduct of Ruthmarie's cheap hair dye, despite the fact that Gemini ordered six dozen fragrant lilies.

"No, there's more. Gladiola thrives on chaos. She's here, in Charming, to ruin you and Howard."

Gemini clucked her tongue. "Why? And why myself and Howard? We're just two normal neighbors, living life."

"That's exactly why. She has a real bee in her bonnet when it comes to happy people. You know how some people thrive on drama? That woman thrives on misery."

All of the old feelings came bubbling up to the surface. Ruthmarie was masterful with her games. "Come to our place for dinner, Gemini. We're having a picnic. You can bring your potato salad." When Gemini had arrived wearing blue jeans and an old t-shirt (Leo was out of town), everyone in attendance stared in shock. The party was a wine tasting event, with local vineyard owners pouring their recent vintages.

Everyone except Gemini dressed for a formal event. "That will teach me to trust the old bat," she muttered. And yet she did. Time and time again.

"It's still unclear why this concerns you. That last time I came to visit you in the nursing home, you told your assistant to frisk me before I left. You were convinced I stole your valuables."

Ruthmarie's mouth twitched, as it always had when she wanted to argue but felt it wasn't the right time. "Do you remember why I was in the nursing home? I was still a healthy woman."

"No, you..."

You're getting ready to argue with a ghost, Gemini Reed.

"Leo thought you made a rash decision. He'd just re-painted every room for you and hired in-home care."

"This young couple moved in next door. They brought me flowers and a nice tuna casserole and told me to call them if I ever needed help. I thought they meant it."

Ruthmarie leaned back in the chair and, as she did, she crossed her legs, right over left. Her signature move when she knew she was wrong but stubbornly wouldn't admit it. It was remarkable that a ghost could seem so human.

"The young bride came over frequently. A pretty thing who always dressed up like it was Sunday. She volunteered to do the dishes and clean the house, and eventually she convinced me I didn't need a caretaker, or to move into your place."

"Leo thought you'd lost your marbles." Gemini slapped her hand over her mouth. "Sorry. That just came out. I assume in death you're more forgiving."

"You would be wrong to assume that." Ruthmarie trained her hollow eyes on Gemini, causing Gemini to shiver.

"As I was about to say, my neighbors did a fine job keeping my house clean and buying groceries, but eventually I needed more help than they could offer. Leo, no doubt egged on by a greedy spouse..."

"Why would I—" Gemini caught herself before she wasted the words and her middle-of-the-night energy.

"Leo had me placed in that end-of-life prison. After my death, those same neighbors sued my estate. They insisted their reputations had been damaged when I was taken from my home, and their care, and placed in a nursing home."

Ruthmarie paused to take a breath. *Was it a breath?* Gemini would have to ask Feather about that.

"Leo and his sister were so stressed, it took five years off their lives."

That time had been a blur, one that she readily put behind her. "Brandon's firm handled the whole thing. That's how he and Sophia started dating. All I remember about the couple is..." Gemini gasped. "Gladiola?"

"You're slow but eventually you catch on. Since she and her husband walked away with next to nothing, she tracked you down after his death. Well, she and her nephew, who egged her on."

"I'll call Chief Boulder in the morning. He'll handle her."

Gemini took another sip of tea. Yes, that scent was just as she remembered it: black licorice and verbena, and as it had on her wedding day, it was giving her a stomachache.

"No, you can't. At least not yet."

Ruthmarie's expression changed from a sour-faced mother of the groom to one of pure, unadulterated fear.

"What's going on? The boogie man chasing you? Or is it the Tompkins' German shepherd?"

Gemini smirked as she remembered the neighborhood tussle to force the Tompkins family to keep Sandman inside so Ruthmarie didn't have to look at him out her window when she did dishes.

"No, it's worse. I'll come back when I have more information."

As she stood and turned, Gemini stared once again with fascination. "Who's chasing you? And how do you escape them?"

In an instant, Ruthmarie dissolved.

Maybe it was time to give up spicy foods.

CHAPTER 14

FEATHER

The scent of aged bourbon and stale smoke tickled Feather's nostrils. On her second visit to The Bleeding Rose, an entirely new set of smells filled her nose. She scanned the room, quickly spotting Alistair Violette lounging in a plush armchair by the fireplace. The flickering firelight cast a sinister glow on his pronounced features, making him appear even more mysterious than he did in their previous encounters.

"Back so soon, chickadee?"

Feather jumped. "Where did you come from?"

Azalea, dressed in a shimmery silver gown and headband with one feather, shrugged, causing the numerous beads around her neck to jingle. "People say I turn up at the worst times. Did you decide to take Captain Monochrome up on his offer?"

Feather was stunned. Not only by the quick

outfit change but also by the amount of time it had taken for the entire Bleeding Rose, apparently, to learn of her conversation with Alistair.

"Yes? No... I'm... I'm not sure."

That was the truth. When Tug said he was going back to the warehouse to work on his big order, she jumped in the car and drove here without giving it a second thought. "When I step through the door, it feels like I'm lost in another time. None of my gifts work and it leaves me off-balance."

It was true; she had no sense of right or wrong. Jayden would know why.

Jayden...

"Yeah, the owner wanted it that way. People don't come to bars because they're feeling good about themselves. The owner arranged it so everyone is on a level playing field. You see those schmucks in the corner?" Azalea pointed to a table with four men who would burst into laughter and then return to silence.

"Yes, I see them."

"They all tried to get into P.I.N.K. as mind readers, reading the thoughts of the recently departed, but Jayden Ko threw them out for lack of ability."

"That's too bad. What are they doing now? Playing a game?"

"They're telling dirty jokes. Funny, ain't it?"

Azalea elbowed Feather, who didn't appreciate the gesture. "Ouch!"

Feather turned again to glance at Alistair, who was staring intently into the fireplace. "Do I have to go through your whole speech again? If so, let's get started. I need to talk business with Alistair."

"You're the star of P.I.N.K., Feather Jones. If something happened to you because I didn't do my due diligence, I'd find myself in a heap of trouble."

It made her uncomfortable when she was publicly praised. Growing up as she did, being the embarrassment of the family, she'd never grown accustomed to accolades. She was glad the poor lighting hid the color in her cheeks.

Azalea clucked her tongue. "I guess you don't have to sign in this once. Consider it your lucky day!"

"Great." Feather started forward, but Azalea stuck out a hand before she could take one step.

"That don't mean I can let you walk around unchaperoned, toots. Follow me."

Feather noticed a table to their left, where a woman peered into a large, translucent ball. As if sensing her question, Azalea cupped her hand around Feather's ear and whispered, "Dorinda's Ball of Wonder. She tells fortunes here three nights a week. They're just inspirational quotes she finds on the internet."

After passing more booths filled with card readers and someone wearing a bejeweled swami hat, they finally reached the fireplace. It looked so much closer when they were standing at the entrance, but now Feather found herself out of breath.

He didn't look up when they approached. Instead, his eyes were trained straight ahead, staring intently at something in the fire that Feather couldn't see. If no one truly had access to their abilities in The Bleeding Rose, he was sure putting on a good show.

Azalea cleared her throat. When that didn't rouse him from his stupor, she slapped his back. "Ya got company, mister. Look alive."

His head snapped up as though he'd just awoken from a trance, and he glared at Azalea as though he was going to physically harm her.

Feather quickly jumped between them. "I told Azalea that I was short on time and needed to speak with you. Don't blame her."

Alistair's body relaxed and his face became serene once more. Something that irritated Feather.

"I've been expecting you."

"Trouble finding a parking space?" Azalea crossed her arms and leaned on one hip. "The Bleeding Rose validates." When Feather shook her head, Azalea continued, "I wanna make sure no harm comes to our Feather here. Do ya promise me?"

Alistair laughed softly. "I can assure you, I have no intentions of bringing harm to Feather or her dear partner, Gemini. Exactly the opposite."

His voice was smooth, like he was giving gardening tips on public radio instead of hiring a hit. Azalea didn't move.

"You've got guests to attend to. While you focused your energy on unneeded protection, a raucous group stumbled in. They've already had too many drinks."

"Huh?"

All of a sudden, the door to The Bleeding Rose swung open and four men in their early twenties toppled in, laughing so loudly the entire room went quiet. "We'll see who has the last laugh," Azalea muttered as she stormed up to confront them.

Feather turned her attention back to Alistair, who had taken the high-backed chair opposite her. He motioned for her to sit.

"I don't know what your game is, Alistair Violette, but no one in the state of Oregon will take you up on your offer. Jayden is well known and loved."

Alistair took a drink from a glass containing something orange. "Feather, you must realize that not everyone is as honest as you. I could get any number of people to do this job. Especially for the price I'm willing to pay."

"Then why me? And Gem?"

"Because you have the most to lose if your mentor is allowed to continue. There is a price on your head, my dear girl."

"I don't believe you." She sat back, defiantly crossing her arms over her chest. The heat from the fireplace caused sweat to run down the center of her back. Or maybe it was her own anger.

"Ms. Ko took the reins of the paranormal organization because she was the most powerful person and the logical choice. After Mr. Beasley, that is."

Feather hadn't heard anyone in their circle refer to him by his given name. It seemed so disrespectful. "She didn't want the job. No one else would take it."

Alistair swirled his drink, causing his ice cubes to clank. "But then you came along, Ms. Jones. When Jayden Ko learned of your abilities, she decided to snap you up before anyone else could."

"Ha!"

Luckily, Azalea was still wrangling the unruly crowd at the front and no one heard Feather's outburst. "Who could possibly 'snap me up,' as you say?"

"P.I.N.K. isn't the only paranormal organization here. Your little band of misfits is just the place for do-gooders like yourself. There is another group, called Renegades of Unearthly Shadows & Terrors, or R.U.S.T. We are much more powerful because we refuse to dampen our strengths by conforming to societal norms."

Despite the fact she was sweating profusely, a chill ran down Feather's back. "I don't understand."

Alistair leaned forward, so close that Feather

inhaled his sickly sweet breath. Her body shuddered, and she coughed violently as she tried to expel the thick substance from her lungs. "Of course you do. It frightens you to think about it because you assumed you were safe because of your abilities. You're not, my dear girl. Jayden Ko is a liar and I have proof. She's been planning your undoing since the first day you joined."

"Oh, I get it. You want me to join your little group. As my first assignment or test, or whatever you want to call it, I'm going to kill Jayden."

"In a manner of speaking, yes."

"And Gem? You're initiating her too?"

"I spend time getting to know those in our group. And you, Feather Jones, are loyal to a fault. If your Gemini Reed is involved, I'm assured you'll follow my instructions." His eyes looked yellow in the firelight. "You don't want her to come to any harm."

Feather's eyes widened. "Are you trying to say I have to join your group and help you get rid of Jayden or Gem's life is in danger?"

Alistair leaned back, swirling his glass again. "Your words, not mine."

Feather hesitated for a moment, her inner turmoil evident in her furrowed brow and clenched fists. She was about to strike a deal with this man, agreeing to end the life of a friend—someone who, like her, had been an outcast before finding others who could hear the dearly departed. "What's your proof? Jayden's the most honest person I know, next to Gem and Tug."

Alistair reached into the pocket of his cape and pulled out two photos. "Recognize these?"

They were the exact same photos Jayden showed her when she told Feather about her new client. Bowls with ghostly attachment. "So? You probably stole them from her desk. Doesn't prove a thing."

"Not my desk. Yours. Jayden took these photos from your purse at the last P.I.N.K. meeting. It was Practice for Beginning P.I.N.K.s night, so all experienced members brought photos of something ancient for the new members. Your partner thought she got a reading on these from the fifth century."

After she'd gone home that night, the photos she'd borrowed from Tug's *Museums of the World* magazines and had framed were missing. She assumed her student accidentally took them home.

Still, it was completely out of character for her mentor. Feather could feel her face heating up. "You'll have to do better. I'm not convinced your finger isn't in this somehow. If one of my best friends' lives is on the line, I'm not prepared to take such a dramatic step without more evidence."

His mouth twitched slightly and, for a moment, Alistair acted as though he'd been caught in a lie. "What if I'm right and you do nothing? Do you want to take that chance? Poor Jayden may face torture from an angry client. So much pain. They won't be as understanding as you, Miss Jones."

Her entire body was likely to go up in flames soon. "You've made your point. Terms first."

"Of course," Alistair replied smoothly, his voice as rich and intoxicating as the orange drink he sipped. "I will provide you with everything you need to complete the task, as well as a substantial sum for your services. In return, I expect complete discretion and unwavering commitment to the job."

Feather weighed his words carefully, searching for hidden traps or underlying motives. She was no stranger to deception, but something about Alistair's charming façade made her stomach churn with unease.

"Deal," she finally agreed, extending her hand to shake on it. Just as their fingers brushed against each other, a familiar voice cut through the tension like a razor-sharp knife.

"Feather? What are you doing here?"

She froze, her heart hammering in her chest as she turned to face the source of the voice. Phoebe Pepper, a fellow member of P.I.N.K., stood behind her dressed in a raspberry sweater and silver wig.

As Feather fought to find words, Phoebe continued, "I come here a lot and I've never run into you."

Phoebe's gaze bore through her like a searing hot knife. Did she know? How could she?

"I don't know what you two are cooking up, but

me and my buddy here need some girl time." Phoebe grasped Feather's arm and pulled until she stood.

Alistair leaned back and folded his hands over his abdomen. "Darling girl, is it your recent faux pas that makes you suspicious of others? Losing your club's ranking over a jealous rage, wasn't it?"

Phoebe lunged at Alistair, caught in the nick of time by Feather. "You don't know anything. It was all a misunderstanding!"

"Let's go get some air, Phoebe." Feather pushed firmly on Phoebe's back.

"You'll return soon so we can continue our conversation, Miss Jones?"

Feather swallowed hard and nodded, refusing to meet Phoebe's questioning gaze.

After they'd left the building, Feather released Phoebe's arm. "Don't pay attention to him. He likes to push people's buttons."

"You know I didn't plan on falling in love with a ghost, right?"

Due to Feather's impressive skills, they'd gone from a Level K to a Level G in the Paranormal Investigative National Organization. Phoebe was working a case where a woman wanted to communicate with her dead boyfriend because she thought he was haunting her.

Phoebe started a relationship with the ghost, who taunted his girlfriend with the news. As soon as the organization found out, they were busted back to K rank.

"I know you'd never do that on purpose."

Feather didn't know her well enough to know whether it was true, but now wasn't the time to argue.

"That guy is bad news, Feather! What are you doing hanging out with him? His R.U.S.T. group was here when I came with my boyfriend." She touched Feather's arm. "Don't worry, this one is alive." She giggled. "I overheard them plotting someone's demise."

Feather gulped. "Did you hear who it might have been?"

Phoebe stared, incredulous. "Does it matter? They're causing harm, not helping like we do. They don't have any respect for the paranormal investigator's creed."

Feather bit her lip and looked away. Everything Phoebe was saying was true.

"Feather," Phoebe continued, her voice cracking with emotion, "if you're thinking of helping these bad dudes, your days with P.I.N.K. will be over. You signed a contract stating you wouldn't use your gifts to end the life of another unless you were in danger. Is that what you want?"

Feather looked into Phoebe's eyes, searching for a lifeline. "I..." Feather whispered, her thoughts tangled like autumn leaves caught in a whirlwind.

"I... I won't do it. I won't let him manipulate me into betraying everything I stand for."

Relief washed over Phoebe's face, but Feather could still see the hurt lingering behind her eyes.

"Good!"

"You won't tell anyone, will you?"

She was relieved that Phoebe hadn't asked for details.

Keep it together, Jones. You don't want to make her suspicious.

"Of course not! What kind of a gossip do you take me for?"

"Sorry. I didn't mean anything."

"Oh, and Feather? Be careful getting to your car. This neighborhood's not safe after nine."

CHAPTER 15

GEMINI

"I'm so sorry, Gem. My casserole took much longer than I expected." Tug leaned over and kissed her lightly on the cheek. Both Tug and Feather seemed to sense she needed a night out, away from the neighborhood drama.

"There's no reason for an apology. I'm just grateful to have good friends who don't mind dining with the neighborhood pariah."

All day she'd tried to think of the right way to tell Feather about her late-night visitor. Ghosts were Feather's territory, not Gemini's.

Would Feather believe her? Of course she would. This was Feather, not some clueless stranger. For some reason, though, the words stuck in her mouth.

"I'm going to work on a more detailed form for potential clients to fill out. To avoid further issues like Mr. Violette." She waited for Feather's reaction.

"Is that really necessary? I get where you're coming from, but people come to us when they're at their lowest. We don't want to scare them away by giving them extra paperwork to fill out."

It hurt Gemini's feelings all the way around. Usually, Feather was more receptive to her ideas. Gemini brought the frosty glass of lemonade to her lips, a large ice cube clunking against her face.

"Gem, I know this drives you nuts when I say it, but I'm worried about you."

Tug set an oblong glass dish on the table and removed his "Tug Bars Official" oven mitts. He and Olive were planning to go big by including merch to sell alongside Tug Bars at the Stuff You Didn't Know You Needed Convention.

Gemini took the metal spoon and heaped a cheesy clump onto her plate. "What do you call this again?"

"Cauliflower cheese casserole. As I was saying, I'm worried about you. Feather and I were talking..." Gemini noticed as his glance shifted to Feather. That was never a good sign. "...and we think you should move in here, at least until the dust settles on your block."

Though she couldn't love them more if she'd given birth to them, sometimes Feather and Tug got carried away with their concerns. "I'll be fine. It's not just me. Howard is in this too. That man has more connections than a solar system. And I told you about the FBI woman—"

"We need to be careful, Gemini," Feather warned, her eyes focused and serious. "Even if we don't entirely believe Alistair, he has a connection to Gladiola Crabbitz and that makes them dangerous."

Gemini nodded in agreement, her mouth tight. The Crabbitz problem had gone from something she and Howard were handling to the focus of the entire warehouse. Not exactly how she planned to handle things quietly. "I understand. We need to be discreet and strategic. Howard said the same thing."

"What if we could find out exactly what they're saying?" Tug asked.

"Babe, I think I know where you're going, and—"

"They're already invading Gem's privacy." Tug gave a giant sigh, one that both women had come to learn meant he wouldn't back down. "You trust me, right?"

"I'm going to start eating now. The two of you obviously have something to work out." Gemini brought her fork to her mouth and chewed slowly, keeping her gaze on her plate before a realization overtook her.

"Of course. That was the whole point of inviting you over."

Tug stood and filled her lemonade to the top. After he set it on the table, he disappeared into the bedroom.

"I thought you weren't going to tell him about Alistair? Did something change?"

Feather nodded slowly. "He wants to get his newest gadget to show you. And he already knows about Alistair." Her eyes were as big as saucers, indicating she didn't want any more questions in front of her fiance.

Tug returned and sat three small, circular objects on the table. Gemini picked one up and examined it. "What is this? A new type of headphone? They're getting so small these days." She sighed before setting it back on the table. "My Sophia keeps insisting that Taurus needs fancy ear-what-the-doodles to listen to his Spanish class. I don't know why I have to keep reminding her what happened to the last pair. How that child fit both of those up his nose will forever remain a mystery."

"This isn't for the ears, at least not directly. I'll place several around the perimeter of their home and we'll be able to hear everything the Crabbitzes say. Heck, we can even hear their phone conversations!"

"I... This makes me uncomfortable. I appreciate your concerns, but for now, Howard and I have a handle on things."

Feather raised a brow and nodded to Tug.

Since Gemini was already feeling a little hurt, this act didn't make her feel any better.

"Do you remember the case we had last month?

It involved the Brothers Whim. They thought their dead Grandpa Gristly was breaking the equipment in their Rumple-Milk-Skin-Care factory."

"Of course. It was one of the more interesting paranormal cases we've had." Feather took a drink of her lemonade. "It turned out to be their cousin Hansel Stews, who was very much alive."

"They sent a $5,000 bonus and a year's worth of skincare products for all four of us, just because we took them seriously."

Feather's eyes narrowed. "You're saying that all it will take to get your neighbor to leave you alone is to treat her like a client?"

She felt a little foolish now that Feather said it out loud, but Gemini had been thinking all day about ways she and Howard could build a bridge with Gladiola. After their recent encounter, she had high hopes.

Feather pulled out a chair next to her friend. "Let's go for a walk tomorrow in your neighborhood. I want to see if I pick up any entities."

Tug, carrying a large bowl filled with colorful grilled vegetables, sat down beside Feather. He reached over and gave her a peck on the cheek.

"That's a really good idea, hon. The exercise will do us good, at the very least."

Feather filled a plate, handing it to Tug before filling another for herself.

"You don't need to worry so much." Gemini

turned her head towards Tug. "Neither of you. I'm perfectly capable of taking care of myself."

They finished their meal in uneasy silence. Gemini was certain now; if she told Feather about her unexpected visitor, her young partner would decide she did, in fact, need to worry about Gemini. Ruthmarie would remain her secret.

"Gem, I will make you a promise. Let me listen in for one week and then I'll remove the devices. If they find out, I'll take full responsibility. I'll tell them I used to live in their home and can't let go."

"Oh dear. That's not wise, Tug. But put your device on for one week, if you must. If you don't hear anything concerning Howard or myself, I don't want to know about it. Understood?"

Both nodded in agreement.

"Now that it's been settled, I want to discuss a new look for the building. It looks so warehouse-y and I've been thinking about hiring someone to make a change."

"What were you thinking? Olive mentioned that she approached you about a fluorescent orange. She's worried the runway from the airport is too close and she doesn't want a collision." Tug helped himself to another spoonful of casserole.

"I'd like to do something in a traditional sky blue," Gemini continued between bites. "When Leo and I owned the hardware store, we always told people it was the most relaxing color. One day I asked Leo how he knew that and he shrugged and said it was the easiest color to mix with the biggest profit margin."

Tug jumped up, startling Gemini. No one ate as fast as that boy. "Wait until you try Feather's dessert creation. She made brownies."

It wasn't that Gemini didn't trust Feather to bake, exactly. It was more that she had heard the horror stories associated with her attempts to use the oven —overbaked, underbaked, too much baking powder, too little flour. It went on and on. "Can't wait."

Tug's phone chirped. "I'm a wheeler dealer. A big time appealer." A rap song from his favorite rapper, Ouchie. Tug said the ringtone motivated him.

Normally, they had a "no phone at the dinner table" policy, but when he was working on an order or she was working a case, things changed.

Tug squinted as he looked at the screen. "It's the prison."

"You'd better take it!" Feather said quickly. She went into the kitchen and returned with a plate of perfectly-arranged chocolate squares. "Gem, you don't have to eat these. Tug insisted I try to bake one more time. He thought it would prove to you that I'm open to suggestions. Like your idea of setting up a screening program for potential clients."

Tug glanced at her suspiciously one more time before excusing himself.

"Good news!" Tug sat down next to Feather and set his phone beside him.

"What is it, babe?"

"After our delivery today, the warden was so impressed that he wants me to come in once a week, maybe even teach a class on nutrition. He's going to pay me!"

"Is that safe?" Gemini asked, fully aware of the irony of her question. "What if you get shanked?"

Tug swatted the air. "Pssh. That's what happens in movies, not real life." He looked up at the clock and frowned. "I told Olive I'd be there in twenty. She's probably making a scene in the parking lot of Charming Acres."

It was time for Feather's phone to ring. As she wandered into the other room to talk, Gemini took a bite of a brownie. Doing her level best to keep her face from showing signs of distress, she reached for her glass. "Mm. So good."

Tug thrust one arm into his jacket and raised one brow. "Isn't she wonderful? Always trying something new."

"Yes, she is! I can't wait until you start giving her baking lessons."

"What?"

"She told me all about your helping her last night. Well, not so much that she told me, but I caught her sneaking in."

Gemini took another brownie and ate quickly.

"She admitted that the two of you had a baking lesson, and I urged her to show off her new skills tonight! You're quite the teacher, Gem!"

With full cheeks, Gemini nodded. She'd really stepped in it now; she couldn't spit it out while he watched. From her own baking mishaps, she recognized the lack of sugar and overabundance of baking powder—at least a tablespoon.

"Help yourself to more, Gem!"

Feather returned to the room with a storm brewing on her face.

Tug's phone rang again and Feather let out a sigh of relief. Olive's angry voice filled the air as Tug kept saying, "I'm leaving now, Olive, I promise."

After he'd kissed both women on the forehead and left the apartment, Gemini mustered up the will to confront Feather. "Can we talk about what happened last night?"

"That's the least of our worries, Gem."

CHAPTER 16

FEATHER

Feather sipped her coffee. "Are you sure you don't want any, Gem?"

"Good gracious, no. This time of night, caffeine would cause me to jump like a frog in a pan. No, I'll just stick to this herbal tea, thank you. What I would like is a better explanation for why we are sitting in the cold and dark when I should be home in bed!"

They were parked on Hazelnut Circle, three houses from the impressive four-story brick mansion where the mayor lived.

"I know you don't like to be out late, so we'll put in an hour to bill for and then we can leave."

"Feather Jones! Are you suggesting we lie to our client?"

Feather's mouth hung open. She wasn't used to Gemini questioning her decisions.

"Cheese and crackers, girl! I'm just teasing you! Of course that Mr. Violette is a nut, and we're going through the motions to make him happy. There's something very suspicious about him, though. I have to tell you, it makes me uneasy."

"I feel the same way, Gem." She stuck her hand in her pocket and massaged the ornament given to her by Jayden the day before. *If anything happens to me, use this to summon help.*

No amount of self-talk made this secret okay to keep. "Gem, I have to tell you something."

"Oh?" Gemini held the binoculars up to her eyes. They were night vision, a gift from Tug. Gemini often mentioned she used them to watch the neighborhood children play kick ball after dark.

"Alistair is trying to recruit me."

Gemini's face eased. "Well, that puts everything into perspective, doesn't it? I'm sure you said no. The less business we have with that man, the better."

It was almost as if her partner knew about her second visit to The Bleeding Rose. "No, I didn't. I—"

"That's Alistair!"

Gemini pointed to a cloaked figure leaving the mayor's gated grounds. He was holding two gnomes, one in each hand.

"Should we follow him?"

Feather was glad she drove this evening. Gemini was too aggressive when she was tailing a suspect. "I'm on it!"

The cloaked figure opened the door of a dark van and got in. It sped away, faster than Feather could turn her car around.

"Pedal to the metal, girlfriend!"

Gemini held onto the handle above the door in preparation for Feather's aggressive driving. Instead, Feather obeyed the speed limit.

"What are you doing? We're going to lose him!"

"The mayor's mansion is notorious for its police presence. I wouldn't be surprised if a cruiser has been here all evening and we just haven't noticed."

Gemini opened her window, letting in the evening's cool ocean breeze. As they drove, she pointed at a car and called, "It's Chief Boulder!"

So much for remaining incognito.

"See? I told you. Besides, there's only one way out of this neighborhood. Up ahead!"

Just ahead of them, slowed by speed bumps, was the dark van.

"Now what? He's going much too slow. He's going to figure out we're following him! Do something!"

Feather picked up Gemini's mug and smelled its contents. "You're not drinking decaffeinated tea, Gem. This is Catastrophically Caffeinated. Olive brought those samples in and you stuck them in your purse, just to be polite, remember?"

"Oh, bugger. No wonder I'm feeling shaky! Oh, Feather! Look!"

They trained their eyes on the windshield. The van was parked in front of them. The driver got out and came around to the back of the van. He opened the double doors, exposing homemade shelves full of gnomes.

"What in the world? Why would he show us? What should we do, Feather?"

"Give me a minute to think!" Feather snapped. "I'm sorry. I didn't mean that. He's obviously showing us for a reason."

The man closed the doors after a minute, got back in the driver's side, and put the car in gear.

"You don't have to apologize. I'm not myself this evening." Gemini drummed her fingers on the dash, annoying Feather further.

"See if you can make out the license plate, Gem. We'll need that information later."

She'd have to think of other things to keep her hopped-up partner busy. "Also, could you make note of where we're going? Detailed directions would be helpful in case we need to come back."

"Your wish is my command."

Gemini retrieved her readers and her small notepad that was mounted on a wooden board with a miniature light affixed at the top. It had been a gift from a client that pleased her to no end.

"A... two... no, is that a three?"

Feather's mind drifted to the real reason they

were here. Alistair's ruse to keep Gemini involved. Her poor partner was a pawn in his game and she didn't even know it.

His words about Jayden bothered her too. Feather had to admit: Jayden hadn't been herself for some time. She'd missed the last two P.I.N.K. meetings, which was totally out of character. There was a strict rule about missing meetings, and each member had to sign multiple forms agreeing to abide by them. Only one unexplained absence was allowed. You could miss two if you agreed to submit to a mind reading, which only Jayden and Capu could administer. If they found you were honest in your excuse for missing the second meeting, you could stay.

But still...

It was no reason for murder.

"Feather! Pay attention!"

"Gem, I told you—"

She couldn't believe her eyes. There was a rifle poking out of the van pointing directly at her windshield. She slammed on the brakes, causing Gemini to scream.

"That's not Alistair! Who's trying to kill us?"

Feather didn't answer, instead putting the car in reverse. Luckily, this time of night, there weren't many people out and about. When she was in high school, the kids joked that they rolled up the sidewalks and put them away. It made doing high school pranks much too easy.

The brake lights came on and the van began to turn around. It was a large vehicle and much more difficult to maneuver on this small residential street.

"What block did you say Chief Boulder was parked on?"

"Fourteenth. No, Thirteenth. No, Fifteenth. I'm sure. It's Fifteenth."

"I want you to take out your night vision goggles and start watching the alleys as we drive by. When you see him sitting in his car, I want you to yell, 'Now!'"

Gemini did as instructed, focusing on the alley-ways. The van driver found them easily and was closing in behind Feather's car.

"Now!"

Feather slowed down, opened her window, and tossed her mug of coffee over the top of the car. It shattered on the road. Next, she laid on her horn.

"Cheese and crackers! The man's sawing logs! Put it in park!"

"That's not safe, Gem!"

"Do it!"

Feather put her car in park and braced herself for the inevitable crash. She hoped her otherworldly friends would visit Tug and tell him what happened. Or maybe she would, if it didn't scare him too much.

Gemini jumped out of the car.

"Gem! No!"

Feather watched in horror as Gemini picked up a decorative rock on the lawn of a nearby home. It was far too heavy for Gemini to lift normally. Over-caffeinated Gemini possessed superhero bravado.

Gemini hoisted the rock on her shoulder and threw it toward Chief Boulder's cruiser. It hit the passenger door and landed with a thud on the ground.

Chief Boulder sat up abruptly, hitting his lights and siren before realizing what had happened.

The black van, which had sped up behind them, screeched to a halt. Feather closed her eyes and held her breath. A moment later, she heard the van speeding away. Before she'd even had a chance to catch her breath, she felt the hairs on her arms rising. "Now? Can't it wait?"

She felt a pull towards her rear view mirror. When she turned on the dome light and looked in the mirror, she recognized the face.

" Grandpa Gristly? The case is done, remember? We caught the criminal in our world."

Grandpa Gristly was a curmudgeon who, despite his demeanor, had nothing to do with the vandalism at Rumple-Milk-Skin.

"You're in some hot water, girl."

"This seems like a conversation that could wait, sir. My partner and I are in the middle of something, in case you hadn't noticed."

"Don't sass me, young lady. I'm only here because I owe a debt. You cleared my name, so this is your payment. The van following you was sent by R.U.S.T. as a warning. Do as you're told, or the next time those shots won't miss."

CHAPTER 17
GEMINI

"No more funny business, Gemini. Those people are professional killers and could have taken you out with one shot while you chewed the fat with the policeman."

Chief Boulder had no idea he'd almost witnessed a murder. When she woke him, he didn't seem concerned either. "Mrs. Reed? I was just parked here to think. Can you come in tomorrow and we'll talk about it?"

He didn't believe her. Feather suggested they regroup in the morning and decide how to proceed after a good night's rest.

Ruthmarie had other plans.

A good cup of chamomile was on her mind after such a stressful evening. Just as she dunked the teabag into her cup, she smelled that familiar smell.

"What is it this time?"

"Could have gotten yourself killed tonight. Doesn't surprise me much."

She didn't bother turning to face her mother-in-law. "From day one, when you told me, 'Gemini is a name hippies give a child hoping she will wave down men on street corners,' I was a disappointment, wasn't I? Utterly disgraceful."

"Your words, not mine. I'm just here to keep you focused on the investigation and not flitting around like a fly."

"Oh, Mother Reed." Gemini sighed as she remembered how many times she'd hoped the old woman would croak. Gemini waited impatiently for Leo to return from the nursing home. "Is she..."

"No," he'd reply with little emotion. Ruthmarie was 104 then, and everyone figured, or at least hoped, she would be dead long before then. Even the nurses who tended to her couldn't believe she'd hung on so long. But Gemini knew the real reason Ruthmarie Reed opened her eyes every morning; she did it out of spite for the rest of the world.

"Tell me what it is you want and then leave me to my tea. I deserve some peace and quiet after the night I had."

"Humph."

Gemini smiled, pleased she'd frustrated the old woman a little.

"You can't turn your back on Gladiola Crabbitz. She's got forces at her disposal, things you can't understand, and... shoot! I think he's heard me!." Leo was such a nice man, but his mother was a bitter, angry woman who complained about everything. Even Sophia, who was the darling of the family, wasn't immune to her wrath.

"Wait! What did you need to tell me?" She turned to find her kitchen empty. "Tug's coming to install listening devices tomorrow, so I'll be just fine. Thank you for allowing me time to drink my tea in my own home!"

The melody of tiny songbirds fighting for meal worms in her backyard feeder woke her. Instantly, Gemini felt the backache, tender forehead, and sore neck of someone who'd fallen asleep slumped over the table.

"Was I dreaming?"

Gemini rubbed the back of her neck and stood, reminded once more that it wasn't the optimal position for sleeping. Glancing down, she realized she was still wearing her favorite rose-print robe. On the table, an empty mug with a teabag string draped over the side gave her the impression that at least some of her recollection was true.

After walking around until her joints were suffi-ciently lubricated, she changed into her butterscotch pants with a maroon-striped blouse. She'd been hesitant to purchase them together, but the young sales associate assured Gemini that, these days, people didn't need exact matches in their wardrobe. She'd be a stylish grandma.

After applying a thin coat of Pink Cloud lipstick and brushing her silver hair, she inspected herself in the mirror and deemed the look sufficient. There was nothing she could do about the bags under her eyes, nor did she really care. An advantage of old age.

Her cell phone was still plugged in beside the bed from the night before, to Gemini's relief. At least something was normal. She picked it up and then put it down. Then she picked it up again, finally touching the preset number two.

"Sophia?"

"Mother! You know Taurus has toddler golf at 10. Why are you calling?"

The image of small children clubbing each other as the teacher tried —in vain— to calm them left Gemini shaking her head.

"I'll be brief. What do you remember about your Grandmother Reed?"

Sophia huffed with irritation. "That's what you found so important? Honestly, Mother, I wonder how your brain works sometimes."

"Just a moment of your time is all, dear."

"She was an awful old goat."

"Sophia! Not nice! I hope that's not how Taurus talks about me when I'm not around."

Though she knew the title was well earned, there

was still a small piece of her that felt paranoid she wasn't included as much as Brandon's mother.

"He loves his Grammie." Sophia moved the phone away from her ear as she yelled, "Tell Grammie how much you love her!"

"Poopy!"

Gemini suppressed a giggle. She knew Taurus found every excuse to irritate his mother.

"Grandma Four-us is here!"

"Was there anything else, Mother? I've got company."

"Oh, right. How nice she's visiting her grandson." Gemini did her best to disguise the hurt in her voice. "Just wondering about Grandma Reed."

"Let me see. I remember when I was little, she and Pop-Up came over for holidays. They brought the cheapest gifts that usually fell apart the next day."

"They were exceptionally frugal. Your father caught them digging through the neighbors' trash on more than one occasion, looking for perfectly good items that had been discarded. I'm sure more than one of your gifts came from those dumpster dives."

"Grandma had the worst smell. It was like... death."

"Formaldehyde. It was her hair dye. And black licorice. I think that was her perfume, but I forgot to ask."

"This trip down memory lane has been interesting, but why are we taking it?"

Gemini could hear Taurus in the background, singing, "Poooopy, poooopy boys and girls, poooopy dogs and cats..."

"That's not appropriate talk for a young man."

Gemini's chest tightened. Sophia would wring her neck if Gemini tried to discipline Taurus. "I found some boxes of her things is all."

"Oh? What did we save? My recollection is that you convinced Daddy to build a nice big bonfire."

Quickly, Gemini wracked her brain for the specifics of any box. "Her clothing, cards you sent her, that sort of thing."

"Just leave them in your garage. I'll pick them up on Friday when I visit."

Gemini's heart fell to her stomach. "Friday?"

"Yes, Mother."

Brandon's mother was lecturing Taurus in the background. If her visits always meant complaints, she could see why Taurus focused on poop.

"I've told you numerous times that I'm having a procedure done at Charming General. If it's too much for you, I'll happily make reservations at the Satin Inn. Brandon has so many points built up, I'll get the Silk Suite for free."

"I didn't forget."

Sophia had a top-secret procedure scheduled.

Every time Gemini asked about it, she changed the subject.

There was a huge ruckus behind her now. Taurus was throwing one of his signature fits, no doubt brought on by his grandmother's unrealistic demands.

"I should go."

"See you on Friday, dear. Tell Brandon's mother I said hello."

SHE WAS RELIEVED to find Feather already in the office. Immediately, Feather frowned as she glanced up. "Spill it, Gem."

Gemini smiled, comforted by the fact she never stood on pretense with her business partner. "I've been feeling a little like you." She swallowed hard, willing the words to come out. "I've had encounters with... a ghost."

"What?" Feather jumped to her feet, the clomp of her heavy boots narrowly missing Gemini's maroon sneakers. "Tell me everything!"

As Gemini explained her experience, Feather nodded in agreement. "I've only had that experience with a handful of entities. They usually appear partially, top or bottom, or translucent. For your first time, I'd say you hit the jackpot!"

It was so nice to know someone wouldn't consider her crazy. "Possibly. It was her message that concerned me."

"I agree. She's got more to tell you though. I'm sure. We could ask..." Feather's eyes dropped.

"Jayden. I know, dear. Tell me what's happening on that front."

"Later, I promise. What happened when she left? Did the room feel cold?"

Gemini searched her mind. "The strangest part of this entire experience is that I don't have any memory of her leaving or what happened after. I know she was afraid."

"Oh. That's not good, Gem."

"Why?"

"Because whoever she's afraid of could easily take her place next time."

Gemini didn't feel the concern she knew she should. There was still a healthy dose of doubt in her mind that the whole thing was just a weird dream. She'd gotten up to make herself a cup of tea and for some reason just fell asleep.

Placing her palms on the desk, she stood. Though she never felt her age, she'd witnessed enough people over fifty who pulled a hip out of socket while rising from the table. As she rose, she felt something crunching beneath her hands. There was a cookie with one corner crumbled. The rest of the perfectly round sweet was preserved.

"What's this doing here?" Gemini was incensed that someone would leave a baked good that didn't originate from either hers or Tug's kitchen.

"Oh, that was here when I came in. I figured you left it."

Gemini picked it up and examined it, bringing it up to her nose. Peanut butter and... what was that? Something metallic? Glancing around the room for signs of anything else unusual, her eyes came to rest on a sealed envelope.

Feather jumped up and retrieved it. "How did I miss this when I was painting?"

She opened the envelope to find a purple card that read, "Are you hungry? No? Let's play first!"

"Gem, toss that cookie outside, now!"

Moving quickly, hips be damned, Gemini took the cookie to the large trash bin outside and tossed it in. She'd no more made it back to the sidewalk when the bin exploded.

CHAPTER 18

FEATHER

"Thank you, Chief. Yes, I do know it takes time for lab analysis. Mhmm... we'll speak again soon."

Gemini swirled around in her fancy chair. "If he didn't think I was crazy when I woke him up to report gunshots, he certainly does now."

Feather lowered her chin. "Gem, are you certain it was the cookie that exploded?" Her low, grumbly tone was nothing like Chief Boulder's, but the dismissiveness was right on track. "There are any number of combustible items in a trash bin."

"It was the same people who chased us away from the mayor's place. R.U.S.T. They are a tight-knit group, and it will be impossible for anyone outside of the paranormal world to track them down."

Feather wasn't sure how to approach Gemini with the news. Nor did she want to. Alistair was going to continue these games until Jayden was dead. No one in their office was safe.

Instead, she changed the subject. "Gem, I don't understand. You want me to do a... séance?"

Gemini set the plate of marionberry rolls on the counter of their break area and poured herself a cup of coffee. Though Ruthmarie hadn't visited in days, according to her, Gemini looked as though she hadn't slept a wink.

"I know how you hate them, dear. But I don't see any way around it. Last night I couldn't sleep. I kept worrying Mother Reed would show up at an inopportune time, like while I was in the bathroom."

Feather nodded. Though she'd never had that experience (luckily), she'd heard from some members of P.I.N.K. who tried setting firm boundaries only to be joined in the bathtub by a pushy ghost.

"Ruthmarie is scared of someone on the other side, someone, I believe, with a connection to Gladiola Crabbitz. Bringing together a group of people, I believe we can put a stop to them both."

"Your plan is to find an informant? That's risky, Gem. Tattle tales face consequences."

Gemini stood and placed her hands on her hips. "I feel like you're teasing me. I researched all of this on that site you sent me."

She'd forgotten all about the article. It was about paranormal investigators and their impact on grieving families. "I didn't realize they spoke of seances. And I didn't mean to tease."

Feather noticed the worry lines on Gemini's face. She'd always been amazed that, for a woman of seventy, Gemini showed none of the typical signs of aging that Feather had noticed in her elderly clients.

"This has really got you tied up in knots, hasn't it?"

Gemini nodded and quickly brought the cup to her lips.

"You know I'll do anything for you. If you think a séance will bring out the Crabbitz' evil alter egos, then let's plan it."

"I was hoping you would say that." Gemini thrust a printed invitation in front of Feather.

"Please join us on Thursday for a séance. Bring a meaningful object—" Feather set the paper down and smiled. "You remembered!"

"The last séance you did for a client, you left instructions for each attendee to bring something that had meaning. They all brought their favorite book, as though they were coming to a book club meeting. The only spirits you were able to drum up were former librarians with a bone to pick over late returns."

Feather continued reading. "Please come with an open mind. Refreshments will be provided. How many people are you sending this to? We have to have a specific amount or it won't work."

"I thought of that too. The rule of thumb, according to your website, is that if you invite ten people, five will show."

Feather gasped. "You're not inviting ten people!" This would be the time they all showed. Then Feather wouldn't be able to contact anyone. That many personal agendas in the room would cloud the air unnecessarily.

"Don't worry, dear. They're either former clients or friends."

"You're having a séance?"

They turned in unison.

"Cassie! I'm surprised to see you here! Weren't you able to make an appointment at the shop?"

Cassie was the last person she wanted to see, or at least close. She wouldn't be happy if Alistair walked through the door either.

"Gem, this is a client of mine. Cassie, this is Gemini Reed, my partner."

Cassie extended a hand, her fingernails painted a pale pink with sparkling crystals on each nail.

"Nice to meet you, Cassie," Gemini replied cheerily. "What brings you clear out here?"

"Oh, I just got my nails done. I had the strangest experience." Cassie pulled out a chair and sat down, flopping a large black-and-white bag on the chair next to her. "Something drew me to your warehouse. I hope it's okay?"

"Tell us about it, dear." Gemini rested her chin in

her palm as she prepared for a long story. Feather found herself bored if the client didn't have a compelling tale to tell. She'd catch herself looking out the window. Gemini, on the other hand, would stay engaged, or at least give that impression until the bitter end. It was a gift.

"It was my grandmother's voice. She said, 'Cassie, girl, you've gotta dump that loser you're a datin'.' That's how my grandmother talked."

The hairs on Feather's arms rose. She helplessly stared at Gemini and pointed to her arm. Gemini nodded. "Cassie, why don't we move up to the office where you'll be more comfortable. We have a nice couch and some massage chairs."

Cassie nodded and followed Gemini. When they were out of the room, Feather opened her mind.

"Cassie's grandmother? Are you playing games with her? You and I both know she doesn't have the gift. Why are you doing this?"

I was testing her to see if anyone could take up space in her head. I was right, unfortunately. Now I know she's in danger. That spirit you're so worried about? It's always looking for new real estate, and whoever brought it into your town has given it free rein. My grand-daughter isn't the only one in danger and you know it.

"Is this séance going to cause more problems?"

I'm not allowed to talk about that. You've already been censured once, let's not try for twice.

"Censured? What does that even mean?"

Her words drifted into the air with no response. Would that mean Feather's paranormal investigations were on hold? She couldn't even ask Jayden because she'd have to explain why she used a young ghost to block out Jayden's gifts.

When she rejoined Gemini and Cassie, they looked relieved to see her. "Feather, sit down with us. I think you'll be interested in what Cassie has to say."

Gemini gave her the "Cheese and crackers! How do we handle this one?" look.

"What's going on, Cassie?"

"Like I was telling *your* grandma, I was hearing *my* grandma. She gave me a list of approved guys to date. Floyd Jensen? Who still lives in his mother's basement and spends his days off playing video games from the '80s? I'm insulted."

"Okay. I get that. What else were you telling my partner?"

"When Twyla was done with my acrylics and I was sitting under the nail dryer, I started hearing more voices. I looked around and nobody else acted like they could hear them."

The color drained from Feather's face. "And what did these voices say?"

"All sorts of horrible things. They knew my deepest secrets, things I've never told anyone." Cassie bit her lip. "I'm not going to tell you either. No weird ghostie-thing can force me."

"You don't have to, Cassie. What else did they say?"

"How they had the power to command someone to set my mom's house on fire. Oh, and if I didn't help them, they would get inside my boss's head and tell him to fire me. They can't do that, can they?"

"You keep saying 'we', dear. Was there more than one voice?" Gemini asked.

"Yeah." Cassie nodded vigorously, causing her long curls to bounce against the table. "It was definitely a group. Mostly men, I think."

Feather thought quickly. If she allowed Cassie free rein, she'd likely fall under the spell of these dark entities. She had to keep Cassie close. "The last time you came to get your hair done, you mentioned needing some time off from your office job."

Gemini frowned.

"You know, now that I think about it, my boss firing me wouldn't be a bad thing. He's such a jerk. Do you think I should go ahead and let the voices talk to my boss?"

"No!" Gemini and Feather said in unison.

"In the back of our warehouse, my boyfriend and his partner make Tug Bars," Feather continued. "When we're done here, I'll give you a tour. It's an impressive operation."

"I bought one of those last week! Well, I meant to buy a candy bar, but I was glad I made the mistake. It was so good! Crazy Cranberry!"

"They just got a contract with the prison and could really use an extra pair of hands."

Gemini nodded vigorously. "Tug's trying to expand, so your paycheck will come from me. I'll pay you twice your office salary."

Feather was grateful once again for her partner. Gemini had no idea why Feather wanted Cassie close but jumped in to make sure it would happen.

Cassie's uncertain look made Feather worry it wouldn't work. "I guess I could. Will you really pay me twice what I'm making at the office? Even though he's a jerk, I make good money. I'd hate to have to stop getting my nails done, or the spray tans I love so much."

Feather and Stevie, the current owner of Featherworks Salon, just had a staff meeting where they cautioned against allowing clients like Cassie into the spray tan booth more than twice a week. They didn't want to be a walking advertisement for raisins.

"Guaranteed. Bring in a pay stub tomorrow morning and I'll set it up for you." Gemini patted Cassie's hand and stood. "Feather will want to take you back to meet Tug and Olive."

CHAPTER 19

FEATHER

Tug, being Tug, didn't even blink when Feather announced she'd found him a new employee. Normally, Olive liked to interview each applicant. Tug figured if they survived Olive's fifteen-page form and hadn't bugged out, they were worthy of working in his business.

"Nice meeting you, Cassie," Tug said, extending a hand.

Instinctively, Feather's protective shield went up. She was used to women throwing themselves at Tug, even though the rational side of her knew Tug would never return the compliments. She'd learned there was a price to pay for dating someone so attractive.

As if on cue, Cassie batted her eyes. "Aren't you a looker? They didn't make 'em like this at the city title office."

Tug grinned. "Would you hold on one minute, Cassie?"

"Well, sure, sugar!"

Feather did her best to keep her eyes from rolling as they waited.

"You never mentioned Tug. New boyfriend, I assume?"

Feather understood what wasn't said. Cassie, like everyone else in the known universe, couldn't understand how someone who looked like Tug would be interested in a combat-boot-wearing, purple-haired woman at least a foot shorter than him.

"No, we've been together for quite a while. Years."

Luckily, Tug reappeared. "Here you go." He handed Cassie a packet. "Please take this home and study it. Tomorrow you'll watch a short video and then you'll have to take a quiz."

Cassie burst out laughing, causing Feather to flinch. Just because she had to keep her close didn't mean she had to like it.

"Oh, you're cute AND funny! Like I would need to study for a test on making protein bars!"

Tug smirked. At least Feather knew it as a smirk. Everyone else thought it was another version of his disarming smile. "You don't need to take a test to make Tug Bars. Olive will train you on that. What I just gave you was the information we give all our employees regarding sexual harassment."

Cassie's face changed color, from overdone

brown to red.

"I have to make sure everyone who works here is absolutely clear on what is appropriate language to use around the boss."

THEY WERE IN BED, tossing and turning. Neither of them could get the images out of their heads. Especially Feather, who had experienced a lifetime of drama, murder, and ghosts all in the span of one week. Facing each other, they opened their eyes simultaneously.

Tug perched on one elbow. "Feath, I've got to tell you something. I went over to the Crabbitz' home to attach listening devices. I heard the garage door open, so I retreated to Gemini's house, where I could decide what comes next."

She nodded and rubbed her eyes.

"While I was standing outside, I found listening devices on her house."

Feather gasped. "Who could've done that?"

"I'm guessing that Crabbitz lady. I was never able to go back to her home. We've got to end this feud before she's hurt. I was waiting to tell her until you and I figured out how best to help her."

"I'm going to make us a snack since we're both still up."

He viewed her with skepticism. "What are you going to... make?"

Though she should have been offended, she was still trying to live down last month's oven fire. The plastic wrap over the chicken should have come with a warning.

"Just whatever's in the fridge, I promise."

She slipped into her cat-shaped slippers, sliding into the kitchen. One of her favorite things to do was slide on the wood floor, and these new slippers were easier to slide in than her socks. It was a childish thing to do, but it made her smile.

After pouring two glasses of almond milk, she bent down, looking for something in the refrigerator that neither needed heat nor electricity to serve: leftover pasta, mustard, two questionable apples, and one egg. Nothing too exciting.

"Oh, wait! Gem sent home some marionberry cream cheese rolls!"

She closed the door and stood on her tiptoes to reach the very back of the counter. As soon as she grabbed the plastic container, the hairs on her arms rose. Turning around slowly, Feather braced herself for whichever entity was making an unexpected visit.

I've got a bone to pick with ye, lass!

In all the years she'd dealt with the dead, not one of them wanted to pick a fight. At least not verbally. They were either confident they were right and wouldn't listen to reason or already agreed with Feather.

She studied this ghost: a middle-aged woman with red hair pinned on top of her head. Several stray hairs hung down around her face and in her large green eyes. On her translucent body was a pale blue dress covered by an apron.

"I don't believe we've met. I'm Feath—"

The ghost placed her hands on her hips and tapped her foot. Feather saw now that she was wearing the lace-up boots she'd seen in 1920s catalogs. "I know who you be. You've been asking my little Millicent to do things that are strictly against the rules. Do you want my sweet girl to get in trouble?"

She certainly didn't resemble Millicent. The young girl was pale, almost pasty. This woman spent some time in the sun, developing a ruddy complexion during her years on earth. "You're Millicent's mother? She always speaks lovingly of you."

Feather smiled hopefully. Her mind had too many windows open and, at that moment, she couldn't remember the anecdotes she'd heard.

"No, I'm not the lass's mam. I'm the family's maid, Maeve McCullovy. Though I took the child to me breast and watched over her 'til her early death." Her hands folded over her chest as she glared at Feather. "She's me charge on this side. Her ma ain't worried about her, nah more than she was in life."

Feather's heart sunk. Even though Millicent was no longer among the living, it was sad that she didn't have the love of her parent after death.

"I'm not sure what you mean, Maeve. Millicent plays games with me, that's all."

She turned toward the counter, standing on her tip toes to retrieve two small plates. She hoped Maeve couldn't read her mind as some of the entities could.

"I was on this earth fifty-two years. Nutting got by me, gal. You've been askin' me darlin' babe to interfere with someone's gifts. That's against the rules. Clear and simple."

"I'm sorry. I really am. I promise it won't happen again."

"You'll see that it don't."

Feather squeezed her eyes shut, as if it would keep the response to her next question out. "Is she... banned from seeing me?"

She heard a loud sigh. "Would if it did any good. The lass has a rebellious streak and she'd sneak off to see ya whether I forbid it or not."

Feather's eyes opened and she clapped her hands together. "Thank you, thank you, thank you, Maeve! I promise I won't ask anything of her ever again!"

"See that you don't, Feather Jones. Or there's more than firm words coming your way."

CHAPTER 20

GEMINI

"Not usually skeptical of your plans, Gemini, but this one doesn't make any sense."

She'd made the decision not to tell Howard about her middle-of-the-night visitor. At least for now. Instead, she'd come up with another plan during her second night of staying vigilant in her kitchen. She didn't involve Feather, worried her partner may not take her seriously. No way was Mother Reed going to sneak up on her again.

Under the guidance of internet experts, Gemini placed two baby monitors on the counter, hung a dozen wind chimes on the upper cabinets, and placed tin foil in the sink. The last one seemed frivolous, but who was she to argue with an expert?

"We have one thing they don't—the element of surprise. They have no idea we're on to them."

"Let me make sure I understand what you've cooked up." Howard motioned for her to sit at his kitchen table. Tonight, he'd made clam chowder and cheese biscuits that were still warm.

She sat, picked up a spoon, and blew on the steamy mixture. "We're going to start monitoring her home. If Gladiola Crabbitz can point a telescope at my yard, then I don't feel a bit guilty about using one of Tug's listening devices to hear what they're plotting."

Howard chuckled. "I fear my devious ways have rubbed off on you, Gemini."

She hadn't thought of herself as so easily suggestible. "I believe it's mutual, Howard. You've done some pretty kooky things at my direction." Spooning the rich broth into her mouth, she groaned. "You've done it again, my friend. This soup is divine."

"Thank you." Howard carefully sawed his biscuit into two equal pieces and spread butter on it before putting it in his mouth. "How are we going about placing this device? Do you think they'll let us in if we come and borrow a cup of sugar?"

"That's the beauty of this plan. Tug says we can attach it to the side of their home and it will pick up everything they say inside."

"Hmm. Interesting. The spy business has changed since my involvement."

Gemini stared across the table at him. "One of

these days, I'm going to ply you with baked goods and force you to tell me everything about your past."

Howard used to be the CEO at Charming General Hospital, but he also maintained relationships with underworld shady characters. Whenever Gemini asked about them, he was always evasive.

"On a need-to-know basis, dear neighbor."

A sharp knock at the door caused them to jump. They exchanged a nervous glance. "Gem, you know that if I don't answer, we'll be up tonight wondering who it was."

Gemini nodded in agreement, though with the Crabbitzes turning the neighborhood against them, there was no telling who might want to do them harm.

She glanced around the kitchen, searching for something she could use to defend herself if necessary. "This mini cast-iron skillet could do some damage."

Hoisting it above her head, she moved silently into the hallway, where she could hear Howard's calm voice. Unable to take the suspense any longer, she decided the element of surprise was her best weapon. She jumped into view, holding tight to the pan with the most menacing look she could muster.

Standing just inside the door was a plump man with a disagreeable face and round glasses. He looked familiar but Gemini couldn't place him.

Beside him was someone who also looked familiar. A statuesque brunette with the body of an athlete, she commanded an air of quiet confidence.

Howard turned when she entered the room. "Gem, this is the FBI agent I was telling you about."

The woman stepped forward and offered her hand to Gemini. "Ex agent, actually. I don't want anyone to think I'm tapping their phone or anything. My name is Maxine Smart. I've heard good things about you."

"I've seen you jogging before. I admire those who can do that."

She shook Gemini's hand so hard it was painful. When Gemini winced, Maxine withdrew immediately. "I'm so sorry. I tend to forget my strength. I still work out at the Portland facility when I'm in town."

Gemini rubbed her hands together as she admired Maxine. Her piercing, steel-gray eyes could be construed as cold, but Gemini didn't get that vibe from her. She was the type of woman Gemini always admired: strong both inside and out but with an obvious concern for others. It was hard to believe this woman was old enough to retire.

"And this is Quentin Zahn. We met him when we dropped off a flyer. Right before Gladiola drove us up to Maxine's porch."

When Gemini knitted her brow, Howard clarified, "His mother is Hetty. The woman with lots of cats."

"Oh! I remember now! Your mother is... very nice."

Gemini stuck her hand out, but Quentin didn't return the gesture.

"Maxine brought Mr. Zahn over to prove to him that we're not conspiring to kill her and eat her spleen."

Gemini erupted in laughter. When the rest of the room remained stoic, she shook her head. "Cheese and crackers! You can't believe that, Mr. Zahn! You told us last week that you're a true crime aficionado. Do I look like that kind of villain?"

"Well," his voice wavered, "serial killers are always the last people you'd expect. And going door-to-door is the best way to find a new victim."

"Quentin visits me frequently to pick my brain." Maxine smiled. Gemini admired her diplomatic way of saying her next-door neighbor wouldn't leave her alone.

"I wanted him to know that, despite the podcast he listened to, *Is Your Neighbor the Next Sock Street Strangler?*, we are quite safe on this block."

Gemini and Howard stared at Maxine, incredulous. She returned their gaze with a knowing glance.

"This flyer was stuck in my door when I came home from the grocery store." Quentin thrust a paper in Gemini's hands. "Maxine and I are concerned."

Dearest fine neighbors,

As you know, our neighborhood has been infected by two amoral homeowners. Because we care about your safety, we've been keeping a close eye and can report they have even more debauchery planned.

Gemini turned away, unable to continue. "I can't read anymore. It's likely to keep me awake again tonight and, if I miss another night of sleep, I'll turn into a zombie." She pivoted quickly. "But not the type that eats spleens!"

Howard finished reading the flyer and handed it back to Maxine. "So our lovely neighbors have decided we run a black market organ operation? That seems a little messy for my taste."

"I know it's ludicrous, Mr. Beachmont. But people like this thrive on outrageous claims and those they bring under their spell. As long as there is someone for them to fear, they easily create a common enemy."

"What can we do about it? When I worked at my son-in-law's law firm, we had several cases of slander. Some were harder than others to prove, but this sounds like a slam dunk."

"I'm sure it is, Mrs. Reed. Unfortunately, if we

stop them now, they'll continue with someone else. We need to end their game permanently."

"I'll help in whatever way I can," Quentin said with enthusiasm.

It didn't escape Gemini that it had barely been five minutes since he'd accused them of horrendous crimes.

"You've come to the conclusion that we're not after your organs, then?" Howard's sarcastic comment went unnoticed.

"Tell us what to do, Ms. Smart. I'm at my wit's end and I don't have anymore worry to spare."

"I'd like to do some surveillance first, before we firm up plans."

"Ya mean spying? I could help!" Howard bounced excitedly.

"No, nothing that devious. Just a friendly neighbor-to-neighbor chat. I'd like us to have another conversation in a few days. Could we do that?"

They all nodded in agreement.

"Good. Shall we say...Tuesday?"

"We can meet at my home. I'm always looking for an outlet for my baking."

"Thank you for your kind offer, Mrs. Reed. I was thinking more about a restaurant, somewhere the Crabbitz couple doesn't frequent."

"Four Cups is nice."

THE GROUP ARRIVED SEPARATELY, each parking in a different lot at Howard's insistence. It did make sense, leaving nothing to chance.

After securing the furthest booth in the back, right by the restrooms, they waited patiently for Ms. Smart's arrival. Finally, she came through the door and waved at the group. She was carrying a folder when she slid in beside Gemini.

"So sorry to be late. We retired FBI have a group video chat and sometimes the old war stories get windy."

She took off her coat and opened the folder. "I went to visit our neighbor. While she wasn't outright rude, she made it clear it wasn't her intention to be neighborly." Maxine chuckled. "In any case, Mrs. Crabbitz was making some coffee and I took the liberty to—"

"Case the joint?" Quentin could barely contain his glee.

"I was going to say look around the living room, but yes, 'case the joint' works too. I took some discreet photos and I'd like each of you to study them to see if they are at all familiar."

Gemini put on her readers and studied the large,

glossy photos. "Better than anything I ever took on my phone," she mused.

The first one was a collection of antique and rare coins.

"Those are counterfeit." Howard sat back and smiled with satisfaction. "Not even close."

Maxine nodded vigorously. "I found that a pattern emerged from all of these. They were all involved in a shakedown of one kind or another. It became clear that Gladiola Crabbitz targeted individuals who had some leverage or influence within the community. She broke into several homes in one neighborhood and then moved on to another." Maxine smiled confidently. "We'll get her, don't worry."

Not involved in paranormal activities at all.

CHAPTER 21
FEATHER

"Cassie has been great. You don't have to worry."

Tug leaned across the table and kissed Feather's cheek.

"I wouldn't have asked you if—"

"Would you stop? I told you, we really did need the extra help. And once I give Cassie directions, she plugs in her ear buds for the rest of the day. I don't have to worry about Olive scaring her off with her detailed stories about her new boyfriend."

"Oh good." Feather let out a rush of air. "It's only until I can figure out who is bothering Gem. Although, the way Cassie's grandmother talked, she's suggestible enough that any evil entity could take control of her. Until such time as it makes sense in my brain, I've got to keep my eye on her."

She scooped a spoon full of chunky beer cheese

soup into her mouth. "Four Cups makes the best soup, don't they?"

Tug nodded in agreement. He was on his second bowl. At least they came here enough that the staff understood his voracious appetite and kept the food coming until he warned them he was finished.

"Have you figured out how you're going to... you know?"

She stared at him quizzically. "No, I don't. Tell me."

Tug leaned forward and made air quotes with his fingers. "K-I-L-L your favorite person after me and Gemini?" He was so dramatic it might have been funny had they been discussing any other topic.

"Shh!" Feather warned. "You never know who's listening!"

"Sorry. You haven't mentioned it in a few days and, whenever that happens, I worry about what you're not sharing."

She should have been upset by his slight, but she knew it was true. When her mind was lost in a case, it went down some pretty scary alleyways.

"I have an idea. Maybe not a good one, but if I could convince Jayden to go into hiding, I could at least buy her some time."

She wiped the soup dribbling down her chin on her napkin and took another piece of homemade bread from the basket. She tore it into chunks and pushed each one into the soup until it was properly absorbed.

The welcome sound of his laughter caused her head to rear up, her bounty dripping down her chin.

"Feath, I don't know much about your world, but I do know that those people can see everything. Won't it be obvious when she shows up for work?" Tug reached over with his napkin and wiped her chin before playfully touching her nose.

"That's the part I'm still sorting out."

She finished her soup and used a remaining chunk of bread to wipe the bowl clean. When she glanced up, Tug was laughing.

"What?"

"You. Eating so intently. One of the many things I love about you."

The hairs on her arms rose just as Tug was leaning across two empty soup bowls to kiss her again. Instinctively, he pulled back. "Go. I can wait."

She nodded as she jumped up and hurried back to the restroom. They chose their dining spots not only for the food, but also for the proximity to the bathrooms, and always private bathrooms. Four Cups had two single-person bathrooms.

As soon as she'd turned the lock, Feather cleared her throat. "What is it? Don't you understand the 'Do Not Disturb' sign I place on your side while I'm in public?"

She waited patiently. Nothing.

"I'm giving you until the count of ten, and if you haven't revealed your name and reason for bothering me, I'm going back for more soup. I won't be taking your calls for the rest of the day."

When there was no response, she began her countdown.

"Ten... nine... eight..."

Feather paused. Her eyes scanned the roomy single-stall bathroom. Clean as usual, with a nice floral soap on one side of the sink and a small bouquet of wildflowers on the other. She observed something new. There was a bottle of fancy hand lotion sitting beside the flowers.

On impulse, she pumped a few squirts of lotion into her hands. She brought one hand to her nose, closing her eyes while drinking in the lilac scent. When she opened them, there was someone staring back at her in the mirror above the sink.

A stern face with tight gray curls framing puffy cheeks glared at her.

"What?"

She jumped back, knocking the lotion off the sink and onto the floor, where the bottle emptied its contents. Feather looked down at the mess and then back up at the mirror. "I'm the one doing the asking, lady. Who are you?"

As soon as she spoke, she sensed a familiarity. "Cassie's grandmother? I did what you asked. She's kicked the bum to the curb. I've even given her a job, or rather, my boyfriend did. I'm keeping my eye on her too."

"Day late and a dollar short. The girl's already been contacted. I checked on her earlier and she's doing their bidding as we speak."

Feather thought fast. "Where is she? We can leave now!"

"She's doing deliveries. Check with your man candy. He can tell you."

"You've got to help! What are they asking Cassie to do?"

There was an insistent knock at the door. "Babe? I hate to bother you, but I just got a text. There's been an accident with my delivery van. We need to check on Cassie."

CHAPTER 22

FEATHER

Feather turned to the mirror, but Cassie's grandmother was gone. She quickly dried her hands and opened the door to find Tug standing watch, looking genuinely concerned. "What's going on?"

"We need to go," he stated urgently. "Now."

She grabbed her bag, pleased with her decision to keep free-floating money in there. When she reached in and pulled out two twenty-dollar bills, she flung them on the table as they ran out. Starla would be pleased with her tip tonight.

"We need to find Cassie," she said. "They've contacted her and she's doing their bidding."

Tug furrowed his brow. "Who? What kind of bidding?"

"I don't know." Feather bit her lip. "But we need to find her before it's too late. This could be bad, Tug."

They rushed out of Four and hopped into Tug's car. Feather's heart raced as Tug peeled out. He gripped the steering wheel so hard that his knuckles were white as they careened through the streets at high speed, narrowly avoiding an accident more than once. His device led them down side streets into a part of town neither was familiar with.

Feather tried Cassie's number, but it went straight to voicemail. "Come on, Cassie," she muttered. "Pick up."

"She's not going to answer. I told her to shut off her personal phone and only use the business cell when she's working. I tried it already." Tug's eyes remained trained on the street and, for that, Feather was grateful.

"I know, but I feel helpless. I'm the one who told you to hire her. If something has happened to her or your delivery van, it's going to be all my fault!"

"When we're home later, I'm going to remind you whose name is on Tug Bars. I do the hiring and firing, and I'm responsible for all of my employees."

Feather dialled the work cell repeatedly until, by some miracle, Cassie answered. "Hello?"

"Cassie, oh, thank god. It's Feather. Are you okay? Are you hearing voices in your head?"

There was a long pause before Cassie spoke. "I'm fine, Feather. Why do you ask?"

"Your grandmother contacted me. She said you've been hearing people—bad people." There was no time to stand on ceremony; Feather would have to explain her conversation with Cassie's dead grandmother later. "What did they ask you to do?"

"I don't know what you're talking about," Cassie said, her voice devoid of emotion. "I'm just doing deliveries for Tug."

"Tug's emergency assistance app notified him that the delivery van had been in an accident."

"I have to go now."

"Wait! Don't hang up!"

Feather felt her stomach squeezing so hard she thought it might explode. "Now what do we do?"

As they approached the 400 block of Dreadful Drive, where Tug's emergency device pinged, they viewed a sickening sight.

Tug's delivery van was pointed at an angle with the front two tires on the sidewalk. One tire was blown and the hood was crushed like an accordion. Smoke poured from an unknown source.

Feather's heart sank at the sight. "Oh, babe. I'm so sorry."

"Let's find Cassie. We can worry about the van later." Tug got out and approached the smoking van. "Cassie? Can you hear me? Help is on the way!"

"There's no way you're doing this alone. Wait for me!"

Feather felt the heat emanating from the wreckage as she surveyed the damage. It looked like the van had collided with something—or someone —with great force.

"The police should be here any minute, as long as my device called them as it should have when it reported to me." Tug jimmied the driver's door open.

"Cassie's purse is still in the van," Tug said, holding it over his head.

"Why didn't I think of this sooner?" Feather fished her phone out of her pocket and connected it the Tug Bars cell. All of Tug's employees were required to share their locations when they were using the company van.

She quickly opened the GPS app and scanned the surrounding area. After a few tense moments, she spotted a blip on the screen that indicated Cassie was in a nearby alleyway.

"That way," Feather said, pointing in the direction of the blip. She and Tug set off as fast as they could, their hearts pounding in their chests.

When they reached the alleyway, Cassie's body was slumped against a brick wall, between an over-flowing dumpster and a flock of gulls feasting on a loaf of mouldy bread. Feather rushed to her side and checked her pulse. It was weak but steady. Last year's mandatory first aid course for Featherworks Salon employees was coming in handy.

"She's alive," Feather cried, relief flooding through her. "We need to get her to a hospital."

Tug scooped Cassie up and carried her back to

the car. After opening the back door for Tug, Feather retrieved a fleece blanket they kept in the trunk for emergencies. She tucked it around Cassie. "Hold her as close to you as you can, babe. She's probably in shock."

Feather jumped behind the wheel and started the engine. She drove with the same urgency Tug had on the way over. Cassie's life wasn't going to end like this.

Tug's eyes were fixed on Cassie, his arms wrapped protectively around her as if he could will her back to consciousness. "Hang in there, Cassie," he whispered, his voice trembling with fear and determination.

Feather's heart ached for her friend, and her mind churned with questions. Who were these people who had manipulated Cassie? What had they coerced her into doing? And, most importantly, why?

The hospital loomed ahead, its fluorescent lights casting an eerie glow across the parking lot. Feather pulled up to the emergency entrance, her heart pounding as Tug carried Cassie inside, her body limp in his arms. The hospital staff sprang into action, rushing to their aid with a gurney and a flurry of questions.

Feather and Tug stood off to the side, watching as the medical team assessed Cassie's condition. Tug's jaw was clenched, his fists balled at his sides.

Feather reached out and placed a hand on his arm, offering what little comfort she could.

A young doctor approached them, her face a mask of concern. "We're stabilizing her now. It seems she's been exposed a sedative. We'll run tests to understand the extent of her condition."

Tug's voice was tight with worry. "Will she be okay?"

CHAPTER 23
GEMINI

According to her skeptical doctor, buying new bed sheets, new pajamas, and soothing music would help ease her mind to reset. "You're working too hard, Mrs. Reed. Seeing your dead mother-in-law is just your brain's way of saying enough." Instead, Gemini tossed and turned until she found no other remedy but to get out of bed.

She shoved her feet into her favorite slippers and wrapped a brand-new lilac robe with pink flowers around her. An app she'd downloaded for sleep instructed her to walk around the room thirty times, repeating, "I'm ready for sleep." After spending as much time walking in circles as she could stand, she returned to bed.

Finally, at 3:00 a.m., when she could take it no more, she left her bedroom and entered the kitchen, bumping her head on the wind chimes hanging from the ceiling. Her doctor instructed her to hang something in the doorway to keep her thoughts in the real world.

If it were daylight, she might enjoy their dulcet tones. Tonight, she found them irritating and, in a fit of aggravation, yanked them off the fishing wire they were hanging from.

"I know you're here, so you might as well make your presence known. I won't let you scare me this time."

Gemini folded her arms across her chest and leaned against the counter. "You've seen to it that I'm awake all night, so obviously I won't be falling asleep any time soon. I can out-wait you, Ruthmarie."

A loud banging in the front yard jolted her. She rushed to the curtain and peeked outside, hoping it was a stray cat and not someone looking to break in.

When she found the yard blissfully free of animals and humans, she closed the curtain and turned around. There, standing in front of her, was Ruthmarie. She was wearing a royal blue sweater with a large B sewn on the front. A long blue-and-white plaid skirt ended just below her knees, and on her feet she wore black and white shoes.

"Bugs and batteries! Will you stop scaring me like that?"

"Why? You don't want to join me on this side?" Ruthmarie cackled.

"I won't answer that, Ruthmarie. You'll take it the

wrong way and torture me for another night. Just tell me why you're here and let's get on with it."

Ruthmarie's eyes widened. "Daughter, you're hurting my feelings. Don't you want to hear what Leo told me?"

It could be a dirty trick. Ruthmarie wasn't above that. When Sophia was four, Ruthmarie called 24 hours before Sophia's birthday to announce that she'd planned a big party to celebrate her ONLY granddaughter's birthday. They closed down the hardware store early and drove to the neighboring town, where Leo's parents lived. During the drive, Gemini struggled to keep her frustration to herself. She'd planned a party with four of Sophia's preschool friends. She'd even made a cake.

When they arrived at Ruthmarie's, there was no party. Taking note of Sophia's tears, they said they'd like to take her out to eat, just the three of them. "To make up for your mother's miscommunication."

"I'm not falling for any more of your tricks, lady."

"Gladiola Crabbitz found your listening device. She is planning to have it reinstalled but with pre-recorded sounds."

"Shoot. I haven't had a spare minute to ask Tug about that. Was there anything else?"

Ruthmarie leaned in close, the smell of formaldehyde and black licorice overpowering. "My granddaughter is keeping secrets. You'll have to be persistent in order to get the truth from her."

Gemini took a step backward, trying to escape both the nauseating scent and Ruthmarie's lack of personal space. The stubborn ghost was having none of it, mirroring her movement.

"Do you have to speak in riddles all the time? Couldn't you just come out with it?"

"Oh dear. You've always been a little slow, haven't you? I'm telling you that my granddaughter is harboring a secret that could bring harm to both of you. Is that direct enough?"

She was taken aback. "Are you saying you are concerned about my... well-being?"

Ruthmarie let out a belly laugh so loud that Gemini's ears rang. She stuck her fingers in her ears and closed her eyes. Maybe if she repeated that sleep meditation, substituting the words, "It's time for Ruthmarie to go away," it would produce better results.

The next thing she knew, her automatic sprinklers were spraying against the siding. She lifted her head and winced, immediately grabbing her neck. The sound of morning songbirds were no longer a comfort. They signaled another night spent outside her bedroom.

"You'd think she could let me lie down for once."

It was time.

"That's it in a nutshell, Howard."

Gemini couldn't decide who she should tell first: Feather or Howard. Feather would want to know every detail, and Gemini had decided she wouldn't be upset at all. Howard would be inwardly skeptical as he nodded in agreement. She decided to go with the hard sell first.

Howard leaned forward, rubbing the knees of his gray khaki gardening pants. His sign that he was struggling for words.

"It's not that I don't believe you. Lord knows we've had some pretty bizarre things happen in this neighborhood. But a ghost? Isn't that Feather's department?"

Howard reacted just as she'd expected. Kind but skeptical.

"This is my first experience with this sort of thing. For this woman who despised me from the moment we met to come back to help me is extraordinary."

"Therein lies the problem, Gem. What if she came back just to toy with you? Do you think that's possible?"

Gemini shrugged. "Anything is possible. It could have been a bad dream or maybe it's tummy troubles."

She stood, straightening her sky-blue blouse before absently rubbing her belly. All better today, thanks to her home remedy of ground ginger, the juice of a lemon, and turmeric. Ruthmarie was no match for special herbs.

"I'd like to proceed as if she were telling the truth. Those Crabbitzes are dangerous. We didn't need my mother-in-law to tell us that. If you don't mind, I'll run this by Feather today. We may just pay Chief Boulder a visit and feel him out for any connections from other communities."

Howard stood as well and folded his arms one over the other. "I could go with you? Other than the garden club meeting at two, my day is completely open."

Though he was often invaluable because of his connections, today she needed Feather's abilities worse than she needed Howard's Rolodex. "Feather is going with me. I'll call when we return."

She couldn't bear seeing her friend's disappointment, so she turned abruptly and left.

Boundaries, Reed. Boundaries.

CHAPTER 24

FEATHER

Light filtered through the shuttered window of Cassie's room, rudely awakening Feather. She glanced over at Tug, who had generously surrendered the faux leather recliner to her. He was seated in a chair with one leg crossed over the other. One elbow was perched on the armrest, allowing that hand to hold his head. It was like he fell asleep thinking about what to do next.

Memories of the previous night slowly resurfaced as her mind came to life.

Charming Emergency Room was packed with broken bones, crying babies, and drunken ramblings.

Feather's gaze fixed on the hospital corridor, her thoughts drifting between the events of the day and the unknown dangers that had targeted Cassie.

Does Miss Rogers have any family that we can contact?

She mentioned an Opal someone, but not as though they were close.

Hours felt like an eternity as they waited for news. They held on to each other tight, afraid if they let go, one of them would fall apart.

Feather realized now was the time to reach out to Cassie's grandmother, or maybe a friendlier connection from the other side. "I'm going to get coffee. Can I bring you some?"

Tug looked at her. No, he looked through her. He knew exactly what she was doing. "Try the stairwell. It should be private this time of night."

If you know Cassie, I need to hear from you now.

An older woman's voice laughed. It was unnerving, given the fact that Feather couldn't see her.

She's not doing well. If you could help me contact Opal, you would be doing us both a favor.

You mean my good-for-nothing daughter? She ran off and left me with her child. Always another man, another adventure. I can't wait until she's on this side. There's no way that self-centered girl will be able to ignore me then.

Feather swallowed hard. *But for Cassie? You want to help her, don't you?*

She returned to Cassie's hospital room with a steaming cup of coffee. Tug's eyes were closed, and his face reminded her of a book from her childhood, one where a sweet little boy slept on a cloud.

He blinked as his eyes adjusted to the harsh lights. "How'd it go?"

"Good. I have a last known address for Opal. I stopped at the nurses' station to give them the information."

Tug took the Styrofoam cup and sipped the coffee before making a face. "Ugh. That's nasty. When we find a good coffee company to partner with, our first stop will be the hospital cafeteria."

She leaned forward, kissing him softly on the lips. "Your poor back must be killing you."

Tug arched his back forward. "Yeah, but it's nothing a few laps around the 8th floor won't cure. We should get some food in our bellies too. I'll see what they consider food in the cafeteria. Do you want to come with me?"

"No, I think I'll stay. Cassie's grandmother wasn't the friendliest, and if she starts whispering in Cassie's ear, I want to be here to fight her energy."

Tug raised one eyebrow. "I never know when it's safe to leave you alone."

"All good. Go!" Feather pushed the air with her hand. "Do some laps around the floor or whatever you need to feel right again."

They kissed one more time.

Tug was barely out the door when the hairs on Feather's arms rose.

"Cassie's grandma? Is that you?"

She's coming! Prepare yourself for a cyclone!

"What does that—"

"Who the hell are you?"

A burly woman with knotted brown hair and bloodshot eyes burst through the door. She marched straight toward Feather and stood inches from her with no appreciation for personal space.

"I'll ask again. Who the hell are you?"

Feather could smell alcohol on her breath. "I'm Feather Jones. A friend of Cassie's."

"I just told the nurse that, from now on, it's just me allowed in here. My girl don't need no riff raff in here trying to steal her personals."

"I'm not stealing anything." Feather's face was crimson, and she struggled to hold her temper. "My boyfriend and I brought her in last night. We found her in an alley. I assume you're Opal Hughes?"

The woman crossed her arms and leaned on one leg. "You 'assume.' What is your game, lady?"

Tug reappeared, using his chin to hold a sandwich in a plastic wrapper while each of his hands held an apple.

"Are you Cassie's boyfriend?" Her words were sweeter than syrup as she swayed back and forth. "She told me about you, Gary."

Tug's eyes traveled from her crazy face to Feather's. It didn't take him long to size up the situation. "Tug Muehler. I'm her boss. Your sister's boss, that is."

Feather rolled her eyes. It was so dumb that this worked every single time.

"Oh." The woman giggled. "I'm her mom. Cassie don't have any sisters, 'least that I know of."

"I have a tracker on my delivery van, so the minute we knew it had been in an accident, we rushed over to find her. The doctor told us last night that she had a brain injury and being in a coma was the best way for her to rest and recover."

Cassie's mother clucked her tongue. "Poor kid."

Like she cares. Opal hightailed it out of the hospital after Cassie's birth. Didn't return until her daughter's eighteenth birthday, when Cassie was going to inherit money from her grandfather.

"Opal, your daughter was being chased by someone."

Cassie's mother whipped around so fast, she lost her balance. Tug sat the food on the bed and moved quickly to steady her, allowing Opal to fall backward into his arms.

"Oopsie. Guess I need a handsome beefcake to get me upright. That is, unless that's not the way you want me to be." She tilted her chin upward, as though she thought he was going to kiss her.

Tug pushed with all his might to get Opal back to a standing position. She patted her pockets and looked around the room.

Ha! The booze bag left her keys in the car! That's okay, gives you time to call the police and report it stolen. She took it from her neighbor's driveway this morning.

"I have to run to the car and get my keys. I'll be right back."

Opal Hughes sashayed through the door and out into the hallway, where she could be heard propositioning a doctor. When she was out of earshot, Feather and Tug searched each other's faces for answers.

"Poor Cassie. That woman is a nightmare! I need a hug, babe." Feather squeezed Tug's muscular body as hard as she could. "We both could use a shower too. Not only are we still in yesterday's clothes, but Opal just reeked of booze and cigarettes. I can still smell it on my skin!"

"What do we do now? I overheard her saying we're not allowed to stay with Cassie any longer." Tug scratched the back of his neck and looked out the window where Opal's backside was splayed out on the car seat.

"And we don't want to risk another confrontation. It's not good for Cassie to have that kind of energy around her."

Wise choice. Opal loves to create a stir.

"You'll let me know? When Cassie is alert?"

"Huh?" Tug's furrowed brow reminded Feather that, as in tune as they were, he didn't always know when she was talking to a ghost.

"Oh, I was just asking Cassie's grandmother to alert me when she wakes up."

Tug picked up his jacket from the chair and took

Cassie's hand in his own and squeezed it. "You're going to come back to us, Cassie. We'll be waiting when you do."

Feather felt slightly jealous that he was so tender with another woman before her jealousy turned to shame. "Cassie, we're rooting for you!" She was standing at the doorway, tapping it with her index finger. "Come on, Tug!"

As they passed the nurses' station, Feather heard the name Stanley repeated in her head. "Wait just a sec, Tug."

She rang the tiny bell on the desk. When that got no reaction, Feather cleared her throat. "Is there a Stanley here?"

All activity ceased and the nurses stared at her. A woman in her 50s with a kind face and faded auburn hair waved. "I'm Lavidia Stanley. What can I do for you?"

"My boyfriend and I came in with the woman in room 112 last night." Feather motioned with her eyes.

"Oh yes." Lavidia looked back over her shoulder. "Poor gal. She's got a long road ahead of her."

"Would you let us know when she wakes up? Her mother is kind of territorial and I don't want to make a scene."

"Who's her mother?"

"Um, Opal. Opal Hughes."

Lavidia's face went blank. Feather thought she'd said the wrong thing. "It's okay. Forget it. I—"

"I babysat Opal when she was a little girl. At least I did until she started stealing from me. Tools, food, perfume—you name it. I don't know how or why she got that way. Her mother was always so pleasant."

After leaving both Tug's and Feather's cell phone numbers, they took the stairs to the lobby. One thing they were both certain of was that they wanted to avoid Opal Hughes at all costs.

CHAPTER 25
GEMINI

The bell over the door sang "Happy Days Are Here Again" as she entered their office. She was planning to surprise Feather with her latest purchase, but the timing hadn't been right.

Feather sprang from her seat and enveloped Gemini in a hug. "I've been so worried! You didn't answer any of my texts!"

Feather's hair was still wet and smelled of fruity shampoo, which was unsettling, to say the least. Feather Jones did not shower before dark, ever. It was her way of relaxing before bed.

Gemini was taken aback by Feather's appearance. Though her partner wasn't a fancy dresser, her look never varied: spiky hair in whatever color she fancied that week, combat boots, jeans, and a shirt. Today, however, Feather's wet hair was pasted to her scalp as though she'd forgotten to comb it. She wore a wrinkled t-shirt with the words "Electric Pickle Trip World Tour" almost rubbed off.

The worst part was the bags under her very red eyes. "Are you all right, hon?"

"I tried calling you a billion times last night. You never picked up." Feather's voice was a mixture of anger and defeat. The combination of the two made Gemini's heart hurt.

When she opened her purse and pulled out her phone, her inbox was full. Nine unread messages.

"Oh dear. I'm very sorry about that. Once I explain why, you'll understand." Gemini clucked her tongue sympathetically. "I'm guessing you spent most of your night awake too? Let's sit down."

"There's been a big development in the Alistair Violette case. But, more importantly, we spent most of the night in the emergency room with Cassie."

Tug came loping through the door with unchar-acteristic clumsiness. He would have knocked a preschool graduation picture of Taurus in a 24-carat, gold-plated frame onto the floor had Gemini not reacted quickly.

"What happened to the poor girl?" Gemini's worried glance traveled from Tug's to Feather's.

"Cassie was in an accident. She was making deliveries when something happened to distract her and she crashed. We brought her to the emergency room and waited all night for word on her condi-tion." Feather nodded encouragingly to Tug, urging him to finish. "She still hasn't regained consciousness. We were hoping to question her."

The doorbell sang again. This time, it was Chief Boulder. "Morning, all." He tipped his hat toward Gemini, who nodded in response. She was still upset with him for treating her like some nut.

"What can we do for you, Chief?" Gemini went over and poured him a cup of coffee and sat it on the edge of her desk. "Have a seat." She did her best to hide her anger.

"Heard your delivery van was in an accident last night, Mr. Muehler. We got three calls from concerned folks on Dreadful Drive. Imagine my surprise when we showed up and found no sign of a driver."

CHAPTER 26

GEMINI

Chief Boulder squinted as he scrutinized Tug's appearance. Just watching made Gemini uncomfortable. She could only imagine what was going through Tug's mind.

"Oh, I have a new employee who got scared when he wrecked the van."

"He just got out of prison," Feather chimed in. "So he was afraid of cops."

Chief Boulder raised an eyebrow at the mention of an ex-convict. "Is that so?"

"Yeah, but he's a good guy," she added quickly. "I'll vouch for him."

"As will I," Gemini chimed in.

The chief hummed, taking a sip of coffee. "I don't doubt it, Miss Jones. But we still need to question him. We found his wallet and some suspicious items near the scene."

"His what?" Tug and Feather exclaimed in unison.

Gemini braced herself for the moment one or both of them collapsed in shock.

"Empty jewelry boxes. And a crowbar. Mr. Carpetia has been a busy man since his release last Tuesday."

Tug's eyes widened in disbelief. "That doesn't make any sense. We're a company that makes protein bars. We don't carry jewelry. Why would Mr.... Carpetia... have any of those items?"

Chief Boulder leaned forward and changed the focus of his interrogation from Feather to Gemini. "The van was completely empty when we got there. The only evidence we found was his wallet approximately 100 feet from the vehicle. Imagine it was teenagers looking for a trophy, unless any of you have other suggestions?"

"My understanding is that the van sat there for hours before you arrived, Chief. An unlocked delivery van is an invitation to thieves, isn't it?" Something about his demeanor made Gemini defensive. He was treating them all like criminals trying to hide a crime.

The chief leaned back in his chair, rubbing his chin. "Two robberies and a missing kid who was just playing hide-and-seek last night in the garbage can. We're a small department, Mrs. Reed. We got there when we could."

It wasn't that she disliked Chief Boulder. Gemini found him to be a reasonable man, for the most part. But something about his tactics made her extremely uncomfortable. "Have you checked the security cameras from the jewelry stores? Maybe someone came upon the van in the hours it sat there, unattended, and decided to plant evidence. It's not a stretch to imagine them setting Mr. Carpetia up to clear themselves."

Feather caught Gemini's eye and gave her a nod of approval.

Chief Boulder touched the tips of his fingers together and stared at the wall. *Had he really not thought of this on his own?*

"What I need now is to speak with Mr. Carpetia to confirm everything you've told me. You have to see this from our perspective, Mrs. Reed. We have a missing driver and some suspicious evidence. We need your cooperation."

"Of course. Whatever you need from me or my employees is at your disposal." Tug's voice was firm. "We have nothing to hide."

Gemini nodded slowly as a new plan entered her mind. "Something just came to me. Mr. Carpetia shared with us that he had acquaintances on Dreadful Drive. He'd been in prison for so long, he wanted to surprise them."

Feather's head cocked to the side and Gemini could almost hear the questions going through her mind. *I have no idea where Gem's going with this, but I'll play along.*

Gemini smiled so hard her cheeks smudged her reader glasses. Chief Boulder was new enough that he didn't yet understand the facial cues she gave when she was getting ready to tell a completely made-up story. "Mr. Carpetia said he wanted to visit a man by the name of Fudge Jameson."

Tug coughed, or rather laughed then covered it with a cough.

"That's a start." The chief jotted down some notes. "Can you tell me more about their relationship?"

"Oh, I wish I could, Chief. In that short time, I only spoke with Mr. Carpetia once. None of us knew him well."

Or at all.

The chief clicked his pen and placed it back in the pocket of his uniform. "As I was going through his record this morning, I came upon an arrest for speeding, and guess who pulled him over? Yours truly. I was working for the highway patrol, in my third year, I believe. Didn't remember much about him, other'n the nice conversation we had about tourists at the beach. Looking at the rest of his rap sheet today shocked the socks clean off my feet. He'd been locked up for nearly fifteen years before his release."

Gemini swallowed hard. "What did he do to be in lock up that long?"

"Killed a coupla dudes." Chief Boulder was nonchalant as he delivered this information. It may have been an everyday experience for him, but the fact that their made-up delivery driver was a real man with a real record was going to take some time to process.

Tug made a pushing motion with his hand. "In the environment he grew up in, it was pretty normal."

"I'd be interested in hearing what he told you during the interview process. You know, when you hired him." Chief Boulder took another sip of his coffee before smacking his lips. "Good stuff."

"Oh, you know, the usual. He got himself into trouble when he was young and, now that he'd been in prison, Mr. Carpetia—Shag—grew up and wanted to make a fresh start. I'm all about giving second chances."

Tug cleared his throat before continuing. He was clearly enjoying this. Too much. "After telling me his story, he said, 'Don't even get me started on the jobs I did in the joint. You don't turn anything down unless you want it to go on your record.'"

Just as they were all feeling comfortable in the make-believe world they'd created, the door jingled again. It had all gone so smoothly, up until then.

"I sure wish someone would have invited me to

this shindig!" Olive's voice was part hurt, part resentful.

She pulled up a chair and sat down as close to Chief Boulder as she could. Today, she wore a tie-dyed t-shirt underneath her Tug Bars apron and, to Feather's dismay, had chunks of her hair dyed in a rainbow of colors.

"Don't think I've met you yet. I love a man in uniform," Olive gushed.

"I haven't had the pleasure of meeting you either." He nodded in her general direction. "Chief Boulder. And you are?"

"Olive Thomas. I'm the co-owner of Tug Bars. Someday, when I'm retirement age, I'll give it all up."

Before Tug could protest that every single thing that came out of her mouth except her name was a lie, Feather socked him in the arm.

"What brings you here today, Chief? Would you like a tour of our factory? I've got some free time."

"I'm just investigating your delivery driver. I'm sure you heard about the accident."

Tug jumped to his feet, his face red. "You really don't have any time, Olive. We've got a huge order, and I need you there supervising our new trainees."

Olive harrumphed and glared at Tug until he noticed.

"Well, Mr. Smartypants, that's why I crashed your private party. We're one short this morning."

Gemini sensed what was coming and flew into

action. "Olive, you and I need to go over the takeout menu. I want to pick up lunch soon and you haven't given me any idea what you'd like."

"At 9:30?" Olive frowned. "Well, you know me, girlfriend. I could always eat."

"When can I interview you, Ms. Thomas?"

Olive stopped dead in her tracks. "Like, for a date?"

The chief's face reddened to the point that Gemini wondered if he was having a heart attack. "No, ma'am. I'd like to ask you some questions about—"

"Olive never met that new employee. We keep her busy in the kitchen while I handle the rest of the staff. She's far too valuable to waste on administrative duties." Tug winked at Olive. Everyone in the room with the exception of the chief knew Olive was putty in Tug's hands when a little affection was thrown her way.

Gemini wasted no time. "Let's go into the break room, shall we?"

As Gemini guided her toward the other room, where thankfully her voice wouldn't carry, Olive paused and looked over her shoulder. "My boyfriend has a police scanner in his bedroom. He says our delivery van was in an accident last night! Wasn't that new gal, Cassie, scheduled? I wondered why she didn't show today."

"No, it wasn't her, dear," Gemini said as she

wrapped an arm around Olive's shoulder and encouraged her to walk.

After settling Olive with a plate of day-old pastries, Gemini scurried back with what was left of her lemon drop cookies and set them on the counter next to Chief Boulder.

"I was just telling Mr. Muehler about the rumors I've heard."

"Really? What rumors?"

"That the four of you are investigating Gladiola Crabbitz."

Gemini fought to remain stoic. "I can't imagine who would spread something like that."

"It was a..." Chief Boulder licked a finger and went backwards in his notebook until he found what he was looking for. "Here it is. Mr. Quentin Zahn. Said he knows everything that goes on in the neighborhood, and he was positive you were looking into Gladiola." The chief chuckled. "Never seen a grown man jump up and down while he spoke with me before. It's kind of nice when someone is that excited to see law enforcement."

Now Gemini could safely roll her eyes. "He's my neighbor. A rather enthusiastic watcher of television mysteries, if you get my drift."

"Uh-huh." He didn't appear to be convinced. "Well, whatever is going on, please leave it to me. I realize they are a bit prickly, but I'm the one with the badge."

Gemini gave him a salute as he grabbed what was left of the cookies and stuffed them into his pocket.

"I'll be in touch soon. Thanks for the coffee and the goodies, Mrs. Reed."

They watched as he walked out the door and got in his police cruiser.

"There was nothing about that experience that made sense." Gemini scratched her head. "Why on earth would he do that?"

"You mean why would he pretend he knew our made-up driver? I can think of a million reasons. The first one being he doesn't want us to clam up before he gets what he wants."

"I'm going to see what I can find out about this Shag person," Feather announced. "Maybe it was a crime of opportunity and he dropped his wallet on accident, or..."

Gemini shifted uncomfortably. "He was there at the behest of someone else."

CHAPTER 27

FEATHER

Since there was no change in Cassie's condition, Feather took the opportunity to visit Jayden. With Alistair's deadline looming, she had to come up with a plan to save Jayden soon.

Ironically, without her mentor's help, she didn't know quite what that plan would be. For the past two days, she'd been wondering if Alistair's dire warning might be true. What if Jayden really was about to bring the downfall of the entire P.I.NK. society? She had certainly been acting strange lately.

Her common sense usually took over from there, reminding her that Jayden had never been anything but kind and helpful to those who asked for her guidance and protection. Today, as Feather pushed the button for the top floor, those feelings battled in her mind. Without Millicent to run interference, she would have to come up with another way to keep Jayden from reading her troubled mind.

"Miss Jones! Always a delight to see you!"

Jayden's secretary, Lulu Rodriguez, was the most cheerful person Feather had ever met, aside from Gemini. A slight woman with caramel skin and bright brown eyes, she had a way of making people feel welcome.

"Lulu! I see you took my advice and got a little pizzazz added." Feather gestured toward her own deep purple locks.

Lulu ran her fingers through her shiny, dark hair newly accented by gold highlights. "Yes! I was just sorry I couldn't get in with you."

"Something just occurred to me. We're having a séance tomorrow night and we're short one person. Would you like to join us?"

Lulu placed her palms on her desk and leaned her head back. "Feather Jones, I could kiss you right here, right now."

Feather took a step backward. That wasn't exactly the response she'd expected. "Um... unfortunately, my partner set this up and then had to back out. If you're busy—"

Lulu's hand shot out. "No, not busy at all! I've asked Jayden for years to include me in these things, but she always says 'It's not wise, Lulu.'"

Feather let out a sigh of relief. "Great! Come to

the back door of the warehouse at seven! I'll send you the address."

Feather walked toward the over-sized door of Jayden's office.

"Oh, you can't go in! She's with a client!"

Lulu was usually relaxed and unflappable, but today she jumped up and rushed to the door before an unsuspecting Feather arrived. Her arms and legs were splayed out as wide as possible, blocking Feather.

"What's going on? You're acting weird, Lulu!"

As if on cue, loud voices emanated from Jayden's office. It was impossible to hear the words, but Feather clearly recognized Jayden's voice.

Feather's gut tightened. She had never heard Jayden raise her voice before, even when she was upset. Something was wrong. Ignoring Lulu's protest, she pushed through Lulu's blockade and opened the door.

Jayden's pale cheeks were flushed as she yelled at a tall, middle-aged man with stringy brown hair standing menacingly close to her.

"Get out of my office, you bastard!" Jayden spat at him.

"Not until you give me what I want," the man growled, shoving her against the wall. "There's no way out for you, Ko. We're taking what we're owed."

Feather's instincts kicked in. She rushed towards the man, aiming a swift kick at his back. If there was one thing that was universal, it was middle-aged back pain.

She may have been small, but she worked out with Tug enough that she possessed the strength of three men.

The stranger's knees buckled as he grabbed his back. He stumbled in a circle, momentarily disoriented. Jayden took advantage of the opportunity and darted towards the door. "Call security, Lulu!"

The man regained his balance and lunged towards Feather. She braced herself for impact, ready to retaliate with all her might, when a shot rang out. His eyes widened as he lurched forward. Feather jumped out of the way, watching in horror as he collapsed to the ground, lifeless.

FEATHER GASPED, sucking in every last bit of air in the room. A sudden surge of adrenaline sent her heart into a wild, frenzied beat. She slowly pivoted towards Jayden, her eyes widening in disbelief and horror. The metallic scent of gunpowder lingered in the air, and there, in Jayden's trembling hand, was the unmistakable silhouette of a smoking gun. Jayden's face was frozen somewhere between a smile and a scream.

Feather was frozen in place, her mind floating somewhere above her body. Jayden's desk, her plush chairs, everything was as it should be. Everything except... the body on the floor. The walls of the room seemed to close in, her vision blurring, and the ground beneath her felt as if it were shifting. She clutched her chest, trying to steady her ragged breaths.

Is this real?

She felt someone push past her. "Honey, you should have warned me this one was a security risk." Lulu's voice was too calm for what had just taken place. She dropped to her knees, feeling for a pulse. "He's gone."

Jayden's eyes were wide. Her posture was stiff, as if frozen in place. The only movement was the hand that held the gun. It uncontrollably twitched at her side. "He was going to kill me, Feather. You saw him — I had no choice."

Nothing about Jayden was making sense: the fact that she let someone else control her emotions, needing a weapon other than her mind, arguing with a client.

"Who is—was—he?" Feather whispered.

"We can talk about that later!" Lulu gave Feather's leg a good shove, forcing her body into the door frame. "The less evidence on you, the easier it is for me."

In the few years they had known each other, she had come to trust Jayden implicitly. But, in a matter of seconds, that trust disappeared.

There was a new problem too. The body on the

floor was going to attract attention, and they needed to get rid of it before the police arrived.

Feather swallowed hard, trying to make sense of this senseless situation. "Okay, we have to think fast. We can't stay here. We need to dispose of the body and get out of the city. Tug can help us with that."

She pulled her phone out of her pocket, but her fingers were shaking so hard she couldn't push the buttons. *How would they keep this quiet?*

Lulu stood, pressing her skirt straight. "Don't bother. In the past, we've used Gary's Restoration. They won the Charming Chamber's Tidy Titan Award six years in a row. There'll be no need to leave town."

Feather couldn't decide if she was feeling shock, admiration, or a combination of the two. "In the past? Lulu, I need more information."

"Later, Feather. We need to lock down the office," Lulu instructed. "Can you lead Jayden into the conference room? She'll be just fine once I get some food into her."

Stepping over the body, she took Jayden by the arm, unsure that a snack would change the poor woman's demeanor. "Come on. I'll get you some water and sit with you until you're feeling better."

As she guided her mentor down the long hallway, she heard Lulu over the PA system. "Code Seven-Seven. Code Seven-Seven."

The conference room was a cavernous space

with a fountain and courtyard sitting outside the doors on the far end. They'd barely sat in the luxurious leather chairs when Lulu appeared carrying two glasses of orange juice and homemade chocolate chip cookies.

She tucked a strand of hair behind Jayden's ear after setting the food in front of her. "Come back to us, boss," she said softly.

"Lulu, how is it that you have a code for murder and Harry's Restoration on speed dial—"

"It's Gary's Restoration. But I can understand how you'd get that confused." She glanced at Feather with a look of concern. "In our line of work, we deal with some shady characters. It comes with the amazing pay and vacations to tropical islands, sweetie. There's always a trade-off."

"Then why is Jayden..."

"Frozen? It only happened once before, when her dog died the same day an assassin was sent to kill her." Lulu massaged Jayden's shoulders with impressive strength. Her act of familiarity with her boss seemed out of place.

"I suspect this has to do with her recent loss of abilities. She hasn't been right since. I'll have some forms for you to sign before you leave, and the D and D office will be calling for a follow-up interview."

"D and D?"

"Deaths and Disasters. It's standard procedure."

There was a commotion in the office, and two men dressed in beige coveralls appeared in the doorway. "How many?" one of them asked, as though he was taking a lunch order for tacos.

"Just one. I'll take you there." Lulu stood. "Don't worry, Feather. We deal with this kind of thing all the time. You'll be okay, right?" Without waiting for a response, she greeted Hal and joined him. "Hal! I thought you quit! How is Margery?"

Their voices drifted off. *Did that really just happen or was it a horrible dream?*

Feather looked down and realized her hands were shaking and, not only that, there were specks of blood on her fingers.

Wiping her hands on her jeans, a sense of dread overtook her. Nothing would ever be the same. Something sparkly caught her eye, and she was shocked to find a business card splattered with blood on the floor. In addition to the blood, the card was covered in gold glitter, creating a spooky combination of gore and gaiety. She gasped as she read it:

Shag Carpetia
Elimination Specialist

CHAPTER 28
GEMINI

"There's something I need to say."

Gemini had been against it, but Feather and Sophia insisted it was important her daughter participate.

"We need one more person, Gem." Feather informed her that Jayden's secretary had an unexpected family situation come up and couldn't join them.

Sophia, on the other hand, grew suspicious when her mother paced across her living room as she sipped chicken broth.

"Out with it, Mother!"

Gemini came to an abrupt halt. "What?"

"You're keeping something from me. Just spit it out so I don't have extra medical issues to deal with. You know how fussy my bowels can be."

"I have an event this evening, with Feather and Tug. They requested that I bring you too."

Sophia crossed one shapely leg over the other and clasped her hands on top of them. "What are we talking, a kegger? Or are they more the boxed wine type of folks?"

"It's a simple office party."

"What kind of party? Are we going to a business-after-hours gathering? I love those!"

It was the most enthusiastic Sophia had been since she walked through the door. Her mystery surgery still hadn't been revealed. Sophia was as thin as a wafer, and Gemini hoped a doctor wouldn't acquiesce to her desire for a concave stomach.

"Its... a séance." Gemini raised her brows and clenched her fists. A complete dressing down regarding her mental competence was surely on its way.

"Oh." Sophia's gaze drifted to the kitchen table, where she'd set Taurus's every-two-month photo shoot photos.

"You don't have to go," Gemini quickly added. "In fact, I don't have to go either."

Pulling her phone from the pocket of her cream-colored slacks, she prepared to text Feather to cancel.

"Wait!" Sophia rose from the chair with startling speed for someone who hadn't eaten solid food in months. "I've always wanted to do one of those! We tried in college, but my roommate, Trixie Belle, insisted we all get drunk first. By the time we started, no one could see straight."

Sophia giggled and then brought her hand up to her mouth, as though she, too, had let loose before thinking it out. "And then last Christmas they did one for the law office Christmas party. I was home sick and missed the entire thing. Brandon said it was a real kick."

"Sophia, this isn't like your college games or a Christmas party performance." Gemini sniffed. "Feather is very good at what she does. An expert in her field."

"I wasn't implying any different, Mother," she said mournfully. A solitary tear welled up in her eye and slowly made its way down her cheek. When Sophia was a small child, she had mastered the art of the tear. Leo once commented, "That famous actress from the forties, Tulip Sloan, has nothing on our little drama princess."

One of Sophia's favorite tricks was to ask friends for a particular number of tears they'd like to see. She would produce exactly that number.

"I'm going with you." Sophia's voice was firm and resolute. "There's no way I'm staying here while you commune with the dead."

Gemini sighed as she picked up her beige purse. "I'll wait for you in the car." Feigning a last-minute trip to the bathroom, she changed her mind and instructed Sophia to go ahead and get in the car and she would join her momentarily. Once her daughter was out the door, she opened the large, catch-all drawer under the microwave. She used her fingers to shove waves of pens, paperclips, small writing pads emblazoned with "Floris, Fealgood and Flem: We do more than you think we can", and colored pencils back and forth until she found it.

THEY WERE the first to arrive.

Gemini shoved two square card tables together without the help of her daughter, who insisted she was too weak from her fast to help. Gemini didn't doubt that.

Next, she opened her large bag and pulled out black tablecloths. According to Feather, everyone in attendance needed objects that would have meaning to the entities.

For her part, Gemini chose a spider-shaped broach given to her by Ruthmarie on the occasion of hers and Leo's fifth anniversary. "I thought for sure my son would've come to his senses by now," she had grumbled as she chucked the small unwrapped box in Gemini's general direction.

Gemini had pondered for a moment, wondering whether it might be an explosive. Chastising herself for such an outrageous thought, she opened the box. It was a surprisingly intricate design: tiny diamonds making the spider's outline with tiny rubies shaping each leg. She didn't have the energy to ask if the stones were real.

Ever since then, she wore the broach when she was angry with her mother-in-law. *A spider, just like Ruthmarie.*

Sophia's item would be a challenge. Though her daughter was curious about the séance, she wasn't sure what kind of reaction the idea of inviting her dead grandmother might induce. For that reason, she was silent the entire ride out to the warehouse, while Sophia gave a detailed account of the many talents of the new nanny she'd hired, including speaking French, German, and Spanish. Sophia was confident Taurus would pick them up by the summer.

Gemini reached into her purse and pulled out the item with sentimental value that she'd brought for her daughter. As Gemini sat the miniature trophy on the table, she suppressed a laugh. It was another memory of Ruthmarie that made her cringe at the time.

Sophia finished setting out place cards and paused in front of her mother, picking up a familiar item.

"Mother, why on earth would you bring Trophy Wophy to a séance?"

"Leave it there, please," Gemini reiterated. "Feather instructed everyone to bring something of sentimental value. We're hoping to attract loved ones who will help us with Gladiola. I remembered how much this meant to you, so that's why I included it."

Sophia whimpered as her form of protest, but Gemini didn't take the bait. Used to her daughter's immature displays of emotion, she continued preparing for the evening by starting the coffee maker and retrieving six cups from the cupboard.

"It brings back so many memories, Mother."

Turning and placing her hands on her hips, Gemini watched as Sophia rolled the three-inch tall silver bear seated on a pedestal of equal size in her hands.

Gemini felt a pang of guilt. Bringing her daughter into this storm was a bad idea. "Come here."

She encircled Sophia's slight frame with her arms and drew her in close. Though they had plenty of differences, the feeling of holding her child in her arms was like no other.

Gemini tucked a few strands of wavy hair behind Sophia's ear. "You were sad that you hadn't won a trophy for gymnastics, so Grammie Reed bought you this. She told you to keep it in your little pocket for good luck."

"Grammie told me to name it, so that every time I went to a meet, I could repeat the name over and over. Trophy Wophy was all I could come up with on such short notice."

"It served you well. You received six trophies and enough medals and ribbons to fill your wall." Gemini squeezed her daughter's shoulder. "Now, let's see what kind of luck it brings us tonight, all right?"

Gently, she removed the object from Sophia's hand and placed it back on the table.

"Ladies! I'm so happy you're here to help!"

They turned to see Jayden dressed in a midnight blue catsuit with matching acrylic nails and a shoulder-length auburn wig.

Gemini found her demeanor odd. Jayden was usually cool and composed; her overabundance of joy was out of character. Almost like she was trying too hard to convince them she was something she wasn't.

"Jayden, this is–"

"Your daughter, Sophia." Jayden moved quickly to Sophia's side, offering her hand before Sophia had a chance to react. "So nice to finally meet you. I've heard many good things about you and your family."

A faint blush colored Sophia's pale cheeks. "Oh, I'm sure my mother talks about me enough that you're over it."

Gemini and Jayden exchanged knowing glances.

"Mother's never mentioned you before, though. What brings you to this fun little gathering?"

Gemini sensed a note of judgment in Sophia's voice. Yes, Jayden looked different than the average woman, but it had no bearing on her character. "Jayden is the CEO of Ko Industries."

"Oh!" Sophia's voice rose an octave. "My husband has done some work for your company, and he is so impressed by your leadership skills." Sophia's eyes traveled up and down Jayden's torso. "I would think a silly game like this would be beneath you. My mother has a habit of thinking everyone likes her theme parties as much as she does."

Jayden nodded without betraying her thoughts. "I'm being harassed by someone from the other side. We're here this evening to figure out who it is and why they're upset with me."

Sophia's eyes darted over to her mother. "You never mentioned anything about that. You said this was a séance just like I had in college!"

"I..."

"There's no danger to you, Sophia. Your mother didn't want to worry you needlessly."

Gemini would remember to thank Jayden later. Crisis averted, Jayden pulled out the chair adjacent to her name card and sat down.

Feather, Tug, and Olive arrived at once, bringing bubbly energy into a strangely subdued room. It only took a minute for Gemini to realize the energy was coming from Tug and Olive, not Feather. Another member of the group who wasn't herself.

"Thanks for setting up, Gem. We had a bit of an issue that I'll tell you about later."

Gemini squeezed her shoulder. "I'm here for you, hon," she whispered in Feather's ear.

Feather nodded. When her gaze fell on Jayden, she froze in place.

"I was the issue," Olive explained. "My man friend was against me going out tonight. It took all the sweet talking Tug had in him to get him to change his mind."

Sophia leaned to one side and then the other, allowing her wavy hair to cascade halfway down her back.

The reason for her signature hair toss became evident when Tug seated himself directly across from her.

"Theodore, I'm so pleased you could join us," she cooed as she offered a limp hand, heavy with two huge diamonds, for him to kiss.

Tug reluctantly grasped her small, pale fingers and shook them. "It's Tug. Nice to see you again, Sophia. Thanks for helping us out tonight."

Jayden glanced from one person to the next. "Thank you all for coming this evening. With all of the energy in this room, we'll be able to combat anything negative. Right, Feather?"

Feather appeared conflicted. If she and Jayden had quarreled earlier, they would surely get past it quickly. Either way, poor Feather was stuck. "We're ready when you are, hon!"

Feather lit two tall, butter-yellow candles, one on each table, and Gemini was pleased her words had brought Feather out of her funk.

"Are we all ready?" Five heads nodded in unison. "Gem, would you get the lights?"

Gemini flipped the switches for everything except the hallway leading to the bathroom and sat down.

Feather took Gemini's hand in hers and motioned for everyone else to copy the gesture.

"Now, I'm going to insist upon complete silence. When I give the instruction, drop the hand of the person on your left and pick up the object you brought with you."

CHAPTER 29

FEATHER

"I want to caution you, there is no 'for sure' scenario. Some loved ones are attached to an object, like the ones you brought this evening. Others attach themselves to a person. There are still others who attach themselves to a location, like Gem's mother-in-law." She nodded toward Gemini, whose daughter opened her mouth to ask about her grandmother.

She watched as Gemini mouthed "later" to her daughter before continuing. "Whoever you're hoping comes forward may not have the ability to manifest here. It doesn't mean they don't want to be with you."

Looking around the table, she was pleased to see everyone listening intently.

Even Jayden.

Feather's smooth, confident voice belied the horrific thoughts still circling her brain. Shag

Carpetia, a man whose wallet was found near their delivery van, a man who may or may not have been terrorizing Cassie.

Then there was the image of Jayden. The face of a woman she'd placed on the highest pedestal—her mentor—completely emotionless as a man lay dying at her feet.

Feather had waited until she was sure they'd removed the body before making her exit from the conference room. When she did, the entire top floor was empty.

She'd paused at Lulu's desk to leave a note. "Please have Jayden call me later! We need to talk about this." When she stood to leave, she noticed a note for her:

> F—
>
> Clear your mind of what you saw.
> It's for your benefit as well as ours.
> Due to this afternoon's events, I'm
> afraid I need to bow out of the séance.
> I've got some loose ends to tie up. Next
> time!
>
> L

"Let's begin."

The words had barely left her lips when the hairs on her arms rose.

Why are you calling me? Are you looking for trouble?

Feather's eyes snapped open. As she glanced around, it was clear she was the only one who heard the voice. Including Jayden, whose abilities far surpassed Feather's.

"Tell me your name. We are all safe, friendly people."

Instantly, five pairs of eyes popped open and stared at her.

"I... I don't hear anyone!" Jayden cried.

Her mentor, stripped of her superpowers, held back tears. Feather was on her own.

"Let's start with your name. Can you tell me at least your first name?"

A hissing sound began at the doorway and moved across the room. When the sound hit Feather, so did a cold blast of air.

I don't answer questions. I ask them!

"You're being downright rude."

Feather looked sharply to her left. She swallowed hard when she realized there was one more person who could hear this voice. It was Sophia. She nodded encouragingly toward Gemini's daughter and hoped she understood.

"I'm assuming you came from some sort of barn-yard situation, because here, in respectable society, we speak to each other politely. Either tell us your name or—"

Two Tone.

Feather squinted. So this was going to be a game. Feather Jones could play too. After repeating his name for the rest of the room, she replied, "Well, Mister Two Tone, it's nice to meet you."

"What year were you..." Sophia paused and mouthed to Feather, "How do I say dead?"

"Dead," Feather replied.

"Yes, Mr. Tone. What year did you die?"

Recently. Unexpected.

"What's he saying?" Olive tapped one hand on the top of a canned good in front of her. "When do we get to use our toys? I brought a can of cherries. My dearly departed husband, Chauncey, used to love a good pie. Trouble was, I hated making them until I ran into my next-door-neighbor, Wilma, at the grocery. She said she always used a frozen crust and a can of cherries. Nobody knew the difference."

It was Tug's turn. "Olive, that's not your husband's name."

"Chauncey was my first husband. We were only married 18 months. He wanted meatloaf twice a week and I hated the sound of his voice. Should have figured that out sooner."

Olive pointed up to the ceiling. "But I guess I spilled the beans. Now you know. At least it wasn't cherries that got you, Chauncey. Unlike my second husband."

"Shhh!" the rest of the group hissed in unison, causing Olive to zip an imaginary zipper across her lips.

"I know that it's frustrating not to hear what's going on. I'll keep repeating the entity's words for you." Feather nodded to Sophia. "Go ahead. Ask more questions."

Sophia cleared her throat and wiggled in her seat with importance. "Are you here because you know someone in this room?"

I thought you were smarter than that. Asking silly questions only brings silly answers.

She harrumphed, causing Feather's chest to tighten. Sophia's short fuse wasn't a secret amongst Gemini's friends.

"You may think I'm a silly woman, but I bet I can outsmart you."

"No, doll, please don't!" Jayden warned.

"You don't know what I was going to say, Jayden. Mr. Tone, I'm going to ask you three questions. You'll have to be truthful or..." Sophia paused and glanced down at Trophy Wophy. "Or my grandmother will come after you. She's not afraid of anyone in your world."

Go ahead then. Ask.

Feather's eyes were like saucers. They were entering uncharted territory, even for her. In all of the training and seminars she'd attended with P.I.N.K. organization members, they were told never to give a ghost an ultimatum that could put anyone in danger. Here Gemini's brash daughter was during her first time encounter with an entity, practically daring whoever this was to hurt those in attendance.

"First question. Who do you know in this room?"

The person who killed me.

Feather thought quickly. "He said the person who cut him off in traffic. Years ago."

Now more than any other time in her life, she wanted someone to know exactly what she was saying without saying it. Her eyes pleaded with Sophia to keep their secret.

"Alright, Mr. Tone," Sophia continued as Feather held her breath. "Why are you still so upset that someone cut you off in traffic?" She smiled slyly at Feather.

"Maybe we should move on," Feather suggested.

"No. You invited me, and I'm going to see this through." Sophia's head wobbled with self-importance. This was her moment and she wasn't letting it go without a fight.

"Ask your Mr. Tone about Gladiola Crabbitz." Gemini nudged her daughter. "What does he know about her?"

She sighed. "Fine. Mr. Tone, how do you know Gladiola Crabbitz? Is she your granddaughter or something?"

You know why I'm here. Tell her. Tell her I'll make sure she pays for my death.

There was a cold blast of air. Everyone shivered.

"Ask what Alistair has to do with this!" Feather pleaded.

"Please do, Sophia." Gemini's face was taut.

Sophia glanced around the table. Her eyes rested on Tug, who smiled broadly and nodded his approval.

I thought you said you could outwit me? I guess you can't, silly girl.

Sophia licked her lips and leaned back in her chair, directing her words to an unseen person in the hall. "Okay. Brandon, honey? You can come out now. I'm very impressed that you set this up on the night before my surgery." She looked around the table and grinned. "You all played your parts very well, and I'm sure my husband has compensated you well."

She placed her palms on the table and lifted herself to a standing position. "We really should get home. I have an early appointment in the morning. Bee, if you made a reservation at that fancy hotel, I'll love you all the more."

The table rattled as the lights flickered. Tug grabbed Feather's hand and squeezed it. She squeezed back, grateful he was there to support her.

This was all just a game to you? Stupid girl. Now I don't have to do another's bidding. Revenge is mine alone!

Sophia grasped her throat as if she was being choked, but no hands were visible.

"Stop! Stop!" Feather yelled. She picked up the polished blue rock she'd brought. "Aunt Cilia, help us!"

Sophia's nails scratched at the table as her eyes bulged.

Gemini climbed on the table, pushing the air—and life-threatening invisible hands—away from her daughter.

"Gem! Put this in Sophia's hand!"

She tossed Trophy Wophy to Gemini, who placed it in Sophia's hand and wrapped her fingers around it.

"Grandma! Help me!" she gasped.

Jayden and Feather joined hands, temporarily putting their issues aside to combine their gifts.

As quickly as it came, the force exited the room, taking the cold air with it.

Sophia dropped her hands and her head fell forward onto the table. Gemini immediately scooted to Sophia's body and cradled it in her arms. "I'm right here, my darling," she whispered.

"How could you bring my poor granddaughter to this circus?"

Feather, Jayden, and Gemini looked up. A dour woman with dark hair and red lips stared at them. She wore a black dress with a white collar, making her appear all the more severe.

She was a fully-formed entity, unusual to witness in a group setting. Usually they were shy, unwilling or unable to share their full forms with a group of strangers.

"Ruthmarie!" Gemini mouthed. "Your granddaughter is here of her own accord," she said. "I can assure you, this isn't a circus. Everyone in this room takes the séance very seriously, and no one wanted any harm to come to Sophia!"

"Ma'am, we had no idea your granddaughter would be injured. She was here to share her energy as a human. Not to be the center of attention," Jayden, who evidently heard Ruthmarie, soothed.

Feather found that statement laughable. Sophia would talk about this day for months and years to come. How she saved a group of dolts from an evil spirit.

"You don't know my granddaughter well if you think this is her last moment in the spotlight."

"Who upset this Two Tone person?" Gemini asked. "And why would he only speak to Feather and Sophia?"

"They decided not to share his words. Two Tone, or Shag Indigo Carpetia, was here to avenge his recent death. Ask your friends Feather and Jayden about that. When I heard the cries of my darling granddaughter, I came immediately."

Gemini looked up for the first time, her daughter still wrapped tightly in her arms. "Cheese and crackers! Nobody here is dim, Ruthmarie. Give us the name of the spirit you chased off. You've had your dramatic entrance."

"Ask Feather," she snapped. "Is that direct enough for you?"

Feather's mouth dropped open. "No... I..."

"DO YOU DOUBT ME?"

The table rattled, causing everyone's objects to bounce. Feather scanned the room for Jayden, but she had slipped out during the fracas.

"You must have immense powers, Ruthmarie. Not many ghosts can travel to different locations." She hoped her quick redirect wouldn't cause questions. Had Jayden stuck around, she would have had backup.

"My precious little rose, are you feeling better?" The change of tone in Rosemarie's voice startled Feather. It was unusual for ghosts to change personalities on a dime. But it was evident that Ruthmarie wasn't like other entities.

"I'm fine, Gram. The other ghostie just shocked me is all." Sophia, too, changed her tone to that of a small child needing comfort. She wiped her face and studied the apparition. "You look good. Did someone do your makeup in the afterlife? You'll have to give me their name when it's my time."

"Sophia!" Gemini slapped her daughter's arm in an uncharacteristic gesture of irritation. "She's a ghost. Your grandmother can take any form she wants."

"We desperately need your help, Ruthmarie. Who is controlling Gladiola Crabbitz?"

"You are a very naughty girl, Feather Jones. I don't have to tell you anything."

"What is she talking about?" Gemini whispered. Feather shook her head. There would be time for that later.

"Okay, you've had your fun. Either tell us about Gladiola or leave."

"She is delightful. Her son is the one you need to worry about. He's just as devious as you, Feather Jones."

Another hot wind pushed through the room, causing the double glass doors to bang open and shut.

"Grammie, could you send me some good vibes for tomorrow? I'm having a little procedure done."

Gemini knitted her brows together but didn't say a word.

"Grammie, dear? You're still here, aren't you?"

Feather glanced down at her arms, which displayed flat hairs. "She's gone, I'm afraid."

"I find it hard to believe my grandmother would just run off like that. We had a little ritual we did every time we said goodbye. She'd say, 'See you soon, kitten!' And I'd say, 'See you sooner, Furball!' It was every time we said goodbye." She crossed her arms and leaned back in her chair. "And I'm not going anywhere until you exit properly, Grammie!"

"She's... got a job in the afterlife." Feather glanced helplessly at Gemini.

"Oh yes. She's been working in the Afterlife Book Club."

"How would you know that, Mother?" A look of recognition crossed Sophia's face. "Oh, right. You said you saw her at home, using all of your supernatural abilities." Sophia made air quotes as she spoke, a sign she had recovered and regained her normal persona.

Feather stood and placed a protective arm around Tug. He responded by wrapping one of his arms around her shoulders.

"Thanks, everyone! I think we should all go home and regroup later."

CHAPTER 30

GEMINI

"What a strange looking man." Gemini leaned in over Feather's shoulder, trying to read the tiny newspaper print from 1885. A man with a long hooked nose and large vacant eyes stared back at her.

"Why don't they enlarge the text when they put these things into the computer? I can't see it either!"

When their internet searches of Alistair Violette turned up nothing, they decided to check with the historical society, on the off chance his family roots gave them some answers.

Gemini looked at her phone. It had been two hours since she dropped Sophia at the front door of Charming General Hospital. Sophia was adamant that she didn't want her mother there waiting.

"You had a terrible experience when Daddy was

a patient here. You know, his coma and such," Sophia had said.

"That's very kind of you, Sophia, but you are my daughter. If you're going under the knife, I'm not going anywhere."

They fought for over an hour, Sophia bringing up any slight she could remember from her childhood and Gemini trying to diffuse the situation by reminding her daughter how much she loved her.

In the end, she gave in, like always.

"The doctor will call you when I'm ready for visitors."

Feather swirled around in her chair, bumping into her partner. "Sorry!"

"That's okay, dear. What do we have so far?"

Feather typed everything on her phone since it was much faster than writing it down, the way Gemini was used to. She did her best to keep up with technology.

"A relative of Alistair's who looks very similar to him died in 1885.This Alistair, who we decided to call A.V., took over Violette Five and Dime when his father passed, eventually expanding to four stores in Portland and the original store here in Charming."

Gemini stared intently at his face. "The resemblance is uncanny. I wonder if Alistair searched his family history and became infatuated with A.V. He copied everything, down to that cape."

Feather nodded and continued. "A.V.'s obituary

says that, since he died without a will and no heirs, his property was sold at a public auction."

She placed her phone on the desk and frowned. "Why would a man who worked so hard to amass wealth die without leaving it to anyone?"

"Someone ended up with his fortune, though it could take us a little bit of time to figure that out, unless we can find a local historian to ask."

They looked at each other and both said, "Patience!" at the same time. Patience Thistle was a retired kindergarten teacher who owned a historic home. She'd been using it as a bed and breakfast, at least until she got into some legal trouble. Everyone was shocked to see her around town just a few months later. "I have good lawyers!" she proclaimed to anyone who would listen.

Since then, she'd been spending most of her mornings at the newly opened Charming History Center. A quirky woman who sing-songed randomly, Patience delighted the librarians as well as the young children in the Charming Public Library for story hour.

When they arrived, Patience was entertaining the children while speaking in hushed tones, "Jump in Jelly, Peter Smelly."

"—and then the mean boys yelled," she whispered, building tension. Her small body hunched forward as she paced in front of the kids, showing them the colorful pages.

Today she was wearing sneakers that flashed different colors with every step. It was easy to see why the kids loved her. Her eyes glistened as she read to them in hushed tones. She was also just about their size.

As small as she was, Patience could very well be wearing children's shoes.

When she heard no answer, she placed a hand up to her ear. "What's that you say?"

Gemini fondly remembered Sophia's childhood story time. She sat on her knees in the front row, transported to colorful worlds. For days afterward, Sophia talked about the stories she'd heard.

Sophia had tried bringing Taurus to the library; they were asked to leave when he ripped the pages out of an expensive travel book.

"It's jelly, it's jelly. It's very, very smelly," Patience sang loudly to a tune only she knew.

> *" Wobble-wobble, don't delay,*
> *Grab a bowl, join the fray!*
> *It might be smelly, but that's okay,*
> *Because jelly makes our day!"*

The group giggled, and some children clapped.

"That's all for today, my lovelies! Now, turn this way," she pointed to her left, "and give that person a hug. Tell them they are perfect just the way they are."

Twenty little bodies turned and hugged each other obediently. As the children stood to find their parents, Patience waved to Gemini and Feather. She danced her way to their spot in the back of the room.

"What brings you gals out today? Checking in for my parole officer?" Patience winked. "Naughty, naughty Pretty Pat got herself into a spat. Now that she has paid her debt, no more mischief, no regret."

"Patience." Gemini was usually able to wait out these songs, but today, she was feeding Leo his butterscotch pudding early and time was of the essence. "Patience, we're here on a matter of historical significance. We're hoping you can shed some light on a former resident."

The face that, moments ago, had been lost in the mindset of a child became serious. "Oh my. This sounds so serious. Who is it?"

"Alistair Violette. He owned—"

"Violette Five and Dime. Yes, I'm familiar with his history."

Patience stared at Feather intently. It was coming back to her; Patience picked one person to focus all of her attention. It must've been a holdover from teaching kindergartners. Feather looked away, rocking on the balls of her feet.

"What do you know about him? Tell us everything!" Gemini motioned for them to sit at the only adult-sized furniture in the room—a table pushed against the wall with several folding chairs.

Patience planted herself beside Feather, irritating Gemini to no end.

"I thought you were mad at me. The last time we spoke, I'd been keeping secrets. I'm very sorry about that. I taught a reading class in prison, and darned if those ladies didn't teach me a thing or two about how to treat others!"

"We *were* mad at you." Feather furrowed her brows. "But we needed information about Mr. Violette more than we needed to stay angry." She glanced at Gemini who nodded her approval.

"OH." Patience wiggled in her seat. "Then I'll tell you what I know before you scoot, scoot, scoot out the door. Alistair was a very unfriendly man. His sister was kind and loving, but once she left the area—"

"We didn't know he had siblings. There was nothing we found that mentioned siblings."

"He had two. A ten-year-old brother named Avery and a twin sister, Alice, who was happily married and living in Portland. When her first child was about to arrive, a girl I believe, Alistair's parents excitedly bought train tickets for the impending arrival."

"Mrs. Pee Pee?"

All three pairs of eyes dropped to a boy with a bowl cut wearing a striped shirt. "His mother said he cut his own hair last week. Used a bowl and everything," Patience whispered before bending down to his level. She took one of his small hands. "What do you need, dear heart?"

"Will you read that story again? Philo was kicking me and I couldn't hear."

Immediately, a flustered mother appeared behind him. "I'm so sorry. He loves your story time so much, he always makes up excuses to talk to you."

She guided the boy away from Patience.

"It's like you're a rock star!" Gemini marveled.

Patience smiled and nodded in recognition. "I'll be the rock star in these little sweeties' eyes any day. You can't imagine how many stories I heard from mothers separated from their kiddos when I was in the big house."

"You were telling us about Alistair's parents."

Feather's cheeks were bright red. Gemini learned this was a sign her partner was tiring of this dance.

"Oh, right. Let's see." Patience looked up at an imaginary book and ran her index finger back and forth until she found the exact spot where she'd left off. She stood and began to gesture as she spoke.

"They bought their train tickets to Portland so that her mother, father, and younger brother could travel. But on the day they were to leave, there was a major rock slide. Tall pine trees cooovered the tracks, while biiiig boulders crushed the rail." Patience made a swoosh with both arms.

"They were told it would be months before it was cleaned up and the trains were running again."

"I'm sure Alistair was upset. He was probably looking forward to some time by himself."

"Quite the contrary, Gemini. Alistair had an unhealthy obsession with his parents. He was forever telling people in Charming that he was his parents' favorite child and would never take that for granted. Sounds more like greed to me."

Patience opened her mouth to sing again, forcing Gemini into action. "We've only got a few minutes before an appointment with a new client. Could you finish up?"

Though obviously irritated, Patience continued. "Alice felt strongly that her parents needed to be there for the birth of her child, so her husband, a steel magnate, hired a coach and driver to bring them, along with Avery."

Patience bent her arms at the elbow and flopped her wrists up and down while she galloped around in a circle. Children were gathering around them, some clapping with enthusiasm.

"Their stagecoach encountered a band of thieves only ten miles from Portland. Everyone in the party was killed, including the stagecoach driver. Their personal effects were looted, so it took a couple of days to figure out who they were because, you know," Patience stuck her tongue out and crossed her eyes.

"Yes, we know, dear."

"Alistair blamed his sister for the deaths of his

parents and younger brother." Patience rolled her eyes. "Obvs."

Patience came to an abrupt halt, much to the dismay of the gathered fan club under five.

"Cheese and crackers! That wasn't at all what I was expecting. And next you're going to tell me that Alistair was devastated, living his life in depression."

"The opposite. It invigorated him to take control of his father's business and run things his way. Where his father had been kind and understood when someone down on their luck couldn't pay for groceries that week, Alistair set a hard and fast rule that all debt was to be paid every Friday. No exceptions.

"His hard line didn't end with customers. Because he blamed Alice for the deaths of their parents, he had her name removed from the Charming birth records, the family bible, and every single photo of school children during the years she attended Charming Primary School. Alistair made darn good and tootin' no one would remember the name Alice Violette."

Gemini tried to picture a closed-off man, of whom they'd found only two photos, with a loving family. "But pretending he didn't have a family was different from actually making sure they were wiped out of history. I don't understand how she could have been erased."

"Easily, Gemini Reed." Patience grabbed hold of

Gemini's arms and began swinging them back and forth as she sang. "In a time before now, I'll tell you how."

She raised their hands above her head and forced Gemini to turn in a circle. "No int-er-net, no tel-a-phone, nothing is known. No pic-tures to—"

"I get it." Gemini dropped her hands. "Thank you, Patience, but I do need to check on my daughter."

CHAPTER 31
GEMINI

Gemini waited until 2 p.m. before storming the gates of Charming General Hospital. She gave birth to this young woman and had every right to comfort her.

Though visitors were usually told to wait for clearance, they waived Gemini through. Everyone knew her after Leo's accident and the subsequent lawsuit against the hospital she'd won.

"I'm sorry, Mrs. Reed. Your daughter was already discharged."

"What? How could that be?"

She looked around for someone she knew. Anyone who could explain this mix up.

"I don't understand. My daughter had surgery this morning. How could she just get up and walk out?"

The sea of nurses walking around in their own

worlds left her feeling alone. Not knowing what to do, she got on the elevator. Her heart raced as her mind traveled back to the time Leo fell into a coma. "You're being silly, Gemini. This isn't anything like that."

Or was it?

Sophia had been so secretive. What if the surgery was serious and she was hiding it from her mother?

The doors opened and she rushed to the nurses' station. "Hello? Can anyone help me? My daughter is missing!"

"Gem?"

Feather appeared from one of the intensive care rooms.

"What are you doing here?" she asked, hating the tears that flowed down her face at the sight of a comforting face.

"I—we—Tug and I are visiting Cassie's room while her mom isn't here. Did something happen to Sophia?"

Gemini motioned for Feather to join her in an unused room. She'd already made a fool of herself in front of the staff on other floors. There was no reason to add to that list.

"Sophia has... has..." She sobbed, trying to get the words out. "She left without even telling me."

Feather's eyes filled with concern. "Maybe she's

back at your place? You did say that she didn't want you to pick her up."

She stared at Feather, feeling every bit the fool. "I never thought of that."

"Give her a call."

Gemini pulled her phone out of her purse and pushed the speed dial button, number 2.

"Hello! This is Sophia Reed Floris! If you're hearing this message, I'm knee deep in activities for my beautiful son. Please leave a message after the tone. Oh, and if you're a salesman, keep in mind that my husband works at the top law firm in the Pacific Northwest and he will crush you like the vermin you are. Have a pleasant day!"

"She's probably resting. You should go home and check."

Gemini sniffed. "I feel so silly now."

"Don't. After that weird séance and your mother-in-law's performance, no one could blame you for being out of sorts."

They walked to the elevator. "Patience called me this morning. She found an article in a society column about Alice Violette Fellows and Captain Thomas Fellows. Their son, Avery, was a world-class magician."

Feather nodded. "Interesting."

"Oh, and Feather, I've been thinking more about the seance. Are you sure you told me everything?"

CHAPTER 32

FEATHER

The news that Cassie had finally awakened both pleased and worried Feather. It was wonderful to think Cassie was recovering. The nurse who called to inform them, a former client of Feather's, whispered that the doctor said she would make a full recovery.

When Feather thanked her for the information, she continued, "Her mother has been kicked out at least three times for showing up drunk and belligerent."

"Not surprised. I can sense you have more to say though."

"The moment her daughter opened her eyes, Opal started in. Not even a 'how are you' or 'I love you.' Just Tug Muehler comes from a rich family and you need to milk that for all you can. We're going to sue Tug Bars for everything they have."

Though she'd been expecting it, the words tumbling out of the nurse's mouth felt like a direct hit to her abdomen.

Luckily, the phone had been on speaker so she didn't have to repeat Opal's sorry words to Tug later.

"We have to go see her, babe," Tug urged after she hung up. "None of this has anything to do with Cassie."

She could always count on Tug to see the good in a situation. "I know. Lavidia said her mother never arrives until around two, so if we can get there in an hour, she can sneak us in."

"What do you mean by that? Why would we have to sneak?"

Tug rested his chin in the palm of one hand, suppressing a yawn. Neither slept much since the accident.

"Opal has banned us from Cassie's room."

"Shoulda guessed."

Tug yawned for at least the millionth time this morning.

"Do you want one of those orange rolls Gem sent over?"

Feather reached into the refrigerator and removed almond milk for her coffee. When she shut the door and stood, she could feel the hairs on her arms bristle against her pajamas.

"Who's there?"

Tug stood and gave her a kiss on the forehead before retreating to the bedroom.

"I'm alone. I don't have the patience to play games this morning."

"You don't have to be like that, Feather Jones."

She was surprised to see Gemini's mother-in-law, Ruthmarie. When she'd appeared at the séance, she looked ten years younger. It wasn't entirely unheard of for a spirit to change their appearance, but in Feather's experience, it didn't happen often. This morning, Ruthmarie wore a blue prom dress with a corsage around her wrist.

"Is this about Gem? Is she in trouble?"

"Now why would I be here about her?" Ruthmarie waved her hand in the air dismissively. "Silly girl. I'm here about your little friend, Jayden Ko."

Feather poured the milk in her coffee and sat at the table, glancing at Tug's uneaten cereal and feeling slightly guilty. "Continue."

The ghost took in an unnecessary and lengthy breath. "Jayden Ko was a young woman who knew she had immense powers but with no way to use them. Desperate for help, she visited a tarot card reader at The Bleeding Rose who offered her a deal she couldn't refuse. Help a pesky ghost who had been bothering said tarot reader with their dying wish and Jayden would have everything she desired."

The thought of Jayden desperate for anything

didn't fit. She was the most chill, most comfortable in her own skin person Feather had ever met. But she knew better than to argue with a ghost. It was the easiest way to get them to clam up. "So Jayden made this deal and had to work with Alistair to find his killer."

"Now you're catching on, Feather Jones. She returned to Alistair with 'proof' and he, in turn, helped her become one of the most highly skilled psychics in the country. The company she built has been successful in part due to the abilities Alistair showed her how to use."

Feather stood, her anger coiled tight. "That's insane. I won't believe it. I've known Jayden for years, and the last thing she would do is hurt someone without just cause."

"Believe me, don't believe me, makes no difference."

Feather cocked her head. "If it makes no difference, why did you put on your prom dress to come and tell me about it?"

White carnation petals fell from Ruthmarie's corsage, changing from white to black before disappearing. "Because your friend is in danger. Alistair's coming for her now that he understands her trickery.

"Alistair, who was sitting one bar stool over from her, took pity on the poor waif. She was desperate to gain entry into the organization, so desperate that she agreed to do anything he asked in return for some pizzazz."

Feather sensed something wasn't right. "Oh, right. Pizzazz, like pulling a rabbit out of a hat? Or maybe turning a frog into a goat?"

"You are a sassy gal. He was right about you. No, Feather Jones, he didn't offer to make her a two-bit magician. Alistair promised that she would have the gift of mind reading, along with seeing the future, and, of course, speaking with the dead. At the time, there was only one other living being with those abilities."

"Capu." Feather nodded knowingly. "He's retired now."

"You can see why it was so appealing to Jayden Ko. There was, however, one catch."

"And that catch was..."

"Jayden agreed to track someone down, a descendant of Alistair's killer, in exchange for all the power she wanted."

Feather frowned. "I don't understand any of this. Alistair died generations ago. If he were murdered, those people would have died long before Jayden was born. And what could he possibly do to help her? Jayden's gifts have been with her since birth!"

Ruthmarie chuckled. "You're not thinking big enough, Feather. Alistair didn't just promise to help Jayden with her gifts. He promised to turn her into one of the most powerful beings in the known world. Alistair is a man of great talent and wisdom. His offer to help her was a gesture of selflessness, and she tossed it aside as though it were trash."

Feather leaned back in her chair, her mind racing. She had never heard of anyone making a pact with a deceased person before. But she knew enough about the otherworldly to believe anything was possible.

"Jayden's no murderer."

"Anyone will kill if the stakes are high enough, girlie. It's a small task, really. There are so many people who would beg for this opportunity."

All she wanted this morning was to enjoy her coffee in peace. Obviously it wasn't going to happen. Something awful occurred to her as she stared at her *Feelin' Detective-y* mug. "Wait, you're telling me that Jayden *already* killed someone in exchange for all of her gifts?"

Ruthmarie danced around the room as though she were listening to music at the prom. "Da, da dee, da, da dum..."

"Ruthmarie! I'm giving you exactly one more minute of my time before I get up and leave!"

"WHAT? Oh, sorry." The apparition whirled around one more time.

"Jayden killed someone..." Feather made a rolling motion with her hand, "and then what happened?"

"No, she didn't. After Alistair bestowed his

wisdom upon her, how to release all of those powers, she used them to trick him."

Gemini never once mentioned Ruthmarie's admiration of Alistair. It could be that, since this was her first experience dealing with a spirit force, she didn't pay attention to those details, Feather reasoned.

"Never give services before receiving payment, that's what my husband always said, and forty years in the paint and hammer business doesn't lie. The descendant of Alistair's killer is still out there, roaming free."

The phone rang, causing Feather to jump and Ruthmarie to disappear.

Tug rushed into the kitchen, his face ashen. "It's Cassie."

On the way to the hospital, she explained everything to Tug. "What does this have to do with Gemini's problem? Isn't Alistair controlling her neighbors?"

"I wish I knew. Ruthmarie, or whoever that was, didn't say."

As they pulled up to the hospital, they were met by a harrowing sight. All of the emergency vehicles in Charming were parked in front of the hospital, blocking the entrance to the parking lot. Tug rolled down his window as they approached the barrier.

"What's going on, Chief Boulder?"

He leaned down and placed his forearms on the

door, causing Feather to recoil. There was something about him that didn't sit right with her.

"A lady just went berserk is the best way I can explain it. Ms. Hughes screamed at her daughter that she'd failed her job and then tried to strangle her."

CHAPTER 33
GEMINI

When she pulled up in the driveway, Howard waved as he walked briskly from his herb garden to meet her.

"It must be important!"

She pulled her purse out of the front seat, relieved to see someone who hadn't witnessed her hospital performance.

"Your daughter stopped by my place earlier."

"Oh?" Gemini raised an eyebrow. "Was she needing help with something? Thank you for looking after her, but I'm home now."

"No, nothing like that."

Howard took a deep breath and looked down at his camel-colored gardening shoes. "She was in a fancy black car with the smoked windows, like the Hollywood types. A man got out and handed me an envelope. He said it was for you, from Sophia."

He pulled the notecard-sized envelope from his pocket and handed it to Gemini. "Didn't give me time to ask any questions."

She opened it quickly and squinted to read without her reader glasses.

Mother,

I didn't want any questions about my surgery, so I hired a car to take me home. Brandon's partner picked up my car and belongings while you were out.

That was an interesting evening. I don't know what kind of theatrical tricks your agency paid for, but they were certainly worth every penny. Nice marketing ploy.

I'll call soon.

Love,

Sophia

For the past hour, as she fed her husband tiny bites, she explained the peculiar story of Alistair Violette, a lonely man who for some reason blamed Jayden for his troubles.

The longer she drug the story out, the less time she had to spend in sorrow over Sophia's harsh treatment.

"A.V. had his sister erased from history. Her baptism record in the church was removed. Alice's school attendance: gone. Even her wedding announcement." Gemini sighed. "For someone to devote that much time to removing their sibling from existence required hate. A lot of hate."

She paused to glance at the swans swimming in the man-made lake just outside Leo's window. "Oh, look! Trudy has almost lost all of her baby feathers! Isn't that something?"

Gemini elbowed Leo in the ribs. Even though it had been years, she still forgot on occasion that he couldn't respond.

"Patience Thistle only stumbled on her existence by accident. Patience helped in the library at the state penitentiary. One of her duties was to help those who chose to create family trees. The only reason Patience Thistle knew anything about Alice at all is because of her prison stint. She volunteered in the prison library, helping other inmates find their roots. In the process of digging up old yearbooks, she found one with a picture of children around a May pole. Alice was the only child she couldn't connect to a family, at least until she found a church bulletin announcing the birth of Alice and her twin brother, A.V."

Gemini paused so she could retrieve Leo's water cup. It occurred to her that Leo was the lucky one tonight. He didn't have to feel the hurt of Sophia's rejection. When she was in college, Sophia had called Leo every morning. This time, her anger wasn't directed at him.

Gemini pushed the straw between his lips. "You're getting so good at this, darling!"

He couldn't suck hard enough to bring anything through the straw, but just the fact that he moved any muscle on command was a triumph to Gemini.

After sitting the cup on a nearby table, she continued. "Patience can be like a dog with a bone, once she finds something to research." Gemini chuckled, remembering their odd visit at the library. "When she called me this morning, I was relieved she wanted to tell me the rest of the story without including song."

"Mrs. Reed?"

Gemini's favorite nurse, Trent always made a point of stopping by Leo's room when he knew she was visiting.

"Trent! I brought you peanut butter-chocolate butterscotch bars. In the usual location."

Trent, a six-foot-five man with strawberry blond hair, picked up the smutty book Gemini was reading to Leo and set it on the bed. "You always make me laugh with your choice of reading material, Mrs. Reed."

"What?" She stood and walked over to the other side of the bed. "Oh, *Garret's Grasp*? Leo's doctor told me that if I could find an activity that made my husband mad in his previous life, I should do it now. Doctor Adams thinks strong emotions will help stimulate his brain."

"Leo had a new visitor yesterday. Your niece, Allie."

Gemini frowned. "Neither of us have a niece with that name. Are you sure?"

Trent shrugged. "Maybe I got it wrong. We were changing shifts and no one had her sign in. She stayed for almost an hour and spoke to your husband about family."

"Hmm. Probably a distant cousin. Leo has many."

Gemini walked back to Leo and bent over, kissing his cheek. "You're such a popular man, aren't you, darling? You always were the more social of the two of us."

"Oh, wow. These smell divine." Trent was already sampling the cookies, much to Gemini's dismay.

"Don't eat them all here. You know your partner is a fan of my baking too!"

"Right. Sorry." He replaced the plastic lid, which made a *whoosh* when it sealed, and sat down on the bed. "I heard what you were saying, about the woman who was erased from history. I may be able to help you. Reminds me of my grandfather. His brother, Gary, moved in with their parents right before they passed. The next week, they were both dead and the will had been rewritten, completely leaving out Grandpa."

"I'm not sure you heard the entire—"

"Grandpa was spitting nails. He went right down to the city building and tore out the page marking

Gary's birth." Trent opened the container and removed one more cookie. "He went to every source in town, removing his brother." Trent chuckled, causing cookie bits to fly out of his mouth and onto Leo's bed. "In fact, it became Grandpa's mission to make his brother insignificant. They never spoke again."

"I guess it isn't as rare as I'd imagined."

"Do you have any siblings, Mrs. Reed?"

"Yes, I do. One brother. We haven't spoken in years, though it's not because we had harsh words. He went his way and I went mine."

"Hmm." Trent wiped his mouth on his forearm, much to Gemini's distaste. Good thing he wasn't performing surgery. "People who carry a grudge aren't the happiest. But you and me, Mrs. Reed, we're practically vomiting joy!"

Gemini glanced at her watch and clucked her tongue. "That reminds me, I have to meet with Howard. While I've been in the middle of Feather's investigation, I've completely neglected my own."

"And which investigation would you be referring to?"

"No time, Trent. Do you mind cleaning up Leo? I really must scoot."

"Go." Trent pushed the air with one large hand. "But I'll expect a full report next time!"

Howard was winding his antique grandfather clock when she arrived. Since Gemini was a half hour late, she didn't bother standing on ceremony. She let herself in.

"There you are." He turned his body away from her and continued his work.

She knew it was a deserved slight, but it still hurt. "I'm sorry. I was feeding Leo his pudding and I lost track of time."

"Evidently." His even tone upset her more than refusing to meet her gaze.

"Cheese and crackers! Just yell at me or something!"

"Have you checked your messages this evening? Or even this morning?"

She fumbled in her purse until she found her phone. Seventeen missed calls. On a day she hadn't just come from the Charming Care Center, that would cause a full-blown panic attack.

"This sounds bad. Just rip the band aid off and tell me." She helped herself to a glass of water and sat down on the buttery leather sofa.

"Our evil neighbors have struck again. This morning after you left, they made the rounds with photos."

Howard opened a drawer in his kitchen reserved for twine, tape, and thumb tacks. He pulled out a paper with a grainy picture and handed it to her.

"What's this?"

"It's us. You and me."

Looking down, she was shocked by the words:

"Our neighborhood has been infiltrated by the wicked. Something must be done!"

Underneath that sentence was a grainy picture, obviously taken through a window. It was Gemini and Howard, and it looked like they were in an embrace. Howard's chin rested on Gemini's head and displayed a serene smile, a contortion his face never seemed to manage.

"How... What..." Gemini's eyes filled with tears, and she felt both rage and shame building inside her. "Everyone is going to assume I'm cheating on my husband. I don't even remember this photo, so how can I defend myself?"

Howard walked quickly to the picture window and shut the shades before returning to comfort Gemini. He patted her shoulders with an open hand. "There are just as many ways to create fiction as there are criminals to create them. Come over to the table and I'll show you."

She set the photo on the table and Howard brought his magnifying glass out of the drawer. "I've been studying this for hours, though I don't know why it took me so long. I guess my rational thinking was clouded by emotions." He handed her the magnifying glass. "I want you to look closely at yourself."

Carefully, Gemini scanned the picture. When she found the clue, she stood and smiled. "Too easy!"

"Aha! Tell me what you see."

"I see a burnt-orange sweater that I don't own. Sophia routinely goes through my closet, and she would flip her lid if she found something that color." A sadness flickered through her at the mention of her daughter.

"Right. Now look at your hands."

She looked through the lens again, this time focusing on the hands on Howard's shoulders. "Those are the fancy nails Feather raves about. Three hours' worth of work and they have to be redone every month. Feather calls them 'acrylic cash in the bank.'"

"Exactly. Not one aspect of that body is yours, save the face. Nor is it mine either. When was the last time you saw me in jeans?"

She breathed a sigh of relief that was short-lived. "It won't matter to anyone else that we aren't these people. We'll have to go door-to-door again and try and convince them. I won't sleep a wink tonight, knowing people on our block think I'm a philanderer." She glanced down at her phone. It had been buzzing all day, but some days she just needed life to be uncomplicated.

"Some of those messages on your phone are from other neighbors. I've been fielding calls all day. I've got an idea that might solve this problem once and for all."

CHAPTER 34

FEATHER

"We're so glad you weren't harmed in the standoff!" Tug took Cassie's bruised hand and lightly stroked it. "When we pulled up and saw all the lights and sirens, we knew it must be Opal."

Cassie nodded. She was still on oxygen and woozy. When her eyes opened, they had trouble focusing. "What happened? My mom was... here? She'd never give up her spot in the Skeeter Schooner Sail. That's her favorite boat race, and Mom's told me more than once it means more to her than any of her kids."

"It's me, Feather." She sat on the edge of the bed doing her best to avoid the myriad of cords and IV lines. "Opal Hughes showed up a few days ago. Today she had a..." Feather paused to check with Tug. He frowned and shook his head. "Opal had a little meltdown. She's gone now and you're safe, Cassie."

A smile formed on Cassie's dry lips. "I'm glad. Mom isn't nearly as scary as my grandma. She yelled at me in the growly voice she used when I was in trouble. 'Kill them, girl! Kill them!' When I refused–" Her head fell backward onto the pillow and her eyes closed.

"Cassie?" Feather looked helplessly at Tug. "Go get a nurse, quick!"

The minute he left the room, Cassie's eyes popped open. "Grandma wouldn't leave me alone. I thought she loved me, but her voice was mean and—"

"You crashed the van to make the voice stop."

"Oh, your van." Cassie's hands grasped either side of her head as though the memory caused physical pain. "I'm so sorry. So sorry..." Cassie's voice faded, and her eyes rolled back in her head as Tug returned with Lydia, the nurse.

After checking her vitals, Lydia turned to the worried couple. "She's been doing this off and on since yesterday. The doctor thinks she'll come out of it eventually. Don't take anything she says to heart. I've seen this hundreds of times before. Her brain is trying to fight its way through the fog and, eventually, the fog will lift altogether." She looked at Tug and smiled. "Just like our beach weather."

"I feel better knowing you're here to look after her." Tug nodded to Lydia.

"Is there something I can help you with? Cassie won't be much help today," Lydia said.

"What was her mother saying? I know she was acting crazy but—"

"She was upset with Cassie for disobeying her. Lots of things strung together that didn't make sense."

"Like?"

"Oh, like how she was going to make her daughter fall in line, or else."

When she was gone, Feather turned to Tug. "Her grandmother was kind when we spoke. Her focus was Cassie's deadbeat boyfriend and her granddaughter's hair. That's not a grandma who tries to get her granddaughter killed."

"You're thinking it's not her grandmother?"

Feather stroked Cassie's arm, but there was no change. She was out cold. "Lydia said she's in a fog. Maybe she's just confused."

Cassie's head turned to one side and then the other before her eyes opened slightly. "Protect them," she whispered before closing her eyes once more.

Feather slid off the bed, narrowly missing two important-looking chords. "We have to go."

"Okay?"

She always appreciated Tug's support, even

when he had no idea what he was supporting. "Come on. I'll fill you in when we get to the car."

All the way to The Bleeding Rose, Feather explained powerful entities to Tug. It just so happened that she'd spent a recent Saturday taking the "Highly Specialized Spiritual Shenanigans" seminar with other P.I.N.K. members.

"Some of them aren't interested in a peaceful afterlife," she explained. "They focus their energy on making changes in our world. Sometimes it takes centuries."

"Centuries? To do what?"

"To become so powerful they can change their appearance."

As they parked in front of the Charming Small Animal Veterinary Clinic, Tug reached for the door handle. "No, Tug. I have to do this by myself."

"What if..."

"I'll be fine. And if you don't hear from me in the next thirty minutes, call the cops and report a burglary."

He nodded solemnly.

As she got out of the car, she noticed Phoebe parked behind them. Though Feather didn't relish another conversation about her fall from grace, she also didn't want to appear rude.

"Phoebe? What are you doing here? The Bleeding Rose is closed until this evening."

"I could ask you the same thing." Phoebe

squinted up at Feather. "I'm just here waiting to pick up my cat, Crunch. They said to wait in the parking lot until they texted."

"Oh." Feather hoped the relief in her voice wasn't obvious. "I have some business to take care of in The Bleeding Rose."

"With Alistair? I thought you said it wasn't open."

"No, I'm meeting Azalea."

Now was the time to make a quick escape, before there were questions she couldn't answer. "I'll see you at the next P.I.N.K. meeting!" She turned and walked away as quickly as possible.

Feather approached the alley door. A homemade sign that read "Shut for now" was taped to the metal door. Ignoring it, she curled up her fist and pounded furiously. "Let me in!"

Finally, the door opened a crack. "Feather? Is that you?"

Feather took that moment to shove her way in. "You know it's me, Azalea."

Still wearing the 1920s party dress she'd had on during Feather's last visit, Azalea clutched the long strand of pearls around her neck. "You sound angry. Did I do something wrong?"

"It's not so much what you did wrong as what you didn't do right."

Azalea scrunched her face up. "Huh? You coming in or not? Because there is some kind of protective field around this place. My ghost senses don't work inside, but out in the fresh air, away from the spell dome, or whatever you call it, my gifts work just fine."

Feather rolled up the sleeve of her shirt. "Do you see that? This system is a fool-proof ghost detector."

Azalea stared at the hairs standing at attention on Feather's arm. "Still don't get it."

"Presumably it's just you and me here. That means one of us is a ghost. I'm pretty sure it's not me."

Azalea's entire body turned yellow, then red. "What does that have to do with anything?" Her voice became a hot whisper, swirling around Feather's head. "I love my job here and I'm staying put!"

"Slow your roll." Feather took a step forward, something Jayden taught her when dealing with entities. Most of them were scaredy cats no matter how hard they huffed and puffed.

Just as predicted, Azalea moved back and regained her lifelike color.

"I'm not here to end your career. I want to know why you didn't tell me about Alistair."

"Feather Jones, I'm insulted that you think I would—"

"Just explain why you're all working for him. And who he's controlling in my world. All this time, I thought my hair-o-meter was off. It wasn't, and Tug was right, again. I'm not crazy— Alistair has created an army of ghosts!!"

Azalea's shoulders fell. "Maybe we keep this between the two of us, toots?"

Her nod was more out of necessity than a pact she was making with a ghost. Feather would worry about that later.

"We have to make this quick. He'll be back soon, and if he catches me, my second career at The Bleeding Rose is kaput."

CHAPTER 35

GEMINI

Gemini threw off the covers and slipped her feet into the soft-as-silk yellow slippers Taurus gave her for her birthday. Tonight, she didn't bother with a robe. She'd been tossing and turning for so long, she'd worked up a sweat.

Though she'd tortured herself for years regarding Sophia's abrupt treatment, Gemini's relationship with Feather taught her that she was capable of relating to a younger generation.

Since Leo had fallen into a coma, Sophia called frequently. Gemini was pleased but also secretly bitter that it took something that extreme to bring her focus to her mother. Taurus was developing a relationship with his maternal grandmother too. Now, all of that was in jeopardy.

After putting the kettle on, Gemini scoured the cupboards for something to eat.

"Top shelf, right in the center. You're such a creature of habit."

By now, she should have been used to her deceased mother-in-law's unannounced visits. Nonetheless, Gemini jumped at her sharp tone and narrowly missed hitting her head on a cupboard door.

"Are you so lonely that you're trying to recruit me?"

Gemini noticed Ruthmarie was dressed in her own wedding finery this evening. A short-sleeved, V-neck satin gown with petticoats underneath that provided a big poof. The old woman was even wearing the same lace gloves and carrying a small white purse. Gemini had seen this picture sitting on Ruthmarie's China hutch the first time Leo introduced them.

"Don't worry, Gemini. It's not your time tonight."

Even confirmation that death wasn't imminent didn't make her feel better. Ruthmarie belonged somewhere else. "Why are you here? I'm cursing myself and I certainly don't need any help from you!"

Ruthmarie's mouth pulled back and her head wobbled. The same old traits she had in life when she wanted her daughter-in-law to know she was the smartest one in the room. "Oh, you can't keep me away from your pity party. I only wish I could partake in the refreshments."

Anger welled up inside her, and she squeezed her fists. "You're about one minute away from me putting on headphones to drown you out, so whatever you need to say, get it over with. I know all of your slights by heart, so I'm going to say this one is 'because of your poor parenting, your daughter is a mess.' Isn't that right?"

Without waiting for a response, Gemini turned back to the cupboard and noticed a box of Bing's Bombastic Chocolate Chippers. They were her emergency stash, for when she didn't have any of her own baked goods readily available. Right in the center of the top shelf, just as Ruthmarie said. Gemini lost her appetite and instead poured herself a cup of tea and sat at the table.

"There isn't a lick of sense that comes out of your mouth. I guess I shouldn't be surprised, though."

Gemini slammed her teacup down, causing most of the tea to spill on her green-flowered tablecloth. "All I've heard from you thus far is the same old drivel. If you're here to make sure I know how much you hate me and how Leo should have married Cinda Prinda, or whatever her name was, you can just go. I've heard it all before."

She turned her body away from Ruthmarie and faced the window. It was silly, pouting in front of a ghost, but there seemed to be nowhere to escape.

Gemini bit her lip to keep from crying. She wasn't giving Ruthmarie the satisfaction.

Gemini's eyes dropped to her cup while she took the last sip of tea. When she looked up again, Ruthmarie's image stared at her through the window.

"Stop doing that!" she snapped. "Your theatrics don't impress me any more than your magic show at the séance."

Ruthmarie appeared in the seat across from Gemini. "You've really got to loosen up. I remember you as a fun-loving girl. Wild and crazy, much to my chagrin."

Gemini opened her mouth to protest, but Ruthmarie reached a hand over the table and sealed Gemini's lips.

"As much as it pains me to say it, your daughter loves you. When I was unable to speak at the end, Sophia would bend down and whisper in my ear that I should apologize to you for my behavior before my death. Obviously, I didn't."

She pointed at her lips while trying to grasp the image of her daughter begging her grandmother for kindness. "I... don't understand. You never said one nice thing to me in the thirty years we knew each other. Why are you telling me this now?"

"Because, dear woman, you're about to make a grave mistake and, since I'm already here, I can't just sit by and let it happen."

Gemini vacillated between thinking she should

just go back to bed and put her headphones on to block this ghost out or listen to the words she'd waited her entire marriage to hear. "What mistake do you think I'm making? Sitting in my kitchen in the middle of the night, talking to a ghost?"

"You're hurt because Sophia shut you out today. You're considering cutting off communication with her and your only grandson."

"Why shouldn't I? Brandon's mother is right there, and she's just the hoity toity woman Sophia connects with. I won't be missed."

Ruthmarie crossed one leg over the other. One very shapely leg that didn't match her middle-aged face. "Instead of focusing on her words, you're not thinking about what she hasn't said."

Gemini squinted as she tried to comprehend these words. It was asking a lot for her to concentrate at this time of night. "She hasn't told me a thing about this surgery, nor has she given me a reliable reason why she had to have it done here in Charming."

"Exactly."

Gemini sighed. "As usual, you're making absolutely no sense."

Ruthmarie dissipated, swirling around her head as a thin wisp of air. "Do you know why I was always so standoffish?"

Gemini swatted at her face. "Stop that! I'm not impressed by your ghost tricks!"

"I was jealous of you, Gemini. You were carefree and made my son smile in a way no one else ever did. Leo quit calling me every day and no longer shared his secrets. I felt like I lost my best friend."

Gemini brought the empty teacup to her lips. "I'm sorry, Ruthmarie. I never knew that. He loved you very much, even if he didn't show it."

"Yes, well, heed my words and all of that ghostly advice." Ruthmarie's voice returned to the harsh tone that normally defined her. "Now, while you're mulling that over, I'm running out of time and you still haven't taken care of business."

"Business?"

"I told you that my temporary haunting ticket was to make sure you were warned about Gladiola and protected yourself. I haven't seen any progress, and if I'm pulled off this job without it, I won't be able to haunt again. A poor review can stall the application process for centuries."

"Well, you put on quite a show the other night at the séance without helping at all. So if you aren't able to earn your badge, or whatever, you only have yourself to blame." Gemini stood and stretched her arms. "I'm going to bed."

"She's always one step ahead of you. Think about it. How did she know you and Howard were handing out flyers?"

"It was a coincidence." Gemini set her cup in the sink. "Good night, Ruthmarie."

"Wait!" She appeared in front of Gemini, though her transparency made her an unlikely barrier.

"I'm not supposed to tell you this, but Gladiola Crabbitz is a pawn in a game she doesn't understand."

Gemini stopped. "Whose game?"

"If you aren't a willing target, those pulling her strings will find another. Like Leo."

Though she was dead tired and struggled to take another step, Gemini's entire body tensed and her pulse quickened. "Why would she attack Leo? You said she likes to cause trouble in the court system, not the care center."

"She's found an ally on our side. Quentin, your neighbor, is a fan of conjuring up spirits." Ruthmarie scoffed. "On our side, we call them Ghostgasmers. Quentin got his spells and gibberish confused, you know, from his pals on the internet. He ended up contacting one of the bad guys instead of the good." She rolled her eyes. "Amateurs make those mistakes. This ghost convinced Quentin he'd have access to everyone on our side, if Quentin would help him. It was the perfect set up for—"

"Alistair. We've met."

Ruthmarie crossed her arms over her ample belly and twisted her face into a grimace. It was the same expression she wore at her son's otherwise-perfect wedding reception. Well, other than her occasional loud sobs.

As she studied this apparition, she marveled at how much of the old, hateful Ruthmarie still existed. The ghost who appeared at the séance was the woman showing her true colors.

"Gemini, you're not listening. It always drove me seven ways to Sunday when I was in the middle of something and you drifted off. You'll have to be very strong soon. He's going to try and break your will. I'M TRYING TO WARN YOU!"

It was at that moment that she experienced her first moment of clarity. "Feather always says when she doesn't want a ghost in her head, she tells them to leave. So that is what I'm saying to you right now. Leave, and never return! I don't care about your silly dresses or your bad memories or any warning you think you have. I'm done with you!"

Ruthmarie frowned. "It's time for my card game with Mother Teresa anyway. She's a terrible cheat." She stood abruptly and dissolved through the window.

A LOUD CONVERSATION taking place outside Gemini's kitchen window caught her attention. She lifted her head, once again feeling that familiar pain in her neck from sleeping sitting up.

Peeking out her curtain, she saw Howard and a

neighbor in a heated discussion. Howard's hands moved up and down as though he was trying to make a point. Gemini opened the window a crack to listen.

"Len, you're taking the word of complete strangers over someone you've known for two decades. Tell me how that makes sense."

"Photos don't lie, Howard. I saw what I saw. You and that woman," he gestured toward Gemini's place, "are turning our nice little neighborhood into a... well... a brothel."

"Brothel." She huffed. "Unreal."

"I've explained to you repeatedly that those photos were doctored." Howard threw up his hands. "There's nothing else I can do. Think about this, Len. See if it makes any sense."

Howard disappeared back into his home as Gemini's phone buzzed.

"Mrs. Reed? This is the City of Charming. We've received some complaints about—"

"My warehouse? I told you people that we're planning to paint it."

"No, ma'am. It's about garbage collection. For three weeks in a row we've received calls that your trash bin is left by your driveway past the allotted time. If this persists, we'll have to fine you."

"What? I bring in my trash bin every Tuesday, after it's emptied." She continued peeking through the window, trying to stifle her anger. These small irritants became monsters when she hadn't slept.

The voice on the other end of the line sighed. "Normally, we would ignore calls like this, but that woman has phoned twice every day for the past two weeks." There was a sound of rustling paper. "City ordinance 412 stipulates that all trash bins be removed from the curbside by 1:00 p.m. on coordinating trash collection days in order to alleviate obstructing the view of drivers on your street."

"It's Gladiola Crabbitz, isn't it? I don't arrive home until at least four p.m., a fact I'm sure she is well aware of."

"I can't—"

"Just send me the fine and get it over with. And while you're at it, fine me for the next month. That way the next time she calls, you can tell her you've taken care of it."

Gemini slammed her phone on the table. On impulse, she marched over and knocked on Howard's door. When it opened, his expression went from irritated to amused. "I didn't realize we were this informal. You know, if the neighbors didn't already think something was suspicious about us, they certainly do now."

Gemini glanced down. She was still wearing her powder blue pajamas and robe from the night before. For once, she didn't care. "We have to come up with a new plan to get rid of that woman."

"Do you want to come in?"

"No, that will make tongues wag even harder. Sit down on your step and let's talk for a minute."

Mr. Beasley, their elderly neighbor who spent most of his time either sitting or standing in his front yard, waved. His other hand held a hose, watering his many colorful petunias. It was a relief to still have him in their corner.

"Call it a coincidence, but I've been mulling over something. We'll throw a party for everyone on the block. But instead of creating a breeding ground for gossip, we'll structure the evening. We're hosting a mystery dinner, where everyone is assigned a character and they can't deviate from that personality all evening." Howard puffed his chest out, obviously pleased with himself.

While it did have a spark of brilliance, Gemini was skeptical. "Won't people just think we're trying to cover up our indiscretions? What if no one comes?"

"I've thought this through. They'll be here, especially when the invitation promises a big reveal at the end of the evening," Howard insisted. "There are too many people to include them all as characters, so in my 1920s vaudeville mystery, those we don't specifically need to target will be given the character of 'audience member.' Everyone on this block likes to throw a good themed party. Remember last summer? Every weekend there were parties. The Blue Party, the Joke Party..."

"I'm warming up to the idea." She wasn't. But Gemini didn't want to hurt Howard's feelings, so she played along. "And what is the big reveal at the end? We've already done our best to convince them we aren't an item."

"The 'evidence' against us consists of Gladiola's fertile imagination and that photo alleging we're a couple."

"Right."

"That's why I've already hired an internet scam expert to track down the real owners of those bodies. Once they appear, it's going to throw a wrench into Gladiola's latest attempt to besmirch our reputations."

Gemini thought about it, and slowly a smile spread across her face. "That's brilliant, Howard. I mean really brilliant. They'll all be excited to come in character, and by the end of the evening, when they're full and possibly a little drunk—"

"I've got two cases of Sassy Lasses wine coming tomorrow. It's more than likely that our guests will be upbeat by the time we make our big reveal."

"This could work!" She bounced, just enough to show her enthusiasm but not enough to appear giddy.

Howard smiled back. "Let's just hope we're better at playing their game than they are."

CHAPTER 36

GEMINI

As Gemini walked home with a new bounce to her step, something occurred to her. Instead of walking up her driveway, she marched across the street, knowing full well and good that Sophia would lecture her for wearing her fancy schmancy slippers outside.

Mr. Beasley was sitting in his usual location—his lawn chair—when she marched up his driveway. A thin green hose lay across his lap and a constant trickle of water made a puddle in his grass. He seemed to be concentrating on it.

A small man with a round face and round glasses, he was the secret retired leader of Feather's paranormal investigators group. They called him "Capu," a name with an impressive meaning that Gemini never could remember.

Around the neighborhood, he was known as the

sweet little old man who sat in his lawn chair and waved to passersby.

When he didn't acknowledge her presence, Gemini cleared her throat. "I suppose you've heard all the ruckus."

"About you and Mr. Beachmont? It's a doggone shame is what it is."

Gemini felt the heat rise to her cheeks. She'd marched over here fueled by emotion and she was already regretting it. "The embarrassment belongs to people who spend time spreading false stories. And I have to say, of all people, you should be the one who used his noodle. You didn't get to the upper ranks of P.I.N.K. by mindlessly following others." After she'd spoken, the air left her sails and all she wanted to do was go home and crawl back in bed.

"I just meant it's a shame that the Crabbitz family are spending all their time and energy trying to hurt you and Howard."

"Oh." Now she felt silly. "I haven't been sleeping well and it's causing me to be short with those I shouldn't."

Mr. Beasley's small head nodded sympathetically. "I have a large extended family, all of whom are notorious gossips. I've reached the point where I'm tired of listening. Now they have to make an appointment to speak with me."

It took her a minute to realize he was speaking of family no longer in the living world. She'd never heard of such a thing, but if he was as powerful as Feather said he was, appointments must be the way it was done. "I marvel at your skill, Mr. Beasley. I'm sure Feather would like to schedule her conversations too."

"What do your relatives say about Gladiola? Can they offer suggestions?"

He turned his back and walked over to the faucet, turning the water off. The ground should have been a river, but it strangely looked dry.

"If you'll indulge me, Mrs. Reed, I have something inside you might find of interest."

He picked up a dark wood cane with two discreet pink strips of tape around the bottom. Gemini knew it was his way of signaling others of his affiliation with P.I.N.K.

Mr. Beasley attempted to open his heavy front door, but with one hand grasping his cane, it was nearly impossible.

"Here, let me get that." Gemini jumped up on his porch and held the door.

"You're still nimble. Impressive, Mrs. Reed!"

"My grandson Taurus demands it."

Once inside, Gemini's eyes could hardly take in all the glass display cases. They were filled with five-inch tall figurines. Each one was a woman of all shapes and shades. Each was posed in a different scene.

The one that caught Gemini's eye was a caramel-skinned woman with bright brown eyes and wavy brown hair. She was crouched over, ready to lift a bar holding heavy weights.

Named "A Powerful Influence," the figurine bore a startling resemblance to Maxine Smart. The exam room was so detailed, it contained medical supplies in the cupboards and a trash can containing used plastic gloves.

"You're quite the collector. I've never seen anything this extensive."

"I've got the largest collection of Careers for Carly in the world."

Gemini examined another one. This time, the doll had platinum blonde hair and held a piece of chalk in her hand, writing on a miniature chalkboard in front of students sitting in desks. "Carly's Journey Begins."

"My daughter Sophia had her finger on the pulse of the toy and doll business. Why didn't she ever beg for one of these?"

Mr. Beasley laughed. "My guess would be the fact that these dolls, though cute, came permanently attached to their stands. They were meant for collectors, not children, unfortunately. My mother was the CEO of the company, far ahead of its time. In order to get her board of directors to agree to a line of dolls who had careers, she had to agree to glue them in place. The irony isn't lost on you, I suspect?"

Gemini shook her head. "No, it isn't. How long

were these dolls in production? By the looks of your walls, it would seem like several decades."

"Only six years. What you see on my walls is every single doll, along with all the prototypes that were never put into production. My mother wanted these dolls to represent what children could achieve. If it wasn't something they could play with, at least they could look at them with admiration."

Gemini moved a few steps at a time, trying to take in as much as she could. When she reached the end of the cupboards, she came to an oblong wooden table topped with a piece of glass cut to size. She glanced down to find she'd been walking on two-tone green shag carpet. Though it was most certainly from the '70s, it looked immaculate.

"Your mother must have been quite an amazing woman."

Mr. Beasley grinned. "She was. All without the support of her family or a board of directors comprised mainly of men."

He gestured toward the table. "Please sit down, Mrs. Reed. Would you like some tea?"

It occurred to her that she was still wearing her pajamas. "I really shouldn't stay. What was it you wanted to show me?"

"Oh, yes." He turned to face a tall oak China hutch and opened a drawer. After rummaging through it for several minutes, in which time Gemini studied the Move Mountains Carly, who bore a startling resemblance to a younger version of herself, he pulled out a crinkled page and sat it in front of her.

Mr. Beasley pulled out his own chair and sat. "Go ahead. Read it."

Gemini was relieved to find the print large enough to read without her glasses.

Mrs. Beasley:

After six years and one hundred and twenty-four Careers for Carly, we have made the difficult decision to cease production. A meeting of the board was held earlier this week, where we took two votes. The first, where we voted on continuation of the Careers for Carly product, was unanimous.

We received an anonymous letter enlightening us on your family's sinister past. The whistle blower threatened to take this information public if we kept you on as CEO.

For that reason, we took a second vote, and then a third. The board was evenly divided, but eventually all agreed it was time you stepped away from the company.

With heavy hearts,
Your Board of Directors

"That's very sad! But I don't understand why you're showing me this."

"My family has a history of coming to the

rescue of those in need. Because we were a high profile family who helped others, it made us easy targets."

Gemini frowned. "I still don't know what this has to do with me."

Mr. Beasley held a finger to his lips and stood. Not a minute later, the doorbell rang.

Sitting there by herself, she was even more ashamed that she'd walked not only to Howard's house but across the street to a virtual stranger's home while still in her night clothes. She needed to sneak out unnoticed by Mr. Beasley's new guest.

"Mr. Beasley, you're such a sweet thing, you probably don't understand what will happen to the price of your home if they aren't removed."

Recognizing the sickly sweet voice of Gladiola Crabbitz, Gemini moved quickly to his kitchen, where she could hear but wouldn't be seen.

"No, Mrs. Crabbitz. We have fine neighbors. Things aren't always as they seem, my dear. It's very possible your judgment has been clouded through no fault of your own."

Gladiola huffed. "That woman tried to poison me! She brought cookies to my door and the next day, both my nephew and myself were so sick we couldn't leave the bathroom. Does that sound like I'm confused?"

Gemini stifled her anger. Not once in her life had she poisoned someone with something she baked.

How dare this woman turn a neighborly act into something evil.

"My nephew and myself have been in contact with an attorney. Your little neighborhood association has unjustly targeted us, and we're planning to sue. That is, unless you'll allow me to join N.A.G."

Gemini maneuvered her body closer to the wall, where another figurine caught her eye. A woman with silver hair and pink lipstick, she wore a stethoscope. The end was pressed to the chest of a small child perched on a table.

"Curious."

As she leaned in closer to examine it, she accidentally knocked the figurine to the floor, where it smashed into a million pieces. She quickly covered her mouth when a gasp came out.

"What was that? Do you have a guest?"

That woman didn't deserve superhuman hearing.

"My guests are none of your concern. I'm sure you'll agree that our homes are sacred spaces."

Gemini peeked her head around the corner where the two neighbors appeared to be in a standoff. Gladiola transferred her weight from one foot to the other, alternately watching traffic drive by and glaring at Mr. Beasley.

"Fine. Don't say I didn't warn you."

The standoff over, Mr. Beasley leaned against the door frame. "Have a wonderful day, Mrs. Crabbitz."

"Those two are troublemakers, and when they finish with us, they'll come for you!"

Mrs. Crabbitz's heels clicked in a quick rhythm as she walked away. That was Gemini's cue to make her exit out his back door. As guilt overtook her, she realized it would take more than brownies to apologize for breaking his priceless figurine.

CHAPTER 37

FEATHER

"I didn't expect to see *her* again!"

Tug pointed to Opal Hughes as he announced the understatement of the day. She was arguing with Chief Boulder and appeared to have completely changed her look. She was wearing a matching bright green jersey and shorts combo. Her hair was pulled back in a tight ponytail.

This woman looked nothing like the person they'd encountered at Cassie's bedside—the Opal who threatened her daughter's life. If it weren't for her gravelly voice, Feather would swear it was someone else.

Opal was throwing a much more docile fit, telling the chief that she'd dropped out of the Regatta in round two when she got the news of her daughter's accident. When she got to town, no one would allow her to see Cassie.

"Nice try," Chief Boulder said. "You bailed out an hour ago, Ms. Hughes. The costume change was creative, though, I'll give you that."

The chief winked at Tug and Feather when he caught sight of them. Opal whipped around and glared at them, causing Tug to throw a protective arm in front of Feather. "We're not here to hurt you, Opal."

"You look like a nice, harmless couple. Could you tell the officer that I'm not who he thinks I am?"

Feather's mouth dropped open as she searched for the right words. "Um..."

Opal sighed. "You too? What's going on in Charming? Is everyone in this town nuts? Makes me glad I left when I did!"

"Opal, we're all very concerned about your daughter. Cassie has been through a lot. You'll agree, right?" Tug was doing his level best to remain calm. A skill he'd perfected.

"Of course! But the nurse who called me said she wasn't doing well. I hightailed it to the hospital and, when I asked for her room number, I was arrested. My baby girl just needs her mama!"

Feather remembered the van Opal fell out of when they first saw her. "How did you get here? Your van has been impounded."

Cassie's grandmother, whatever your name is, I need you now!

Opal pointed to the bench behind her, where a weather-beaten man who looked like he'd never seen a tube of sunscreen raised his Styrofoam cup in response. "Howdy, kids."

"I have to hand it to you, Opal, getting an actor this quick is impressive." Chief Boulder was calm as he nodded to the officer standing beside Tug. "Now I just need the two of you to leave. If I have to arrest you again, the judge won't be so generous with the bail money."

The officer guided Opal by the shoulders as she protested. "I'll sue you! Every single person in this godforsaken police department!"

Feather and Tug followed them outside, where Opal burst into tears. She buried her head in the man's chest as he tried awkwardly to comfort her.

"There, there. It's not so bad. I haven't seen my young ones in four years. Their mamas think I'm a bad influence."

"Yes, you did mention that on the ride up," she sniffed. "Me and Cassie aren't close, but when they called to say she was in the hospital, I did everything I could to get up here from Florida."

"She ain't lying. Opal paid me $400 and the use of her schooner for a month to drive her. And she don't know me from Adam."

She's here hoping to scoop up Cassie's inheritance while my granddaughter's knocked out.

How do I stop her?

One of these people isn't really Opal. Are you getting the picture yet?

CHAPTER 38

FEATHER

Feather's car careened down the windy bricks of Buttercup Way, narrowly missing Mrs. Aycock's prize-winning indigo hydrangeas. The hydrangeas were, after all, a traffic hazard. The six-foot tall bush and dinner plate-sized blooms hung beyond the clearance of her driveway. Citations for cutting her shrubbery went unpaid.

"The last six accidents on this block were initiated by Mrs. Aycock, so I guess you get a freebie," Gemini joked.

Feather would have found it funny if it were any other day. She knew her partner was doing her level best to keep her mind somewhere other than the road as she hung onto the top of her seat belt for dear life.

Glancing over at Gemini, she noticed she was examining her brand new pink blouse. The green apple pattern made the perfect accompaniment to her green slacks. Gemini had an enviable way of making outfits out of clothing pieces that didn't seem to go together. "Very cute outfit, Gem."

"If I die today, at least I'll go out looking festive."

Feather laughed in spite of the serious situation. "That you will. I'm sorry for the crazy driving, but we have to hurry, Gem. If we don't get to Jayden before the cartel does, her goose is cooked."

"Tell me again how you know this, and how Opal is involved? You lost me somewhere between Alistair isn't Alistair and Jayden shot someone in her office. Which, by the way, you should have told me sooner."

Feather took another corner at high speed, causing the car to momentarily lift off its wheels. "Alistair is a ghost with a lot of power. He can change his human form to match anyone he wants. The ghost of Ruthmarie at the séance? That wasn't her. You said yourself she can't leave your house. It was Alistair."

Despite all the unusual circumstances they'd encountered in Kindred Spirits Detective Agency, this one was hard to comprehend. "What was Alistair hoping to accomplish?" Gemini gasped when a horrid thought occurred to her. "And why was he only speaking to my Sophia? Is she in danger too?"

Feather wasn't a fan of Sophia's, both for the way she treated her mother and her general attitude toward others. "I don't think so."

"Maybe it was a bad idea to bring me along. I should try calling Sophia again. Besides, Howard and I were in the middle of something."

When Feather called, Gemini was having coffee with Howard, discussing the peculiar turn at their party. Maxine's confession threw a wrench into their success story; one that was supposed to end in Gladiola's apology. Feather had barely listened as Gemini told the story. It would have to take a backseat for now.

"There is an emergency, and I need you with me. I promise, as soon as we warn Jayden, you can call your daughter."

Not realizing her phone hadn't hung up, Feather heard the entire conversation.

"Maxine, you bear a striking resemblance to a figurine—"

"Who was that on the phone?"

"It was Feather. She's my partner, Maxine. She needs my help with something. I'm sure I'll be right back. In fact, I should run home and get the batch of cookies I made last night for her."

"We have to go RIGHT NOW, Gem! There's no time to waste!"

Gemini picked up the phone. "I'm sorry, love. Didn't realize you were still there. I'm at Howard's. Just tap your horn when you're in the driveway."

The unwelcome sound affectionately known as "mechanical nose with a cold," also known as

Feather's horn, honked persistently in her driveway.

A small child was riding her baby blue trike in and out of the gutter. She was oblivious to the impending doom speeding towards her.

Feather jammed her foot on the brakes as hard as she could and both women held their breath until the car came to a complete stop. Only then did the child glance up.

She shielded iridescent brown eyes with a chubby arm. "You're noisy!" The child stood and turned her trike around, heading back the other direction, just as carefree as she had been minutes earlier.

Feather glanced down at her forearms but said nothing.

"Cheese and crackers, Feather! We'll be of no use to Jayden if we die in a fiery car crash."

"Sorry!"

"I know we're in a hurry. But let's make sure we don't have an accident. A dead child isn't worth—"

"She was already dead. It was another one of Alistair's tricks to slow us down." Feather could tell by Gemini's expression that things still weren't adding up. "Tell you what, start a timer and I'll put all my cards on the table. It will take both of our minds off the drive."

Gemini pulled out her phone and played with it for a moment. "I started the timer. Or maybe it's the calorie counter. They shouldn't put so many gadgets on these things. No one could possibly use every single feature."

"Gem!"

"Let's think positively that I did set a timer. For the next minute, I want you to explain why Sophia isn't in danger, why my presence was mandatory, and what kind of danger Jayden is in."

The car slowed slightly, something Gemini was extremely thankful for.

Just as Feather opened her mouth to speak, they hit a speed bump that nearly knocked Gemini into the dash. "Oops," Feather remarked in the understatement of the year. "My ghost senses have been working overtime lately. I can't get through a single night without being awoken by an entity. Yet I walked into The Bleeding Rose and—nothing."

Gemini knitted her brows together. "What are you saying? That your arm hairs are on the fritz?"

"I was starting to wonder. But then I remembered my early training to join P.I.N.K. Jayden taught me to trust my gift. If I was in a ghost situation and there was no ghost, either it wasn't really a ghost or—"

"Someone put a block on you!"

Feather smiled at her. "You know me so well, Gem."

"Not well enough, apparently. I had no idea you were struggling so much. By the looks of your driving, it's far worse than anything I could have imagined."

Feather wasn't offended. It was true; she wasn't normally a reckless driver.

"When Jayden shot the man in her office, the hairs on my arms were at full attention. Everything about that situation was strange." She glanced over at her partner, waiting for her reaction to that shocking revelation.

Feather's momentary distraction almost led to an accident when they came upon another vehicle at high speed. Luckily, just as they were about to crash into the back of a very expensive bumper, the other car took off from the intersection, completely oblivious to the near-miss behind them.

"Sweetie, you may want to—"

"Slow down. I know. I wish I could, Gem. Jayden's life depends on our reaching her home as quickly as possible."

Gemini pondered their conversation, trying to come up with something to distract Feather to prevent a full-fledged accident. "It doesn't happen right away when someone crosses over, does it, dear?"

"Huh?" Feather's eyes left the road momentarily. "No, not usually. We were at the hospital when Cassie's mother was hauled off for making threats against her daughter and my hairs stood. I thought it came from Cassie's grandmother. She was there, in the room, but someone else was there too."

She'd eased her foot off the gas just enough to allow Gemini to breathe easy. "Today we were at the police station when Opal appealed to see her daughter. Only this time, Opal looked totally different. She was calm and collected. That's when I understood what was happening. Alistair was hopping around from form to form, trying to keep me—and you—from discovering the truth."

Gemini's eyes darted back and forth. "This is what happened... to poor Cassie too? She was possessed?"

"She fought it the whole way. Wrecking the van was the only way she could make it stop. The voice of her grandmother, who was really Alistair, was guiding her to kill Jayden. I think Gladiola Crabbitz is also Alistair's doing."

"Oh dear. He's much more powerful than the angry ghosts you've dealt with before."

"I went to The Bleeding Rose and had a heart to heart with Azalea, who is a ghost by the way," Feather continued. "She admitted that Alistair wants control of Jayden because she is a descendant of his killers. One of many. By controlling her, he thought he could force her to do his dirty work. But she refused."

Gemini shook her head in disbelief. "There is

something to be said for occupying our time with mindless television instead of revenge, isn't there?"

Feather nodded. It wasn't that she was angry, because Gemini knew right away when that happened. It was more a sense of defeat, and that hurt her partner's heart. "Where's Tug? Not that we need a man to help us, but he's always handy for the heavy lifting and such."

"He had an emergency at the factory. He's been putting in so many hours for the big order at the prison, I hardly see him. And now, when I need him the most..." Feather's voice broke.

"Oh, honey." Gemini stroked her arm. "You're both just stressed right now. Don't hold it against him."

Feather wiped her tears away and bit her lip.

"What's important now is that you understand we can't trust anyone. Jayden is in terrible danger. Because we can't communicate telepathically, I need to warn her that Alistair has placed a hit on her. The man she killed was the first one, but there are more coming. Opal maybe?"

"Can we circle back to 'the man Jayden killed?' You need to fill in the rest of the page."

"The whole thing was so crazy, I didn't know how to start." Feather's voice was calmer, and for that, Gemini was immensely grateful. Maybe today wasn't going to be the untimely end for the green apple blouse after all.

"The secretary, Lulu, made it seem like it was a common occurrence in their building, but when I saw Jayden with a gun in her hand, she was shocked. I mean, really shocked. I don't think she knew he was coming. And Alistair controlled Shag Carpetia's mind. He was sent to clear evidence from the van after Cassie's crash, and then he was sent to kill Jayden. Unfortunately, Mr. Carpetia is also a member of the salmon cartel—the real Mr. Carpetia."

"And now they want their own pound of flesh."

Feather nodded as she took another corner at high speed.

"Could you use both hands on the wheel, dear? It would make me feel so much better."

"Azalea said the cartel are heading to Jayden's place right now, so we have to warn her. We've lost our connection and that scares me the most. Jayden and I communicated telepathically forever. It feels like I've lost her."

Gemini sighed with relief as Feather's left hand joined the right on the steering wheel. "Maybe it's some sort of roadblock Alistair put up on you both?"

There was one more sharp turn and, this time, Gemini was ready for it. She gripped the handle above the door and closed her eyes.

Feather's voice quivered. "She's been so good to me. I can't let her down. We've got to come up with a plan, just in case."

"If there's one thing we excel at, it's figuring things out on the fly."

"Have you been to her home before?"

"Never. She's very private and I try to respect that."

"We'll tell her we have an important message and it's time sensitive. That would make her open the gate, wouldn't it?"

Feather shrugged. "Maybe. We'll need something a little more compelling than that."

"I've got it!" Gemini snapped her fingers. "My neighbor, your grand poo-bah."

"Capu," Feather corrected her.

"Yes, Capybara. He has this marvelous collection of dolls. His mother was the CEO of the company and—" Gemini caught herself before she went on too long. Twenty seconds left. "He has collectibles. If Jayden were to think *he* was the target, she'd be instantly concerned."

"Yes, Gem!" Feather banged her hands on the steering wheel.

They turned left on Beachbum Avenue and then a quick right on Gilded Cat Drive. Instantly, the car rode like it was driving on butter. The black top looked brand new as they drove past mansion after mansion.

"Cheese and crackers! I never knew there were so many rich people here!"

Feather laughed. "You mean, like you?"

Because her large settlement from the hospital and Leo's stroke weren't topics she enjoyed, she rarely thought of them. "Oh. I guess you've got me there."

They pulled up to a large wrought-iron gate with a fancy J on one side and a K on the other. Feather rolled down her window and reached over to push the speaker button.

"Feather Jones and associate. We need to speak to Jayden about—"

Before she'd had a chance to tell the story she and Gemini concocted, the gates squeaked as they slowly parted.

"Maybe we were overthinking this," she remarked.

Jayden's home sat on a hill hidden from the main road. Gemini enjoyed the view. Raised gardens, each with a theme, were lined with trees. Blueberry and blackberry bushes framed a strawberry bed and, standing just behind it, a large apple tree. When they finally reached the home at the end of the lane, they gasped. Jayden's home was like something out of an architecture magazine.

Two stories tall and shaped like a boat, the portion of her mammoth home that was shaped like a hull contained huge windows that stretched from the ground up to the second story.

"What in the..." Feather began. The closer they got, the more concerning the scene became.

Through the large windows, they were able to see it was buzzing with activity.

Someone wearing a pink lab coat and pink rubber gloves approached their car, adjusting black-framed goggles as Feather leaned her head out. "Phoebe? What's going on?"

Phoebe Pepper leaned down and peeked in Feather's window. Now Gemini could clearly see the letters P.I.N.K. emblazoned on the right side of her chest.

"You shouldn't bring your grandmother to a containment, Jones. This is confidential. What if she blabs to her bridge club or whatever?"

Gemini swallowed hard. She'd never get used to people assuming she was Feather's grandmother. She didn't feel any older than forty. Maybe fifty when her arthritis flared up.

"This is my partner. Gemini, this is Phoebe. Phoebe, Gemini."

"Oh, I remember now. You're the one who caused the..." Gemini stopped before she said too much. Feather told her that Phoebe caused the group to lose their G Level because she'd taken up with a ghost. "I've heard you're very thorough." Gemini sat back, feeling relieved.

Phoebe didn't respond. Instead, she tapped the window with one gloved hand. "We need a break. Ten of us have been at this for almost four hours.

Could your partner stay in the car while you help with containment?"

"I'm not ready. I haven't passed that exam level yet."

"Oh, really?" Phoebe crossed her arms and barely contained a smirk. "The great Feather Jones has a kryptonite and it's good old Level R?"

Gemini leaned across Feather, needing this game to end. "She has test anxiety, dear. Much different. What happened to Jayden, and what are you trying to contain?"

CHAPTER 39

GEMINI

Jayden's circular bed sat on a podium in the center of the room. A very large walk-in closet was the only space without windows.

As Gemini stared at the dramatic ocean view, doing her best not to snoop, a P.I.N.K. member nudged her side. "Push that button to your left."

Without looking, she shook her head. "No. I don't understand your containment process, but I refuse to touch anything. This is someone's private living space."

Feather had convinced Phoebe to allow Gemini inside by bringing up a recent visit to The Bleeding Rose if Phoebe didn't comply. Once they were alone, Feather explained that Phoebe was still trying to get into the good graces of the group and had been soliciting members to make paranormal contacts on her behalf.

"Poor dear," Gemini had clucked. Gemini let go of the seat belt strap for a moment as she gave space to feelings of resentment. Sophia didn't deserve to be at the center of their case. She'd only come to the séance out of curiosity, not to connect with a spirit. This was Feather's mystery and Gemini's was back with Howard and Maxine. "Watch out!"

The member frowned before shrugging her shoulders. "Suit yourself." She pushed the button herself, causing a low rumble in the room.

"What's happening? What did you do?"

"Just watch." They pointed to large shades rolling slowly over the windows, just as a movie theater curtain would lift. When the shades reached the floor, Gemini realized she could still see the ocean without any problem.

"Those are amazing!"

"Right? She's got all the best stuff. I wish I had her cash."

"All right. Everyone freeze and drop whatever is in your greedy little hands."

Gemini's hands rose over her head, and she turned around slowly. Men and women in black suits filled the room, tackling P.I.N.K. members to the ground and removing whatever was in their grasp.

When a tall man reached her, she blurted, "I'm not one of them. I'm just here because a friend was called in and she didn't have time to take me home."

His eyes traveled up and down her body, causing her to wish she could turn away. "Turn your pockets inside out, ma'am."

Women of the World green slacks no longer had pockets. *Didn't everyone know that?* She searched through every single one until she found this pair. As she turned them inside out, two used tissues and a hard candy dropped to the floor.

"That's it?"

He seemed disappointed, like taking someone his mother's age to the ground was his only wish.

"No, sir. As I already mentioned, I'm just here as an observer. None of this is any of my business."

When his shoulders relaxed and he allowed his eyes to travel across the room to another potential victim, she asked, "What is it you're looking for exactly? I can assure you, this group has been quite thorough."

"Ko Industries Level Four Security. Our sources informed us that Ms. Ko may be in danger. We're here for containment."

What is left to contain?

Gemini glanced around the room, where samples of everything, including Jayden's toothpaste, had been taken.

"Who called you?"

CHAPTER 40

GEMINI

"Go about your days as though nothing has happened."

Gemini couldn't imagine how that could happen, given Jayden Ko's disappearance and their unsettling experience at her home, but when Feather dropped her off, she gave that stern warning.

When they gained entrance to Jayden's compound after signing a privacy document, there were at least a dozen people wearing pink lab coats, collecting evidence from every room.

"Where is Jayden?" she'd asked after Feather drifted off. As of yet, she hadn't received a satisfactory explanation. Gemini grabbed the arm of a passing pink coat and held firm before asking again. "Where's Jayden and why all the fuss?"

"Unclear." The pink jacket shook free of her hold and examined her jacketless appearance. "Right now, we believe it's a crime syndicate related to the elimination of one of their own."

"This must be what Feather referred to in vague terms."

Pink Jacket's eyes widened. "Jones told you everything? That's against protocol."

"No, she didn't!" Gemini protested. "I heard her mumbling about an...unfortunate event in Ko Industries. That's all I know."

Pink Jacket nodded in a way that made it unclear whether she really believed that explanation.

"How do we find her?"

It was at that moment the FBI swarmed the place like an invasion of black beetles. "On the ground!" they barked, training their weapons on several pink jackets. Gemini watched with equal parts fascination and horror. Just as she was lowering herself to the ground, she heard a familiar voice.

"We need to get out of here!"

She whipped around to see Feather standing in front of a secret door, one painted the same color as the pale blue wall. She motioned furiously for Gemini to join her.

When they were safely in Feather's car and bouncing through the stubbly wheat field behind Jayden's home, Gemini spoke first. "Why would the FBI show up? Does it have something to do with the man Jayden killed?"

Feather didn't answer.

FEATHER WASN'T at work the next morning. Though Tug assured Gemini she was under the weather, Gemini sensed something more.

The next few days were a whirlwind of planning for Howard's Flappers, Fizz, and Fatalities Mystery Dinner. Without a sufficient explanation from her partner, Gemini was left with more questions than answers, but she needed to focus on supporting Howard.

Howard insisted on paying for catering, with explicit instructions on how and when the four-course meal was served. There were invitations to be made, food to be planned, and decorations to be purchased.

Everyone in the neighborhood received an invitation detailing the theme of the evening, with the stipulation that they were participating in a game, and as such, their attendance implied an agreement to stick with the script. This was Howard's ingenious idea to keep people from bringing up the photo and their ideas about its origins.

Quentin and his mother were Gary Gangster and Ma Pumpkin. Mr. Beasley was nightclub owner One Eyed Wally. Gemini and Howard were Pinky and Bean, a ventriloquist team with

Howard acting as the wooden dummy. Each person was given a brief backstory and were encouraged to dress up and really get into their roles.

As the date of the party approached, rumors swirled about the impending event. Some were excited, others skeptical, but most were curious enough to attend. Even Gladiola, assigned the character of Bourbon Betty, had RSVP'd.

The night of the party, the house was decked out in a noir theme, with dim lighting and jazz music playing softly in the background. The guests arrived in character, creating an exciting buzz. The only no-show was Maxine Smart.

The couple from the doctored photo, whose names were Don and Sherrie, were hidden away in the laundry room. The entire meal was served to them on a folding table covered with a black cloth. Howard apologized profusely, but they were eager to clear his name and pleased to receive a meal.

He hoped that the jazz music playing from the other room would filter in, creating somewhat of an ambiance.

Two chalk outlines in the middle of the room were the talk of the evening. Everyone stayed in character as they spoke, even Gladiola Crabbitz, who wore a black-beaded flapper dress and a matching headband. She spoke with a nasally accent, staying in character as Bourbon Betty. "I just saw the victim last week," she read off the invitation. "She told me she had a secret."

As the night wore on, guests mingled, questioning one another and searching for clues. Mr. Beasley, dressed as One Eyed Wally, was the most enthusiastic as he delivered drinks to each guest. "I was so lucky to get this job after losing the last one," he mentioned to several guests. "Glad the owner of this joint didn't ask why."

The atmosphere was electric with suspense, punctuated with laughter as guests tried to stay in character while also trying not to giggle at the absurdity of it all. Howard winked at Gemini who nodded in support. He was right. Having a party was the perfect medicine for their broken community.

Howard and Gemini gave a ventriloquism performance to uproarious laughter. When the time came to reveal the "murderers," Howard blew an exotic Koori Buck Horn he'd been gifted by a shaman in Indonesia. This was the cue for Don and Sherrie to make their entrance.

"As you know, this evening was all in good fun," Gemini began. "But it was also an opportunity for us to clear the air about a certain photo."

Don and Sherrie appeared wearing the same clothing they had in the photo. "We are actors, plain and simple, who were paid to pose for this magazine ad," Don announced, clearly relishing his role as the star of the show.

The room filled with gasps and murmurs as the truth came out.

"Wait, so you guys aren't...?" Quentin began, trailing off.

Howard's entire home grew so quiet, the sound of his water softener, housed in the basement, could be heard creaking and groaning. "And now you can clearly see that we aren't involved in a relationship. Not only that, all of the rumors about us are blatantly false."

"Are you going to reveal the killer?" Hetty asked. "I got all dressed up for nothing. Figures."

"The real killer is—"

Howard was interrupted by the doorbell. "The evening hasn't ended yet. Dessert and coffee will be served on the back porch! Don't worry, it's covered and heated, so those of you in thin costumes will be plenty warm. I'll reveal the killer in ten minutes."

The mood of the evening returned to its previous jovial state as the guests filtered into the backyard. Gemini searched for Gladiola, unsure of her reaction. "She must've snuck out during the big reveal."

Hetty caught Gemini's arm. "Can I have them start bagging up the leftovers? Quentin promised we could take them home."

Gemini nodded, stretching her neck to see who was at the door.

By the time she'd reached the front room, the door was open and Howard was deep in conversation. "Maxine! It's not too late for dinner; we still have plenty of food!"

"You'd better make sure Hetty hasn't cleaned us out," Gemini muttered.

"No, I've already eaten, but thank you. I knew you both would be here this evening." Maxine turned toward Gemini and continued. "My friends at the Portland Bureau sent me some disturbing information. Is there somewhere we could sit down and talk?"

CHAPTER 41

FEATHER

Feather squeezed her eyes shut, trying hard to contact Jayden. *I know you're in trouble. I'm here, Jayden. Just tell me where you are and I'll find you.*

Nothing. Not even the opportunistic ghosts who tried to take advantage of her when her defenses were down.

Even more concerning was Tug's message:

One of the ovens went out. It stalled production and we have to get this order finished before tomorrow. Don't wait up.

Love you to the moon, babe!

She was all the more grateful when Gemini knocked on her door with a basket of fresh blueberry muffins.

Feather fell into her arms before she'd crossed the threshold. "I'm so sorry. I didn't mean to shut you out. I was just overwhelmed. Usually, Tug and I talk things out. I never realized how much that kept me calm. And I'm worried sick about Jayden. I wish I could contact her."

Gemini placed a comforting arm around Feather's shoulder. "We'll find her. We just need to keep brainstorming."

A loud rumble reminded Feather that she hadn't eaten all day. As she inhaled one muffin and then another, Gemini waited patiently.

"Maybe we should try and sneak back in to Jayden's place?" Feather said between voracious bites. "The FBI has to have left by now."

"That's one of the things I came here to tell you, hon. Remember when Tug found a listening device attached to my home? It wasn't Gladiola Crabbitz's doing. It was the FBI. Our neighbor, Maxine Smart, placed it there."

"What?" Feather paused momentarily, allowing crumbs from her mouth to fall to the floor. "Why you? Do they think you're a spy?"

Gemini chuckled. "No, hon. Nothing like that. You could have knocked me over with a feather when Maxine told me the problem was an ancestor of mine. Apparently, great-grandfather Obbediah Plum was a master thief. He befriended the wealthy and then stole their jewels."

"And they think you have them?" Feather

brushed what was left of the muffins from her shirt. "That's not a reason to bug your place."

"They received intel that I was selling the jewels, and they wanted proof so they could return them to their rightful owners."

"Oh. Well, I hope you explained you're loaded and you don't need to do that."

Gemini guffawed. "Oh, hon. You always cheer me up. I did ask Maxine for the names of these families. She gave me one that sent chills up and down my spine."

Feather swallowed hard. "The Violette family?"

Gemini nodded. "There is some evidence that Obbediah Plum and his associate broke into the home of Alistair Violette, expecting no one to be there. Instead, they found Alistair in an upstairs bedroom and shot him dead."

Feather's mind swirled. "He wants you to pay for his death, Gem."

"Possibly. If so, he's certainly not tried too hard." Gemini forced a laugh. "He needs to take ghost lessons from your Millicent."

Alistair's insistence that she kill Jayden didn't make sense when she had easier access to her partner. "Someone has been protecting you, Gem. I'm not sure who, though. You mentioned that Obbediah had help. Who helped him?"

"I was getting to that. It was Jacob Ko, Jayden's great-great grandfather."

"That makes sense. And Jayden didn't have protection because she didn't need it. By the time she was in danger, it was too late to call on anyone to use their powers."

"What if we got some help?"

"Help? From who?"

"You aren't going to like my suggestion."

Feather studied her friend's face. "Chief Boulder? You want us to go to the police with this? They already think we're the kooks who run a shady business."

"I do hate it that you've learned to read my thoughts, dear. It's an invasion of my privacy."

"Sorry, Gem. It's a byproduct of my many hours learning under Jayden."

Gemini put her phone on speaker after dialing his personal number. He answered on the third ring.

"Mrs. Reed! What can I do for you?"

Gemini took a deep breath. "Chief Boulder, I need your help. My friend Jayden has gone missing and we think a... ghost might be involved."

Chief Boulder was quiet for a moment. "I'll be there as soon as I can. Believe it or not, it isn't the craziest thing that's happened to me this week."

Feather nodded.

"In the meantime, I need you to tell me everything you know."

Gemini and Feather detailed everything that had happened since Jayden's disappearance.

When they finished, Chief Boulder cleared his throat. "Let me get this straight. Your friend is missing and a whole bunch of people know but haven't reported it to law enforcement. But the two of you are positive she's been kidnapped by a ghost."

Feather shot Gemini an "I told you so" look.

"No, that's not it at all, Chief. When the head of a giant company like Ko Industries goes missing, there is going to be some kind of information lockdown. When I worked for my son-in-law, we had several clients who asked us to draw up directives for just such occasions." Gemini frowned and shook her head, making Feather smile for the first time today.

It was obvious to Feather that her partner was making the whole thing up.

"I'm with you on that, Mrs. Reed. I know you ladies specialize in tracking down things that go boo in the night, but my deputies won't find it funny if I ask them to find an outlaw ghost."

Feather was angered by his oversimplification of her chosen profession. Not once had she or any of her cohorts in P.I.N.K. mentioned seeing an entity the way he described.

"No, sir. This is Feather Jones. Jayden wasn't kidnapped by a ghost. But whoever has her could very well be influenced by one. Her life is in danger if that's the case."

"I'll repeat my question. What do you want us to

do about it? Officially, we don't even have a missing person!"

He did have a point. Was she going to risk her standing in the paranormal community by going public?

"I have a contact who may be helpful. Could I call you after that?"

"Yup."

After hanging up, Feather felt uneasy. "Chief Boulder doesn't believe a word we said, Gem."

CHAPTER 42
FEATHER

Four Cups was buzzing with the electricity of an exuberant crowd. Feather scanned the booths filled with noisy children and animated adults until her eyes came to rest on the arm of Lulu Rodriguez, waving enthusiastically.

"Hey, girl! I was surprised when you called!"

"Why?" Feather slid into the booth, unprepared for Lulu's cheeriness.

"Because I figured you would be in the fetal position, worried about Jayden."

Her comment caught Feather off guard. "Aren't you? She's your boss."

Lulu crossed her arms and leaned forward onto them. "Of course I am." She motioned for Feather to meet her in the middle. "I know where she is."

"You do?"

Feather had no sooner sat back down when Lulu

motioned to her again. "Where is she? Who are her kidnappers? Her life is in danger, Lulu. We can't wait another minute!"

Lulu leaned closer, her secretive tone dropping an octave. "She's safe, girl. Calm down. She's being protected by the same people who set up her 'kidnapping'."

Feather blinked several times, trying to make sense of this information. "What do you mean 'protected'?"

Lulu leaned back, calling the waiter over to order a couple of their signature Four Extras Mochas. Four Cups made no secret of their signature drink, listing all ingredients on the menu: cinnamon, nutmeg— just a dash on top to add a delicate spiciness, cardamom, vanilla, and a pinch of sea salt.

Once he was gone, she continued. "Jayden's life was in danger, Feather. And if they discovered where she was, she'd be dead within an hour. Jayden's disappearance is a carefully orchestrated event."

"From the drug cartel. I know. But why hasn't Ko Industries issued a statement? Or at least pretended to search for her?" Feather found herself becoming increasingly upset. Though Jayden was her mentor, she'd assumed, wrongly, that their relationship had grown much closer.

"Because they know that the shareholders will panic if they hear even the suggestion of trouble. If something happens to Jayden, Ko Industries will crumble. Let's be honest, Jayden is the only one who had the balls to run that company properly."

Feather was stunned. "So she's not being held hostage?"

"No. But she can't come back yet. Not until we get everything sorted out and make sure her enemies are dealt with. We think there is a mole in P.I.N.K. helping the other side."

"Can I talk to her?" Feather's mind was spinning.

Lulu shook her head. "I'm sorry. That's not possible right now. But she is safe, Feather. I promise."

Feather's phone buzzed. "It's my boyfriend. I'll be right back." She practically jumped from her seat and ran out the front door.

"Babe? Where are you?"

"Olive and I are trying to get the factory back in order."

"Why? What happened?"

"Oh, just another employee going off the rails. He turned over the tables and threw most of our prison order on the floor. I'm starting to doubt my ability to judge a qualified employee."

Her chest squeezed tight. *Alistair.*

"Babe, are you safe?"

"Perfectly. I promise. But Olive and I will be here all night. We've asked a few other employees to stay late to help."

Feather Jones knew differently. No one in her life was safe. "Babe, you know I love you..."

Tug chuckled. "That's usually followed by a 'but.'"

"No, I just want you to be careful. Don't trust anyone right now, even me. If someone acts odd, treat them as the enemy. Lock yourselves in the office until the police arrive."

"Feath, you're scaring me!"

There were muffled voices behind him, causing Feather to tense up. "Tug? Are you okay?"

"Peachy. Olive had to cancel her date for this evening, causing her to feel..."

The phone changed hands. "Feather? I told the boy I'm feeling like a cactus at a hug convention. Everybody knows to be on their best behavior right now."

"Okay, got it. Tell Tug to remember what I said."

She returned to the table where a spicy aroma arose from two steaming mugs. "I'm afraid I'll need this to go."

Lulu's face was downcast. "Really? I don't have much of a social life. I can't talk to anyone about my job, and any time I've tried socializing with people on other floors, they treat me like a pariah. Jealous of my position, I guess."

Feather shook her head, frustrated, both by Lulu's situation and Jayden's. "This is ridiculous. I can't just sit here and do nothing."

"I know it's hard, Feather. But you're going to have to trust me."

Feather huffed. "If we can't talk about that, can we at least talk about what happened the day I visited? I've been there a hundred times before and I've never witnessed a..." She paused, unsure what she should say out loud.

"A containment," Lulu finally added. "Yes, they do happen often. This one was different, though." Once again, she leaned forward and motioned for Feather to do the same.

"Jayden's had some assassins sent her way recently. They've come in all forms, from a coffee delivery to someone from the second floor." Lulu paused to roll her eyes. "Those guys on the second floor are always doing stupid things. It wasn't a surprise that one of them had allowed himself to be controlled by an evil being. I caught him before he entered Jayden's office." She nodded solemnly. "Containment."

Feather nodded, though she wasn't convinced. Ever since discovering Alistair's ruse, she didn't know who to trust. "Why didn't she tell me? I could have helped her!"

"If she would have involved you, opened your mind to the evil fighting her, they would have a chance to destroy you too."

"Wait—what you're saying is that Jayden's mind

has been closed for business to keep Alistair out? That makes so much sense!"

She thought back to all the odd interactions she'd had with Jayden lately, from Jayden being unable to read her mind to her strange behavior at the séance, to the murder. "Fine. But if I don't hear from her soon, my detective agency is going to find her. With or without your help."

"I understand." Lulu's face softened. "But Feather, please try to have some faith. In Jayden and in the universe."

CHAPTER 43

GEMINI

Gemini leaned against the headboard of her bed, relieved to be at home. The events of the past few days had left her mentally and physically exhausted.

Her gut hurt when she thought about her assignment in Jayden's home. Maybe it was her age or upbringing, but snooping through someone's private room without looking for anything specific seemed wrong.

Her head hurt when she thought back to Sophia's strange visit and departure. She'd tried phoning her for days, but her daughter didn't pick up. Eventually, her voicemail filled up. She'd become more and more convinced that either Sophia was dead by the hand of Alistair Violette or Mrs. Floris had finally succeeded in cutting Gemini out of her daughter's life.

Next, Gemini called Brandon with no response. The legal secretary at Floris, Fleagal and Flem said Brandon came in every day, but she was instructed not to give any further information. "Is my daughter safe?" Gemini cried.

"She's fine. I'm a mother too, Mrs. Reed. I promise you, when she's ready, you'll hear from your daughter."

Gladiola was uncharacteristically quiet. At least that part of her life was going better.

Just as she considered picking up a book to take her mind off her troubles, her phone rang.

"Sophia? How is your recovery going?"

It was silent.

"Sophia? Are you still there? I've been worried sick. Whatever it is, I'm not going to be angry with you."

"Grammie?"

"Taurus! Sweet boy!" She began to sob, relieved that at least her grandson still loved her. "I've missed our talks. Did you go to school today?"

"No. The new nanny forgot to take me. But Granmuvva Four-ust is here."

"Oh." It was just as she suspected. She was being frozen out. "Sweetie, can I talk to your mommy?"

She heard muffled conversation before the phone hung up.

"I'm not going to cry. I'm not going to cry."

Eventually, she cried.

She was just about to drift off to sweet sleep. Her thoughts were filled with images of her and Leo, dancing in the moonlight under hanging baskets of fragrant blue flowers. He, whispering in her ear as she hummed softly.

Someone was tapping on her leg. *No! Please! Just one more minute!*

The tapping continued until her eyes flew open and she sat up quickly—too quickly. When her head stopped spinning, she focused on the unwelcome apparition at the foot of her bed. "What are you doing here? It's not the middle of the night, is it?"

She blinked slowly, hoping it was just a bad dream. Ruthmarie was dressed in her favorite party dress, the one Leo said resembled lettuce covered in tiny black aphids.

Nope. No dream.

"Why are you here?" she repeated. After Feather's revelation that Alistair could change his appearance to resemble any entity, Gemini was skeptical that the ghost in front of her was really Ruthmarie. "Did you forget that I'd asked you to leave permanently? If so, I'll refresh your memory."

"They're all working together now. You need to go into hiding!"

It was hard to know just how much to share with Ruthmarie. Though they'd had more meaningful conversations than they ever had when she was alive, Ruthmarie was still standoffish. "We've got her right where we want her."

Ruthmarie's hands snapped to her hips. "I recognize that tone, Gemini Aries. You're making fun of me."

She bit her lip. If this really was Alistair, the last thing she needed was to tip her hand. "It's Gemini Reed, Ruthmarie. I haven't used my maiden name since my wedding day." Gemini took a deep breath and cleared her head after her rude awakening.

"He's set a trap and your friends are the bait."

"What do you want me to do about it?" If this were really Alistair, she wasn't going to make it easy.

"You need to find Tug and Olive. Now!"

A loud banging on her door jolted her. "Who is that?"

"No! Don't answer! I mean it, Gemini!"

Now she was really in a pickle. How did she know which issue was the trap?

Another set of urgent knocks—no, bangs—made her jump out of her skin. This time, they didn't stop. Though she was rarely afraid living alone, this shook her to her core. Gemini pulled the shades apart just a slit. The only visible part of her front porch was the cement slab that stuck out. If it were a large group of people energized by Gladiola, she would see them.

Wrapping her daisy-print silk robe around her and cinching it at the waist, she slipped into her slippers, remembering she needed to clean them thoroughly before her daughter visited.

She stepped cautiously, avoiding the squeaky boards. The knocking continued.

Ruthmarie moved in front of her, but Gemini already knew this trick and walked right through her.

"Leo needs you!"

"Nice try."

A weapon. There was a bat under her bed, but it was too late to turn around. That's how all those horror movies she'd watched with Leo began; the victim turned away from the killer only to be bludgeoned to death.

Gemini glanced around, her eyes searching desperately for anything to defend herself. She had a cast iron skillet, but it was doubtful she could raise that above her head.

Tiptoeing into the kitchen, she opened the dishwasher. Two dirty bowls and a plastic lid. Not exactly fear-inducing. In the silverware holder was a large knife she'd used to cut a cantaloupe. A dirty knife would do the trick.

She swallowed hard. The closer the got, the more frantic the knocking became. Her fingers tightened around the knife handle. The threat of salmonella had to scare an intruder, didn't it?

Counting to ten, she flung the door open, knife over her head.

"Gemini! Thank goodness!"

"Chief Boulder? What are you doing here at this hour? And why wouldn't you just phone me?"

"This was too important for a phone call, ma'am."

Her heart rate was returning to normal, affirming that it wasn't her time. She opened the door wider and sighed. "Now that you're here, I'm concerned that Gladiola has done something to Howard."

The look on his face made her wonder if she'd offended him. "Chief? I'm going to change into my day clothes and we can confront her together."

As she turned to return to her bedroom, he grasped her arm. "Ow! I can assure you that isn't necessary!"

"Don't worry about what you're wearing. I can assure you, fashion is the least of your worries."

She turned around to see he was holding a weapon, and it was trained on her.

CHAPTER 44

FEATHER

Feather found her violet fuzzy robe and curled up on the couch with the remains of her mocha. Just as her eyes became heavy, she heard the familiar sound of a ball rolling on the hardwood floor. *Millicent.*

"I promised your caretaker I wouldn't involve you in my sleuthing, Millicent. And our usual playtime is..."

Feather paused when she entered the room. Her little ghost friend wasn't alone. Her caretaker, Maeve, held Millicent by the neck. Millicent's stockinged legs moved back and forth, as though she was running a race in midair. "What's going on? Put her down. Your beef is with me."

Millicent reached a hand out to Feather. "Please help me!"

Though she knew Millicent wasn't in danger, at

least physically, she felt a strong urge to yank the girl away and hold her tight.

"You don't get it, do you?" The woman's eyes glowed yellow. This wasn't the same ghost that appeared before, a woman who loved and protected Millicent even in death. "If I can't have Jayden, then I'll have you."

"Why? Isn't this whole performance about a vendetta you have? Go find something constructive to do on your side and leave the living world out of it." Feather moved closer, but Alistair in the form of Maeve stood his ground, still holding tightly to Millicent.

"I've tried. Gemini Reed is protected. Jayden Ko is missing. Using you as bait will force them to bend to my will."

"So holding Millicent by the neck is going to get you closer to your murderer? It doesn't make any sense."

Alistair's gaze moved from Feather to Millicent, who was still in running mode. He dropped the girl to the ground and she scurried off. "Thank you, Feather!" she called, disappearing through the wall.

"Good! Now, let's figure out who has your jewels and how we can get them returned to your family." She swallowed hard, aware that she was offering to help Alistair carry out his vendetta.

"You're going to make a phone call."

She pulled her phone out of her pocket and it lit

up immediately. A number dialed automatically as Feather put the phone to her ear. What was she going to say to this poor person? That she was interested in luring him to his death?

"Hello?"

His soft, soothing voice sounded familiar.

"Capu?" It couldn't be. She almost dropped the phone but somehow managed to hold her composure. "I'm sorry. I... meant to call someone else."

"No, sweetheart, you didn't."

Feather paused while she tried to comprehend his words. "Why would Alistair involve you? Are you related to his killers?"

"My mother had her own doll company from 1940 to 1946. I'm sure you know that a woman in that decade faced insurmountable odds to succeed."

"Yes but—"

"Our family has dark roots. My great-grandfather, Seamus Beasley, ran a burglary ring. He gave the men who carried out the burglaries a nice cut of the profits."

"Your grandfather worked with Jake Ko and Obbediah Plum?"

"They worked *for* him. When Alistair tracked down my mother, she made a deal. He would help her start her company and she would turn her son over to Alistair, to train as an assassin. Of course, Alistair wanted to create an assassin to kill every single descendant of those men."

Feather's head was swimming. "You're a trained assassin?"

"No. When my mother was forced out of her company, she felt betrayed. We went into hiding, and I learned I had gifts that she encouraged me to use to help, not hurt, people."

"Your mother was willing to give you to..." her voice trailed off. "To someone else, to complete a deal?"

"I'll never know, dear Feather. Either way, we avoided his wrath. I grew up in hiding and my mother lived a full life."

"You're the one whose been protecting Gem."

"I am."

"Tell him to meet us!" Alistair sneered. Feather had forgotten about him.

"He wants—"

"I know. I'll be there soon."

She would have to think of a way to stall him while she came up with a plan to keep him safe. If something happened to Capu, the entire organization would come after her.

"Oh, and Feather? Don't worry. Everything is working out just as it should."

CHAPTER 45

FEATHER

The Crabbitz's home was chock-full of familiar faces. Gemini was tied up in the corner, back-to-back with Howard. Quentin lay on the couch, his arms and feet bound in front of him. Hetty's hands were handcuffed to the refrigerator. Patience Thistle hummed an unknown tune as she sat bound to a kitchen chair. The only two people missing were Tug and Olive. At least that crisis didn't involve ghosts.

"You'll sit over here," Gladiola instructed, pointing to the wooden chair next to Patience.

Feather sat down obediently and clasped her hands behind her. It wasn't worth fighting.

"I don't know why I'm here, why I'm here, dear," Patience sang in a whisper voice.

"I'm not going to tie you up, honey. I'm Gladiola Crabbitz, by the way. It's just lovely making your acquaintance, Feather Jones." Gladiola smiled and touched Feather's arm, causing Feather to jump. "You're the star of the show!"

Feather gulped. "What does that mean?"

The doorbell rang and Gladiola's high heels clacked on the hard wood floor as she rushed to answer it. "Come in! We've been expecting you!" Her high-pitched voice sounded like a chair being dragged across a floor.

"You guys havin' a party?"

Opal's vacant-eyed boyfriend fell through the door, with Chief Boulder appearing behind him.

"You'll be seated on the floor, next to the couch." Chief Boulder pointed to the only open space in the tiny living room. He clasped his hands together and nodded slightly. "We're ready now."

"I'm the only one you need, Alistair. Let the rest of them go."

As soon as Feather uttered those words, Gemini wriggled to get free. "No! I'm just as guilty as you, Feather!" she protested. "Alistair, I'm the only one you need. My mother-in-law is right; I was evil from the get-go."

"Gem, you don't know what he's capable of!"

A hot blast of air swept through the room. "Neither of you are ruining my fun!"

Feather strained to keep her eyes open as an act of defiance. His silly tricks weren't going to scare her.

"You're all here because you've wronged me."

Quentin was sweating profusely, even though he was the only one in what could be considered a comfortable position. "Excuse me, sir. But I don't even know who you are. I have a podcast called *Boo's Talking* where we explore paranormal activities. If you're actually a ghost, I'd love to invite you on."

Patience stopped her song abruptly. "Booze talking? Shame on you for glamorizing the drink!"

"Told you it was a dumb name, boy!" Hetty chastised her son.

"It was you who brought me back with your gibberish." Alistair moved close to Quentin's face. As Quentin shook his head back and forth, his eyes closed. "Jayden and her cohort banished me after she reneged on our deal. I should thank you, Quentin, but you continue to conjure lost souls who get in my way."

Quentin's eyes popped open and a smile crossed his face. "I did that?"

"How many times have I done told you to do the weightlifting instead, boy?" Hetty added with disgust.

"Silence!" Alistair shouted so loud the house shook as Quentin's lips disappeared, leaving him mute along with his mother, Hetty. Not one to go down without a fight, Hetty kicked furiously, trying to somehow injure the apparition.

"You'll be playing for my side once you cross over.

But for now..." Alistair flicked a finger and Hetty's legs fused together.

Alistair moved on to his next victim without remorse.

"Patience Thistle. Poor little waif. You've been trying to fight me off, haven't you?" Alistair used a long finger to touch underneath her chin, forcing her face upward. "After you uncovered my story in the prison library, I thought your simple mind would be easy to enter. But, alas, silly songs kept me from controlling you. Crazy like a fox, eh?"

"Helpers, helpers, we stand tall and true,
There's always something good we can do.
From morning 'til night, in sunshine and rain,
We help, we share, again and again."
Alistair rolled his eyes. "Ugh. So nauseating."

Patience continued singing softly until her lips, too, disappeared. Left without her only coping mechanism, tears rolled down her cheeks. She hummed a loud and mournful tune.

Alistair grinned as he zeroed in on his next victim. "Howard Beachmont. Up nights trying to find ways to foil poor Gladiola."

Every pair of eyes shifted to Gladiola Crabbitz, who was mindlessly dusting a lamp.

"The woman has been mine for decades, dear man. Your efforts were all for naught. However, the mystery dinner was amusing. The couple you invited to foil Mrs. Crabbitz are now under my control. Oh, dear. What a sad mess you're in. They'll be presenting proof of your harassment to the police tomorrow."

Howard's lips dissolved as his eyes widened in terror.

Alistair spun in a circle, his face sickly serene. When he stopped, he looked the next person straight in the eye. "I've been waiting for this for a very long time."

CHAPTER 46

GEMINI

"Gemini Reed, my darling woman." Alistair whipped his cape around and bowed in front of her. "You've been such a delight. Using my ability to become anyone I wanted, like the angry Ruthmarie Reed you encountered at the séance, was just my warm up. Opal Hughes was a rather unappealing form to assume, but I'll address that when it's Feather's turn."

"Woah," Opal's boyfriend remarked. "You guys-es town has the gnarliest welcome committee!"

Alistair whipped around and the man's lips dissolved. "Your mind frightens even me. But there will be plenty of time to use you in other ways!

"Where was I? Oh, yes. Gemini Reed is about to become my next little solider. Won't that be fun?"

Gemini vigorously shook her head.

"True, there is a dome of protection around you,

dear woman, but we're all here to witness my true strength. Nothing can keep me out forever!"

Feather stood and took one step before Alistair froze her in her tracks.

"Mrs. Reed gives the impression that she is a do-gooder, always helping others. But the one person she refused to help was her mother-in-law."

"That's not true!" Gemini protested, her cheeks burning.

Alistair's form changed into a middle-aged woman, dressed in a pink maternity dress, holding a screaming infant. "My precious baby boy."

"I already know Ruthmarie can't leave my home. You aren't fooling anyone."

Alistair as Ruthmarie pointed a finger at Gemini. "You are the reason Leo is stuck in that care center! If you hadn't pushed him to seek experimental care, he'd be at home in Fassetville, where his friends could visit him every day."

It was true, Gemini had pushed Leo to try the experimental treatment. She'd told Feather the whole story when they first connected. Even though he was left speechless and unable to walk, the treatment cured his illness. Gemini made the right decision. "If we'd stayed there, Leo would be dead. The doctors told us so. The real Ruthmarie knows the truth."

Instantly, his form changed into a 50ish Ruthmarie, dressed in a sleeveless white blouse and blue jeans. Her roller-filled head was bound by a blue kerchief.

"I have an idea. Let's play 'Gemini's daughter hates her.'"

Gemini's face twisted in pain. "She doesn't hate me," she replied weakly.

"You forget, I can see your thoughts. I may not be able to end your life, but I can make it miserable. Tell everyone why you can't see your grandson!"

Though tears cascaded down her cheeks, Gemini remained silent.

"Stop attempting a noble front, woman! Sophia Reed Floris is hiding from her mother because Gemini Reed is an embarrassment!"

Gemini refused to look at him, instead training her gaze on the carpet next to her.

"Here's a good one. We went on a week-long camping trip once. You hated that I was there and didn't make it a secret. We were all tired and a little cranky by the end. Well, *you* were cranky, Gemini Aries."

Howard used his pinky to squeeze hers, for which she was thankful.

"There was a family in the space next to us with a whole bundle of unruly, dirty children," Alistair/Ruthmarie continued. "And they kept sharing candy with Sophia. She was sick for a week afterward."

Gemini glared up at him through her tears. "Yes,

Alistair. My daughter was sick. So sick, in fact, that she was hospitalized. All because I insisted she play with the children who were obviously poor. Is that what you wanted me to say?"

"No need to get emotional, Gemini. I can make all of these hurts go away. Every single painful memory you have as a parent—gone in an instant! All you have to do is avenge my death. Make amends for your great-grandfather Obbediah by killing Jayden Ko."

The room was silent, with the exception of a cuckoo clock chirping to remind them it was midnight. Gemini bit her lip and glanced from one face to the next. They weren't judging her; it was just the opposite. She felt an inner strength blossoming from their energy.

"No, thank you. While those memories hurt, they are what makes me who I am today. I'll keep them, if it's all the same to you."

Feather felt her lips unseal at the same time movement returned to her body. She jumped from her seat, wrapping her arms around Gemini. "Leave her alone, Alistair! She's not responsible for anything that happened to you! None of us had anything to do with your parents' and brother's deaths."

Alistair bent close to their faces, releasing a putrid smell. "Feather Jones. Such a disappointment. You were going to be the crown jewel of R.U.S.T.

Instead, you let your silly emotions get in the way. I learned early on that I had only myself to rely on. My sister was the apple of our parents' eye. Well, until young junior came along. The accident that killed them was no more accident than your presence here today."

"Are you trying to convince me that you caused a train accident?" Feather shook her head in disbelief. "No one has that much energy."

"I didn't cause the train accident, no. Alice's husband insisted they attend the birth of the wretched child. I was ill with scarlet fever and that selfish woman didn't care. I begged and pleaded with them and, finally, my father locked me in my room. He was tired of my pleas."

For a brief moment, Alistair showed an emotion besides hatred. His transparent eyes glistened with tears.

"That must've been very painful for you, Alistair," Gemini said.

Alistair's eyes returned to their previous, hard look. "No, Mrs. Reed, you're mistaken. The arrival of the coach presented an opportunity. As I gazed at them out my window, loading gifts for Alice's child, an anger welled up inside me. It was a heat that melted me from the inside. Before the coach left, my energy loosened the wheels on their coach."

Though most of the captives had no mouth, there were groans of disgust.

Alistair stood, his eyes sweeping the room. "You dare to chastise me? Any of you would have done the same. I led a happy life, free of the bonds of family. I died a wealthy man." He made a sweeping gesture, one that tightened the restraints on everyone. They all whimpered in pain.

"If you were happy, you wouldn't be here, in this room. You wouldn't have to silence us."

Feather watched as Gemini swayed back and forth. There was a physical pain in her eyes. "Gem, you bought us all of that expensive furniture because you've been in pain, haven't you?"

"Silence!" Alistair's voice boomed. He motioned toward the patio door, sliding it open. "I was forced to find someone willing to carry out my orders. You may enter now."

All eyes were trained on the open door as Phoebe Pepper appeared, wearing a burnt orange R.U.S.T. jacket. There was an evil glint in her eye that Gemini hadn't noticed back at Jayden's home.

Feather gasped. "That's why you seem to pop up wherever I am! You've been following me! I can't believe you sold us out!"

"You made it too easy, Feather. Alistair promised I could spend eternity with my ghost love, Nigel." She nodded toward Alistair with devotion. "My one and only. No P.I.N.K. leader was going to keep us apart! All I have to do is avenge Alistair's murder. It's too bad you're so soft, Jones. You could have anything you want."

"Never!"

"The chief isn't a coward, are you?"

His previously silent demeanor reanimated. "No sirree. I don't have trouble getting rid of someone if they need gone." He moved to the center of the room and pointed his gun directly at Quentin's head. "This one first?"

Quentin whimpered softly and glanced over at his mother, who had tears in her eyes.

"Chief, I'll let you decide the order. What if you made it look like they got into a showdown? Yes, that's what I'd like. Find more weapons and we'll place one in each hand." He giggled, a sickening sound in the midst of their terror.

Alistair's form dissipated into a cloud that swirled around Feather as it hissed, "If only Jayden were here. This would be the perfect ending for all of you!"

The front door swung open and two figures appeared. "Well, I think you're in luck."

CHAPTER 47

FEATHER

Mr. Beasley, wearing a maroon knit sweater over a white shirt, looked like he was ready to attend a fireside chess game and not about to take on a formidable foe from the other side.

Jayden, on the other hand, wore a shiny silver catsuit with midnight blue accents. Dark red lipstick covered her lips. The CEO of Ko Industries and fierce leader of P.I.N.K. was back.

"I'm here now. You can let the others go," Mr. Beasley said calmly, smiling at Feather.

"This is *my* game and we'll play it the way I want!"

Gladiola's appearance changed, each feature dissolving to reveal Alistair's purple outfit. Next came Chief Boulder, then Opal's boyfriend. One

Alistair was an Alistair too many. "We're ready for you!" they said in unison.

Jayden and Mr. Beasley joined hands and closed their eyes, producing a bright light around themselves. Feather had never seen anything like it before, but she felt the strength of their bond, a compassion stretching toward every living being in the room.

Soon, other entities appeared. Ruthmarie, then Millicent and Maeve, and finally a woman who shared Cassie's features but who displayed wrinkles and gray hair.

The room filled with light, Feather's restraints disappeared, and Jayden motioned for her to join them. It was almost impossible to find them through the bright light. "Reach out, doll! I've got you!"

Feather stuck her hand out blindly and felt Jayden's firm grip. It was as if she'd done this a thousand times before. She closed her eyes and thought of every person in her life whom she'd used to create her family of choice: Gem, Olive, Jayden, and, of course, Tug. All of the times they'd laughed over Tug Bar names, the cases she and Gemini worked together, and their unwavering support. And Jayden, who brought her into P.I.N.K. and didn't care that Feather was a broken, imperfect being. They all taught her that love was meant to be forever.

When she opened her eyes, Alistair was gone and Gemini was rubbing her wrists.

Opal arrived, rushing to untie her glassy-eyed boyfriend. "What happened?" Her eyes searched the room before landing on Chief Boulder. "I'm going to sue the pants off you and your nutty department! Arresting me for doing nothing but driving into town, kidnapping me, and—"

The room shook with another loud and abrupt entrance. "FBI! Hands in the air!"

CHAPTER 48
GEMINI

"Can we please start from the beginning? None of this is making sense."

Lucky for them, Chief Boulder was dating the owner of Four Cups. She usually arrived at 5:00 a.m., so opening up a half-hour early didn't bother her. She even pushed two tables together so all the victims could sit beside each other.

"Sure, Gem." Tug smiled at her reassuringly. "Let's start from the beginning. Gladiola and her late husband were career criminals. They moved into a neighborhood and stole valuables from garages and through open windows until people started to get suspicious, and then they moved on. That made her the perfect mind for Alistair to use, but I'm getting ahead of myself."

"Which explains her suspicion of everyone," Howard chimed in.

"Right, and I jumped to the conclusion that she placed a listening device on your house, Gem. But that wasn't her. That was the FBI." He nodded toward Maxine, who cleared her throat.

"We'd been tracking Gladiola for months before her trail went cold. When her nephew, Eli, who had been in prison for burglary, was released, we figured he'd move in with his former cellmate who had moved to Charming. Then, as luck would have it, on a jog around the neighborhood I noticed a familiar face. Every day, I tracked who came and went from her home, hoping to bust a burglary ring. Mrs. Reed and Mr. Beachmont were always at their door. I assumed, wrongly, that the two of you were somehow connected to their crime ring."

Gemini harrumphed. "You FBI types should figure out just who you're dealing with *before* you start listening in."

"Yes, I'm very sorry about that, Mrs. Reed. If it makes you feel any better, we only picked up conversations you were having with... your dead mother-in-law. I get it, sometimes it's nice to pretend we have someone to talk to."

Gemini crossed her arms and leaned back in her chair, squinting hard.

"Moving on," Tug continued. "Ko Industries contacted me about a partnership with the Charmless State Prison. At least I thought that was the reason. Instead, when I went for our meeting, Lulu asked if I would help keep Jayden safe." He turned toward Feather and squeezed her shoulder. "Knowing what she's done for the love of my life, I immediately said yes."

"You're so brave, babe." Feather stared at him with admiration.

"Unfortunately, that's when things got weird. Cassie wrecked the delivery van and Ko Industries informed me that she was in danger."

"And that's where I come back into the picture," Maxine said before taking a sip of her mocha. "Shag Carpetia was also on our radar. He and Eli Crabbitz served time together in the federal penitentiary. We were pretty certain the two of them were involved in jewelry heists in the area. We followed Shag to Ko Industries where we were sure he was planning his next heist and waited, but he slipped out undetected."

Feather swallowed hard. She couldn't bear to look at Jayden.

"His body was discovered yesterday, alongside the murder weapon. Phoebe Pepper did a poor job of removing her prints. She was already in our system because her prints were found at the scene of another murder six months ago. Ms. Pepper murdered one of the guards on Shag and Eli's cell block. Wish we knew why."

CHAPTER 49

GEMINI

Tug tucked a blanket around her neck as though she were her grandson. She didn't mind. "I'm just fine, dear. Really. You and Feather get some rest."

Normally, when they offered for her to spend the night, she was annoyed. Why would they think she couldn't take care of herself? But tonight, or rather this morning, she needed to be around those she loved, even if they were all asleep.

"You're family, Gem. Sleep well."

"It's funny, isn't it?" she said sleepily.

"What's that?"

"Alistair believed having loved ones in his life was a source of pain. For us, it's a superpower."

Tug bent down and kissed her forehead. "That's right. We fit together like the perfect recipe, each person bringing another ingredient."

"You'll make that bar soon."

She fell into a deliciously deep sleep, dreaming of a holiday gathering with everyone she loved. Leo cut the turkey while Taurus stuck his hand in the mashed potatoes. Tug and Feather prepared side dishes as Olive oversaw them.

Gemini awoke to the smell of something baking. Her stomach grumbled as she tried to decipher the time of day and when she'd eaten last. There was a hint of sunlight coming in through the shades, alerting her to the fact it was late afternoon. "I won't need Ruthmarie to keep me awake tonight."

Tug had taken the liberty of returning to her home to pick up clothing and toiletries. It was one of the perks of sharing her house key with friends.

Her favorite lavender slacks and lilac and pink top were laid out on the chair as though she'd asked an assistant to do so. Slipping out of bed, she made her way to the bathroom to shower away thoughts of their shared trauma. Tug insisted they install a fancy showerhead that pulsed three different ways. Feather complained for weeks until she tried it. "You need one, Gem! You'll never want to leave the bathroom!"

"Feather was right. I'm not sure I want to get out."

"Well, you'd better."

Gemini grabbed the shower curtain and peeked her head out. "Ruthmarie! How is it you can leave my home now? And why? I don't appreciate your showing up when I'm indisposed!"

"I come with urgent news!" Ruthmarie was dressed in the skirt and blouse she wore to Sophia's christening. Gemini remembered it distinctly because the frilly blue blouse scratched Sophia's delicate little face, causing her to fuss every time her grandmother attempted to hold her.

"I don't think I can handle any more drama. Let's talk in a week or so, after I've recovered."

"No, we have to talk now."

Regretfully, she pulled the fluffy towel off the shower curtain and began drying herself. A momentary sense of dread passed over her. What if Alistair were up to his old tricks?

"How do I know you're really Ruthmarie?"

"Because I don't have the bells and whistles of the evil models. In fact, I'm here to say goodbye, among other things."

Gemini stepped out of the shower with the towel wrapped around her body and stepped onto the small rug, almost nose-to-nose with Ruthmarie. "What do we need to talk about? Something else I did wrong?"

"No. I'm sorry I've been giving you a hard time, Gemini. It's the only way I know how to be." Ruthmarie sighed. "You've given my Leo the happiest years of his life, and I appreciate you for that."

Gemini wished she could hug the old woman. It

was somewhat ironic that these feelings came so long after Ruthmarie's death.

"Feather explained that you were the one protecting me. Well, you and my neighbor, Mr. Beasley. Is that the reason you appeared in my kitchen?"

Ruthmarie nodded and smiled proudly. "My actions regarding your well-being earned me an invitation to the event of the year. Marilyn Monroe is having a big cocktail party next weekend and—"

"What was it?"

"Huh?"

"What was so important that I had to end my relaxing shower?"

"Oh, right. Your little rift with Sophia. She's not mad at you. In fact, she really needs you right now."

Gemini folded her arms. "If that were true, wouldn't she answer her phone when I called?"

"I've got to go now. I won't see you for many years. Take good care of my son! And regarding your daughter, listen with open ears and an open heart." Ruthmarie dissolved into nothingness.

"Wait! You're talking in riddles again!" Gemini was a little sad, thinking that she'd never see her again. Just a little.

As she was dressing, her phone buzzed. *Sophia.* She took a deep breath and thought of Ruthmarie's words. *Listen with open ears and an open heart.*

"Darling daughter? How are you?" Her voice was as bright as she could possibly muster.

"Mother, could we video chat?"

No time for pleasantries. That wasn't a good sign. "Whatever it is, I love you, dear."

In a matter of seconds, they both appeared onscreen and, as soon as Gemini glanced at Sophia's precious face, she gasped. "What have you done?"

"I knew you'd hate it!" Sophia sobbed.

It took every bit of self-control Gemini had. "Sophia, your beautiful nose has... changed. It no longer looks like your father's. It was perfect, but it's still a part of you and I'll love it just the same." *Good, Gemini. Excellent, in fact.*

"Brandon's mother has been making comments about my looks ever since we married. I'm too thin, I'm too fat. I'm ugly, I'm too pretty. I can never please her."

"Her opinion doesn't matter, sweetie."

"I know that now. I let her convince me to get a nose job. I thought if I did it in Charming, then, I don't know, you would talk me out of it?"

"Oh, Soph."

"No, it's not your fault. You had that séance and everything. How could you know? And after it was all over, I couldn't bear to face you."

"Why? Don't you know I'll love you forever?"

Sophia was crying now. Real tears. Perhaps she

hadn't even been trying. "Yes, I do. You and Daddy have always loved me."

"Sweetheart? I'd like to come visit you this weekend. We could go shopping, and to that gelato shop you like. Taurus could show me his latest karate moves!"

Sophia nodded eagerly. "Yes, please!"

There was a light knock at her door before Tug called, "Breakfast is ready!"

"Okay! I'll be out in a minute."

"Where are you, Mother? Do you have a lover now?"

"Don't be ridiculous. Your father is my one and only. But I do need to go."

"Mother?"

"Yes, dear?"

"I love you."

CHAPTER 50

TWO MONTHS LATER

"You'll all remember Mrs. Gemini Reed from last month's live podcast episode taped at The Bleeding Rose. 'Vicious Violette, a Vampire in Disguise' has broken all records for podcast downloads. At least the ones I know about. Today, we're at the grand opening of her detective agency."

"It's not a grand opening, Quentin. It's the unveiling of our mural."

Gemini was slightly irritated that Quentin chose today to record his next episode. Since he'd won a Best in Ears award for his episode about Alistair's family history, a slightly skewed version where Alistair was actually a vampire, Quentin was always bugging her for another interview.

"Can you tell us more about your experience

with the vampire? Last month, you left off with the arrival of the FBI."

There was only one way to get rid of this nuisance. "Quentin and his mother jumped into action and saved the day. I'm sure he can speak better to his heroic actions."

Quentin let out a little giggle. "Oh, yes. I'd forgotten about our role."

"You really should interview your mother too. She was instrumental in our rescue."

"Did I hear my name?" Hetty, dressed in her best flowered housecoat and a headband with plastic flowers attached, nosed in between them.

Quentin's face turned a shade of red Gemini hadn't seen before. "Yes, my mother. She, um..."

"If you're gonna talk about the day my legs disappeared quicker than my boy on laundry day, I should be front and center."

Gemini took this opportunity to rush off, hearing Quentin's voice in the background, "...I've always been interested in becoming a vampire slayer..."

Their office was filled to the brim with employees and local dignitaries. Even the mayor, who'd had no idea he was included in Alistair's plans, attended.

"We've got a new Tug Bar flavor called United." Cassie, dressed in all black with her hair pulled back in a ponytail, held a silver tray containing small samples. "It is a mixture of cocoa, nuts, chocolate chips, cranberries, and chocolate protein powder. Everyone contributed one of their favorite ingredients. Mine was the hazelnuts."

"Good job, sweetie!"

"Thanks, Mrs. Reed!"

"How is your mother doing these days? You haven't talked about her lately."

Cassie's gaze fell. "She married her boyfriend."

"Oh, I'm sorry, dear. He did seem a little... lost."

"Not the guy who brought her to town. This guy's name is Ripper. Mom thought he was only interested in her money. You know, the settlement she got from the city of Charming."

"I'm aware." Gemini was on the citizen's council that offered her $25,000 for her bravery in the hostage situation. Opal asked that they include a plaque and the deal in a sealed envelope, avoiding an embarrassing lawsuit for the city.

"Yeah, she was worried about him, but it turns out Ripper is loaded. His family makes Rip Chips Potato Chips. She proposed to him after that."

"We shouldn't expect to see her for a while then?"

Cassie grinned. "Nope."

Gemini playfully pinched her arm and moved on. Jayden and Feather were giggling in hushed tones. "What did I miss, ladies?"

Feather turned around and hugged Gemini. "We were just talking about Capu's figurines. Did you know his mother had the gift of sight?"

"I don't understand. She could see? What's so special about that?"

"The woman was a psychic, able to see decades beyond her years. That's why all of her dolls were representative of women who would play a role in her son's life."

She thought back to the day she hid in Mr. Beasley's kitchen and broke a figurine. One looked like Maxine Smart. Another looked just like her. "That makes sense! Now I want to go back and study the rest!"

"He has one for Olive called Still Kicking. Carly is kicking her foot above her head." Jayden burst into infectious laughter.

"Accurate. So accurate." Gemini nodded to Tug and Olive, who were standing on a stage made especially for this moment.

"Thank you all for coming today. My wonderful fiancée, Feather Jones..."

There was an audible gasp.

"Yes, we're engaged." Feather's face was beet red. "We hadn't formally announced until—" Tug looked sheepishly at Feather. "Today, I guess. Sorry, babe."

Feather shrugged.

"Anyway, my beautiful Feather is talented in so many ways, and she wanted to create a mural that encompassed all the good in our community. So, we'd like to present the Kindred Spirits of Charming."

Olive pulled a cord, which dropped the thick canvass cloth, exposing a colorful wall. There were small storefronts with familiar faces lining the brick street. Maxine Smart jogged by in her running gear as Mr. Beasley, in his maroon sweater, waved. Cassie, Olive, and Tug sold Tug Bars to passersby. Jayden, in her trademark catsuit, tossed glitter above her head. The mural included everyone in the room, even Chief Boulder, who had recently found his way back into the good graces of the community.

"What about you and Gemini?" Chief Boulder asked.

Gemini walked up to the mural and pointed to two transparent figures in the background. "We're right here, behind the scenes. Feather thought that, as we looked at it every day, we'd be reminded of our role in the community."

The mayor stepped forward and raised his glass of punch. "To our Kindred Spirits!" Everyone followed suit.

Feather and Gemini embraced as the guests milled about. "I think we need a break from sleuthing."

Feather pulled back and stared at her in shock. "What? We've finally hit our stride!"

"No argument there." Gemini smiled slyly. "Just thinking that we may need a little extra time to plan a wedding."

ALSO BY JOANN KEDER

Piney Falls Mysteries

Welcome to Piney Falls

Saving Piper Moonlight

Tales of Naybor Manor

Lavender's Tangled Tree

The Twisted Stitch Society

Kinundrum

Charming Mysteries

Oceanberry Blues

Tangerine Troubles

A Lime in Time

Emory Bing Mysteries

The Case of the Half-Baked Bing

The Case of the Rootbeer Bungle

The Case of the Fudged Features

The Case of the Chunky, Funky Monkey

The Case of the Clairvoyant Carrot

The Case of the Vegan Vixen

The Case of the Cream Cheese Caper

Pepperville Stories

The Story of Keilah

Secrets and Sunflowers

Franniebell and Purple Wonder

Be the first to hear about new releases! Sign up for my newsletter here:

http://www.joannkeder.com